# The Wizard of god

*A retelling by*
*Stephen Roy and Brooke Gale Louvier*

*To all who travel the long, winding road through the land of god.*

*Thanks to Gabe Robinson, Shannon Josey and Sara Crawford for their help editing the book.*

*Special thanks to Rebecca Hall for coming along with us on this journey. It wouldn't have been the same without you.*

# TABLE OF CONTENTS

"Come to the edge, he said. We are afraid, they said. Come to the edge, he said. They came to the edge, He pushed them and they flew."
— *Guilliame Apollinaire*

"My father says almost the whole world is asleep...everybody you know, everybody you see, everybody you talk to. He says that only a few people are awake and that they live in a state of constant...total...amazement!"
— *Joe Versus the Volcano*

# CHAPTER 1

# THE STORM

*"Now is the winter of our discontent."*

— WILLIAM SHAKESPEARE

There is a place, before you wake into complete consciousness, where everything seems new. This is the place you briefly visit when morning is introduced to you slowly, when the day is not yet abruptly shoved into your lap, yelling and demanding your full attention.

Grace came out of that place steadily as she woke without the need of her alarm clock. Remnants of the dream she'd been walking in lingered like the scent of smoke on her clothes after a campfire. Not a tangible plot with clear faces or meaning, but drifting colors, lights, and an overwhelming feeling of peace.

She checked the clock and realized she had overslept. It was Sunday: the one day out of the week her sense of duty overcame the wild growing notion to run far away. She stood up, walked to the window, and drew back the old-fashioned, blue-and-white-checkered curtains. Faint sunlight streamed through the window, enough to reflect through the framed glass mosaic hanging over a window-pane. The light formed a tiny rainbow on the wall above her bed as it passed through the colored glass. She looked back at the dull, late-winter Texas landscape outside. Fields of dry, brown grass spread out before her. A straight road dotted with old farmhouses disappeared into the distance beyond her view. The clouds shifted and made the beam of light disappear. Grace turned away from the window, and the weight of the day rushed onto her.

She looked in the mirror next to her bed and smoothed down her frizzy brown hair with her hand. The bags under her large brown eyes were evidence of another restless night, though the dream had been a great relief.

*BANG! BANG! BANG!*

"Grace!"

A loud knock on her door and her aunt's irritated voice interrupted her introspection.

Grace sighed. "Come in."

Her aunt Emily burst through the door holding Grace's small black-and-white mutt. She placed him on the bed, and he shook himself off.

"You need to keep Terrence in here. I caught him chewing on a pew leg again."

"Sorry," said Grace dryly. "I mean, I don't know how he keeps sneaking into the sanctuary."

"Well, make sure he stays in here," Aunt Emily said through gritted teeth. "People are arriving to worship, not to be jumped on and licked!"

Grace petted her dog. "Well, we'll both be out of your way soon."

Her aunt frowned. "I don't want you *to leave,* just keep him under control. I don't know what has gotten into you lately. You seem so short-tempered. Please don't be late for church. The weatherman is calling for bad thunderstorms, so make sure you close all your windows tight!"

"Okay," she mumbled as her aunt turned and walked out of the room.

Grace looked out the window again, desperation building inside her. She could see dark gray storm clouds, framed by the curtains, churning and growing in the western sky.

Every time a storm blew its way past the tiny house and church, an ache would form in Grace's chest. She didn't remember much about her mom, but she remembered how she got excited when storms came, jumping up and down like a child about to have a birthday party. She would grab Grace's hand and whisk her outside. They would huddle together on the porch, her mother's warm arm draped across Grace's bony shoulder.

"Storms are the way the universe tells us we are smaller than we think we are," she'd whisper. "So small but so loved."

Grace's mother believed the world had more color in it than the average person could see, no matter how dreary the weather or how bad the day.

Her mother was an artist.

She'd create art out of anything she could find—shards of beer bottles, dried flowers, and plastic doll dishes Grace had cracked in half while playing.

Grace rubbed the smooth glass pieces of the mosaic her mom had given her before she was sent away. It was a figure of a man, arms lifted above his head. He stood in an archway but seemed to hold it up as if he were part of it. As she stared at the figure, a hodgepodge of broken material, she couldn't help but think it felt like the sum total of her life. She slipped on a pair of black dress pants and a green button-up top with a tan jacket, dabbed on some light make up, and headed out the door.

Grace stepped outside of her small apartment connected to the church building, the one that used to house the old janitor before lung cancer took him. She had recently moved there from her room in the farmhouse to try to find some space and freedom. She didn't have to pay rent on her aunt's condition that she never missed a service. Her uncle was the minister, yet her aunt was really the one who called the shots in the small country church that had been standing longer than any of them could remember.

Grace noticed a blue moped sputtering down the road, stopping at the entrance to the church's driveway. A girl jumped off the bike and tore off her helmet, letting loose a mass of auburn curls, which stuck up in the damp air. She watched the girl lift up the lid of the seat and slam it back down, cussing loudly as she did so.

"Are you okay?" Grace called out from across the driveway.

"Yeah, I'm fine. Of all the damn places to break down!" She lowered her voice at the last part but Grace could still hear her. The girl zipped up her leather jacket and opened her seat up again, rummaging through it.

Realizing the girl didn't want any help, Grace walked up the stairs back into the old, peeling church. As she found her spot on a pew near the back, Grace looked around at the congregation. Families trailed in with their squirming children, forcing smiles onto their faces for another week of songs and sermons on right and wrong. These were good people, and Grace knew all of them by name. They chatted afterwards about small things, and Grace genuinely cared about them, but not enough to stick around for small talk.

A man sitting a few seats down on her left was someone she didn't know. He looked about mid-forties, with soft brown hair with silver flecks. He sat alone, looking sad and slightly nervous. His eyes were red and bloodshot, and he was blinking rapidly.

Chords from the old organ began to reverberate through the sanctuary. Everyone stood. Grace mindlessly mouthed words to old songs, hymns about far-off glory and walking on streets of gold.

Her mind drifted off while she went through the motions. She sat down with the rest of the congregation and listened to her Uncle Harry's sermon about avoiding temptation, peppered with a few cheesy jokes.

"Now why do we take communion?" he asked no one in particular. He pointed to the words carved in the wooden plaque sitting on the communion table,

"The table says so!" He chuckled to himself. "Do this '*In Remembrance of Me.*'"

His gaze seemed zeroed in on Grace as he continued. He winked at her.

"We must obey our Lord! This is why we eat and drink."

Grace smiled slightly and looked away, gazing out the window. She noticed a man walking down the road. He was tall and lanky, and as he got closer she could tell he was relatively young. He carried a large backpack and wore a funny-looking hat, which was barely staying on his head in the strong wind. She imagined he was a wanderer, a free spirit traveling the open road, happy and content, going nowhere in particular. She envied him and longed for the freedom he had.

The gray clouds had now turned an ominous dark purple and seemed to be chasing the traveler down the road. She thought she heard the faint sound of distant thunder.

Grace turned her attention back to the front of the church where her uncle was still speaking. She noticed movement coming from the side of the church that led to her room. She strained her neck to look. A tiny black-and-white face was peeking through the door. Terrence! A wave of panic swept over her.

Before Grace could do anything, the dog trotted under the communion table to the left of the pulpit. No one seemed to notice, as the long white tablecloth covered him nicely.

Her uncle continued. "Before we take communion, we must have clean hands and a pure heart."

Grace watched as the communion plates began to scoot to one end of the table. A faint growl came from under the table. The growl was followed by a quick flurry of black and white. The table-cloth flew off the table, and tin plates containing crackers and little cups of red grape juice splattered to the ground. The dog appeared from underneath the tablecloth, cheerfully devouring the crackers he had cleverly fished for.

The congregation murmured. Aunt Emily took action and stood up, pointing at Grace. "Get that dog out of here!"

"I'll get him," Grace said awkwardly, barely holding her laughter in.

She rushed up to the front. Juice covered the floor and had splattered on the fallen white tablecloth. It looked like the aftermath of an actual blood sacrifice. By the time Grace grabbed him, Terrence had eaten most of the tiny wafers. Crumbs clung to his furry face. Grace picked him up and he licked her, unaware he had just consumed something sacred. Her uncle stared, his mouth gaping open, not sure what to do next.

Most of the congregation had stayed in their pews and were chattering about the scandal. Aunt Emily stalked behind Grace as she carried Terrence back into her room, stroking his soft black head.

"Grace, if you can't keep that dog where he belongs, I want him out. There is no room for a dog in *church*!"

Grace buried her nose in her dog's fur. She looked up at her aunt, knowing what she had to do.

Steadily, calmly, she responded. "I mean, if he is not welcome, then neither am I."

Her aunt frowned at her. "Don't be ridiculous! That's not what I meant…" She paused, staring at Grace disapprovingly. "We'll talk about this later. There is a bad storm coming fast, and we may have to usher people down into the church's basement. Lock that dog in his kennel and hurry back to help!" Her aunt turned and walked away quickly.

Grace put Terrence down on the bed and lay down beside him. A panicked feeling formed inside her stomach, overwhelming her.

Thoughts began to form in her mind, and she couldn't keep them out this time.

*Loser. You will never get out of here. You are too dependent. It's pathetic. You will never be free. You're just like HER...*

Outside the wind was howling, matching her stormy emotions. Terrence stuck his wet nose toward her face, concerned.

"I need to get the hell out of here," she said. "I wish there were some kind of place where I could escape..."

Through the dark voices invading her mind, Grace could hear the faint whisper of her mother, how she had held her during similar storms,

*So small but so loved.*

The building shook in the wind. Grace turned to look out the window behind her. The sky was dark and it looked like dusk even though it was the middle of the day. Small tree branches and leaves swirled in the wind. She saw her aunt and uncle frantically ushering people into the basement.

She turned her back to the window, fixing her eyes on her mother's piece of art. She wondered how her mother had created something so beautiful out of so much pain.

"Show me," she said.

*CRASH!*

Grace stumbled back as a massive tree limb crashed through the glass in the window. She screamed and tried to jump out of the way, but tripped and felt herself falling. Shards of glass flew past her face. She felt a sting, a loud thump, and then nothing.

# CHAPTER 2
# THE TABLE

*"Hunger steals the memory."*

— LOUISE ERDRICH

Grace was aware she was moving, spinning. It reminded her of the first and only time she had rode the hurl-a-whirl at the state fair when she was eleven. She remembered closing her eyes and opening her mouth—no scream coming out—and wanting desperately for it to stop. Her corn dog and lemonade beat against her gut in protest and eventually ended up all over her favorite sunflower print shirt.

A deafening roar flooded her ears. She was falling, down, down, deep into a bottomless black abyss. She couldn't make sense of what was happening; she just wished the motion would stop. She felt as if she was somehow moving between multiple dimensions. In one sense she was still in her bedroom, while at the same time she was moving through a nightmare.

Blurry, disconnected images raced through her mind. Her life was passing before her.

*I can't be dying.*

*I'm too young!*

*There's so much more I need to do.*

*I want to get married, have a family.*

*I want to get out of Texas, see the world!*

*I am not ready...*

*God... Please!*

God? Panic gripped her. What if she *wasn't* ready? What if everything she had believed had been wrong? What if her growing doubts had sent her here? What if...

Her thoughts abruptly stopped as she noticed the roaring noise had ceased. Everything around her, the room itself, shuddered and then...stillness.

Maybe she wasn't dead after all. Dots of light began to appear randomly in front of her, and she realized her eyes were open. She felt the rough wooden planks of her floor on her back. She felt something sharp and pulled her hand back towards her quickly.

*Ouch.*

She then felt something wet and warm on her cheek and heard a low whimper. Terrence. She was definitely still alive.

Grace blinked rapidly as she slowly sat up. Her head ached from the fall, but other than that she seemed to be in one piece.

Terrence stood by, looking up at her and wagging his black tail, not seeming bothered by anything.

She looked down at her hands and realized she was fine, apart from a small drop of blood on her index finger where she had touched a shard of broken glass.

*Her mother's mosaic.*

Oddly, the tree limb was nowhere to be found in the room. Everything else seemed in place besides the mosaic. Grace stood up and looked out the window, rubbing her eyes in disbelief.

"What in the world?"

She ran across the room and flung open the front door. Shock hit her chest and she gasped.

This was not the dreary landscape of west Texas.

Everything about this place was...*alive.*

She was standing in a quaint village with small cottages lining a brown-and-tan cobblestone street. In the center, directly in front of her view, was a patch of green grass that appeared to be the town square. The grass was the greenest Grace had ever seen. It was so vivid it seemed like it was a living creature, happy and vibrant.

Flowers lined the square: tall orange snapdragons, deep-purple lilies, bunches of lacy white baby's breath. In the center of the square sat a long banquet table, covered in a white tablecloth, which stretched out from one end of the square to the other. Wood crafted chairs, too numerous to count, were pushed under the table. The table was covered with serving dishes, blue-and-white china, and carved wooden bowls. Fresh-picked flowers dotted the center in large china vases. The table was roped off, with small pillars at regular intervals every few feet, like a museum display. Grace exhaled.

"They must be having a wedding or something,"

She spoke to Terrence, who was already bounding onto the stone street. Grace cautiously stepped out the door after him, looking around at the houses. Thick brown curtains were drawn in the little cottage next to her.

"Where is everybody?"

Terrence looked up longingly at the table and Grace made her way over to him. She inhaled and was overwhelmed by a mouth-watering, savory fragrance. Although all the dishes were covered, she could pick out distinct smells of roasted garlic, basil, and fresh rolls. Her stomach growled in anticipation.

"Hello? Is anyone here? Where am I? Whose food is this?"

No response.  The cottages appeared unoccupied, as if the town had been suddenly deserted.

The brightness of the air, the color of the flowers, and the scents of the food formed an enchanting combination that drew Grace to step over the ropes and sit down on the closest wooden chair. She drew her chair in and looked down at the empty plate before her.

She should have felt awkward, being in this strange place, but it seemed like the most natural thing in the world.

"If this is only some sort of dream, I may as well eat."

As she lifted the cover of the dish in front of her, steam rose revealing a perfect-looking garlic-studded roast surrounded by red potatoes, pearl onions, and bright orange carrots all dripping with juices. She knew she had made the right decision.

She grabbed a large wooden serving spoon and heaped meat, potatoes, and vegetables onto her plate. She lifted another cover, revealing rolls, still warm as if they had just come from the oven. Grace served herself fresh salmon, roasted with a honey ginger glaze, and grilled asparagus drenched in butter. When her plate was full, she picked up her fork.

Just as she was about to take a bite, she heard a voice behind her.

"Stop!"

With mouth wide open and fork in mid-air, Grace froze. She dropped her fork and turned around, startled.

A woman stood directly behind her. Grace didn't know where she had come from or how she had snuck up on her so quietly. She was tall and attractive with a cold glare. Her head didn't have one blonde hair out of place; it fell neatly on the shoulders of a gray suit jacket. Matching pants and black heels made her look city-sharp and out of place in this quaint village.

"Get out from behind there!" the woman scolded Grace, as if she was a child.

Grace immediately stood up and stepped back over the rope sheepishly.

"I'm sorry.... I didn't know."

All at once people started coming out of the houses that surrounded the square. A small crowd formed around the two women. Several were dressed in odd-looking uniforms.

"Everything okay, Linda?" a man in uniform asked.

"This girl was about to eat from the table!" Linda announced.

Gasps could be heard through the gathered assembly.

The woman called Linda looked at Grace angrily. "Who are *you* to think you can eat here?"

The question caught Grace off guard. "Um, I'm Grace. I was just hungry. I think I'm lost. Where am I and who are you?"

"We represent the godvernment," a uniformed man offered.

"The what?" Grace asked.

Linda ignored her question. "Nobody handles or touches the food on this table. Can't you see it's roped off? If you need food, we have a work-for-food program you can enroll in."

"What? I don't want to work. I mean, I don't even know how I got here. Where is here?"

The crowd began murmuring upon hearing the strange young woman's question. Grace noticed the townspeople not in uniforms were all dressed simply, in plain cuts of old-fashioned-looking fabric, mostly brown, grey, or black. All the women and girls had their hair tied back in taut ponytails. Expressions on the residents' faces ranged from curious to confused to fearful.

A little boy who looked about five with enormous eyes and two missing front teeth snuck up behind Grace and reached under the rope, grabbing a roll off her plate with quick hands. He stuffed it into his mouth eagerly. A man, presumed to be his father, grabbed the boy by the arm and pulled him away from the table.

Linda glared at the boy's father then turned back to Grace.

"This is sacred ground. This table is an important part of our heritage and traditions. The food is purely symbolic, it is not to be actually eaten!"

"As it is written, 'Someday we will eat from this table, but not now. Now we must work.'"

"Look, I *am* sorry," Grace pleaded. "I didn't know any of that! Please tell me where I am!"

A thin-haired man with an upturned nose and round glasses stepped out of the crowd and addressed her.

"You are in god."

"Excuse me?"

"You are in gawwwwwd," the man replied, sounding it out the second time in a condescending tone.

"God, like *God*? God? Am I dead? Is this heaven?"

Grace shook her head in disbelief.

Linda looked at her suspiciously.

"If you are not from god, where did you come from?"

"Uh... Texas."

A loud murmuring continued through the crowd.

"There is no Texas in god," the man with the glasses proclaimed.

He stepped closer to her and smiled. "You are obviously lost, young lady."

The people around them nodded their heads in approval.

"Now here is a true and wise man of god," Linda remarked proudly, facing her flock.

"Okay..." Grace spoke up, still confused. "Well, um, do you have a map? Maybe it could show me how to get back home?"

The man chuckled. "Why would I have a map? I'm not lost!"

Several in the crowd chuckled as well.

"I do have something *like* a map, something that tells me everything I need to know." He reached into his pants pocket and pulled out a small leather-bound book. Oohs and aahs could be heard coming from the onlookers. He flipped it open and began to read, but from his eyes Grace noticed it appeared as if he was reciting from memory, not actually reading.

"Someday we will eat from this table, but not now. Now we must work." He closed the book.

"Okay, I get that, thanks for reminding me. Now please take another look at your map-book and tell me how to get back home," Grace said, exasperated.

"See here now!" said Linda. "You will never find your way to this place you call *home*. We really should get you started filling out the paperwork."

"What paperwork?" Grace said, confused.

"The required citizenship paperwork, of course!" Linda replied, annoyed at Grace's ignorance. Linda continued, "We will process you quickly so you can get to work ASAP! The quicker you get to work, the quicker you will earn your food vouchers."

Grace interrupted Linda and said in a loud voice, "I don't want to join your group, and I don't need your food vouchers! I just want to go home!"

Linda narrowed her eyes. "I don't know what it's like in Texas, but this is the way we do things here. This is how we have *always* done things. If you won't cooperate, I can't help you. And without my help, you will surely starve!"

At that, she turned and marched away, the crowd parting to make way for her.

Grace stood there with a stunned look on her face. She had no idea what to say or do next.

The man with the glasses drew near and spoke to Grace in a gentle voice. "The road out of town is that way." He pointed. "You may be able to get back home if you follow it."

"Okay, thanks." Grace whistled for Terrence, whose belly was being rubbed by a group of adoring children. He jumped up and ran to her side.

She started walking down the path, ignoring the stares of the crowd, her head spinning from all that had just transpired.

Grace walked for some time until the houses, the old church, the table, and the people grew faint in the distance. The path soon led into an enormous open field of tall grass, which made following it very confusing at times.

"Great. I have no idea where we are *or* where we are going," she huffed to Terrence.

Her faithful friend at her side, she walked on for what seemed like hours. In the far distance, Grace could see hills and trees. It was beginning to grow dark, and the landscape hadn't changed much. Anxiety began to creep into Grace's heart as the sky darkened and she still saw no sign of civilization.

As the path wound around a large boulder, she saw some lights in the distance.

"Just in time. I hope these people are nice." Terrence wagged his tail excitedly.

As they approached the town, she could see in the fading light that the village looked familiar. As soon as Grace saw the town square, her thoughts were confirmed. She stopped in her tracks.

"We've been walking for hours...in circles!" she said, exasperated.

Terrence leaned against her leg to console her.

Looking down at Terrence, Grace sighed and said, "Oh well, at least we have a place to spend the night. Who knows, maybe we'll wake up and realize this has all been, like, a weird dream."

As they entered the familiar town, she noticed houses lit from the inside, but the square was empty.

She walked past the table, noticing it was still full of all the same dishes. She looked around to make sure no one was watching before leaning over the rope and touching the side of a dish. It was still warm. Grace wondered at the strangeness that had occurred hours earlier and why they would have a feast like this if no one was allowed to eat it. She noticed a loaf of bread peeking out from under a towel. Her stomach growled. She grabbed the bread quickly and a bottle sitting next to the breadbasket and rushed back to the church to hide.

*SLAM!*

The door of the church echoed in the sanctuary. With her heart pounding, she stopped to listen, and then breathed a sigh of relief once she realized no one was coming after her for stealing the food.

She collapsed onto the floor against the wall, shoving bread into her mouth hungrily. It was still warm, crusty on the outside and soft on the inside. It filled her mouth and belly, and she closed her eyes, feeling a strange sense of peace.

She opened the bottle and gulped the liquid inside, not caring what it was. Wine! It was sweet and fruity and it warmed her insides. She caught herself smiling.

Terrence whimpered, and she gave him a piece of bread.

Grace took another swig of wine and laughed out loud at the irony of it all.

*BANG! BANG!*

Grace's heart nearly leapt out of her chest. Someone had come for her. Terrence barked.

"Shhhh!"

She looked around, anxiously searching for a place to stash the bread and wine. Someone must have seen her steal it from the table.

*BANG! BANG! BANG!*

The knock came again, more frantic sounding.

Grace quickly swallowed and got up, wiping the crumbs from her mouth; she shoved the rest of the loaf and the bottle under a pew.

She looked through the window and saw a figure standing by the door. In the moonlight, she recognized the man with the round glasses from earlier. Grace cracked open the door.

"Hello?"

"Hello, Grace from Texas," said the man. "Don't be afraid, I'm here to help you." He was wearing a long coat and a wide-brimmed hat as if he didn't want to be recognized.

Grace opened the door a little wider.

"That's nice of you, but I don't think anyone here can help me," Grace said, trying not to tear up. "I think I'm having some kind of terrible nightmare and hope to wake up soon."

"You are a strange case for sure. I saw you grab the bread and wine and run into this old abandoned building."

"What do you mean 'abandoned building'?" Grace asked, flustered. "This is my church!"

"What is a church?" the man asked.

Grace looked down, shaking her head, and then buried her face in her hands.

The man continued, "I don't pretend to know how to help you myself, but I can tell you about someone who can. I know someone who can answer your questions, and who knows all the answers."

"Who?" Grace asked, looking up at the man with tears now beginning to fall down her cheeks.

"The Wizard."

"Wizard?"

"Yes, The Wizard of god."

"Can he tell me how to get home?" asked Grace, wiping her tears.

"If anyone can, it's him."

"Where do I find him?"

"He lives in a place called The EC."

"Okay...um, well, where is this place?"

"I've never been there, but I'm told it's a long journey. It won't be easy finding food, because you aren't part of the system. But the good news is there will be plenty of water along the way. This is the land of god: the land of a thousand springs."

"Okay, but how do I get to this EC place?" Grace pleaded. "Does your map book show the way?"

"No doubt, but to be honest, I really can't make heads or tails of it anymore. But that's no matter. There is only one path out of this town anyway. Just stay on it and I'm sure you'll eventually find your way."

"But I already tried that path and ended up walking in circles." Grace swallowed hard.

The man continued, "Nobody has had the courage to eat from the table in a very long time. You are special, Grace. This is why I have come here tonight. There is a reason you are here. Just start walking and soon you'll find what you seek. There is much evil in god but also incredible goodness just waiting to be discovered. I believe you have eyes that will recognize the difference. Good-bye, my dear."

With that the man with the round glasses smiled, hurried out the door, and disappeared into the darkness.

Grace shut the door, walked to her room, and curled up on her bed. Total exhaustion had hit her, and all she wanted to do was sleep. Terrence curled up close, resting his head on her arm. "What would I do without you, boy? Maybe we will wake up tomorrow and this will all be over."

Grace opened her eyes, startled. She sat up too fast, looking around the dark room.

A whimper came from near the window, and Terrence stood on his hind legs trying to see out. As she stood up and walked over to the window, she heard whistling through the broken glass. She saw light beginning to form on the horizon, and she guessed it was just before dawn.

Grace could see the town square from the window and noticed a man walking around the table pushing some kind of cart. He was whistling a tune that sounded familiar, but she couldn't place it. Her heart was still beating fast from being startled awake, but the tune had a strange calming effect and soon she began to feel a bit better.

She watched the man. He appeared to be dressed in laborer's clothes, so she guessed he must be a servant. From the cart, he lifted up dishes and set them on the table. Even from her window, she could smell the food, and the aroma instantly brought a smile to her face. As soon as the table was filled, he walked away, wheeling his cart, and was soon out of sight. The whistling grew faint, and Grace wondered yet again if she was dreaming. Still very sleepy, she lay back down next to Terrence and quickly drifted off again.

# CHAPTER 3
# THE POLE

*"Truth isn't always beauty, but the hunger for it is."*

— Nadine Gordimer

Bright sunlight streamed through the broken glass and onto Grace's face. She opened her eyes and squinted for a few moments before noticing Terrence sitting by the door, waiting to go out.

Grace stood up and looked out the window at the table, remembering the mysterious man with the cart.

Grabbing the remainder of the bread she'd taken the night before, she broke off a big piece and stuffed it in her mouth without thinking. She washed it down with the last few sips of wine.

She laughed to herself, feeling a little giddy from the wine.

"We're still here," she said to Terrence, handing him what was left of the bread.

She ran her fingers through her hair, brushed the crumbs off her clothes, slipped on her shoes, and headed out the door.

Stepping outside, she saw people coming out of houses and busily walking from place to place. A few of the people stopped briefly to look at the table in the square, which was filled with fresh food.

She said hello to a woman coming out of the house next door, but the lady quickly looked away.

Grace looked down at Terrence.

"Let's get out of here, boy. We're obviously not wanted. We need to get home."

She started down the path that led out of the town. Oddly, she wasn't anxious about traveling the same path as the day before. Today was a new day and she felt ready for anything.

She was surprised by how good she felt. Maybe it was the night's sleep or the resolution in her mind that this was real and she could get through it. Perhaps it was the growing sense of adventure she was feeling. Maybe this was just how people who drink wine with breakfast felt.

As Grace exited the town, the road seemed much easier than the day before, and Grace was enjoying the scenery, despite being surrounded by rather bland fields. Every blade of grass that swayed in the breeze gave her a little thrill. She could see a forest in the distance and knew that it was where she was headed.

As Grace approached the edge of the forest, she saw something odd sticking up out of the ground in the field to her right. At first she thought it was a skinny tree with no bottom branches. Drawing nearer, though, she realized it was not a tree, but a man sitting on top of a small platform attached to a pole. Terrence gave a friendly bark, and Grace called out a greeting.

"Hello."

The man sat still, cross-legged, his gangly arms hanging loosely with his hands on his knees. He appeared to be close to the same age as Grace. He had a pale, boyish face with freckles and blond scruff on his chin. His reddish-blond hair was matted into messy dreadlocks that stuck out from under a green corduroy hat. His eyes were closed. He looked familiar, like an actor she recognized from a movie but couldn't remember which one. Grace stood directly below him and tried again.

"Hello?"

The man opened his eyes. They were a piercing blue but had a vacant look to them.

"Heyyyyyy!" he said, surprised, but pleasantly. "Wow, I wasn't expecting to see anyone else here. Who are you? Did you come to bring me a message?"

"I'm Grace. Um, I don't have a message, I'm just traveling through. Mind if I ask what you are doing up there?"

He grinned, and one dimple appeared on his freckled right cheek.

"I'm Hayden. Good to meet you, Grace. Man, this is pretty trippy. I'm sorry, I just thought I was the only one here in this place... Weird! I am up here because I want to be above the earth. You know, transcend the here and now." He spread his arms out and smiled.

Grace looked at him quizzically. "What do you mean?"

Hayden began to talk, moving his arms wildly, causing the pole to wave back and forth a bit. Grace was amazed he could still keep his balance.

"I was hoping to find balance, get it? This is a way of getting rid of my own thoughts and becoming a part of something bigger. Like Voltaire said, 'Meditation is the dissolution of thoughts in eternal awareness.' I want to be eternally aware, you know?"

"So, do you live here?" Grace asked.

Hayden thought for a moment.

"No. I mean, I haven't always. It's all pretty hazy. I can't remember much from *before*. I was thinking maybe I went over the edge. You know, down the rabbit hole! I was hoping I'd find out who I am by meditating, you know, like maybe if you go deep enough in, you have to come out the other side somehow, right?"

His voice trailed off, and he stared as if he was looking right through Grace.

"So, is it working? Do you know who you are?"

Hayden shook his head and refocused on Grace. "You know, I know my name, so that's cool. Every time I feel like I'm reaching the light on the other side, though, I end up losing my balance and falling off. I hurt my head pretty badly the last time."

He felt beneath his hat and winced.

"It's a good thing I have so much padding up there or I could have caused some serious damage!" He laughed to himself, a goofy-sounding chuckle, which immediately made Grace smile.

Hayden held out his arms straight to keep the pole from wiggling and continued.

"You're the first person I have seen since I've been here. Once in a while some birds come by. I love watching them. Except once a crow landed on me, and I took it to be some sort of omen or something, you know, like the universe speaking to me. It made me think of Poe's 'The Raven'. I thought he was going to start telling me, 'Hey dude, you're screwed,' that I would *nevermore* transcend the earth or something. Then you came along, so it must be a good sign."

Grace smiled slightly. "Is that why you asked me if I had some kind of message for you?"

"Yeah, exactly. I figured you came here to tell me something. You look like the kind of girl I should listen to."

Grace laughed. "Well, I think I am just as confused as you. But maybe you should come down?"

"Yeah, I guess it's time then. I may need your help, though. I don't want to fall on my head again. Really can't afford any more brain damage, you know."

Grace stepped closer and put her hands on the pole to steady it. Looking up at the platform, she figured it was about eight feet off the ground. She hoped he wouldn't hurt himself trying to climb down.

"Okay. Ready?"

Hayden carefully uncrossed his legs, got on his knees, and slid down off the platform. He grabbed Grace's shoulders to steady himself.

"Thanks!" Hayden said, brushing dirt and leaves from his baggy cargo pants and multicolored patchwork coat.

"Hey, where are you heading, Grace?"

"Well, I am trying to find a er...um...a Wizard. I am hoping he will tell me how to get back home."

"So, this guy is like a spiritual leader, huh?"

"I guess so."

"So you are lost and can't find your way home. That sounds like a bummer for sure. Hey, I am too! Sweet! I am coming with you."

"Well...okay, sure. Why not?" replied Grace, feeling relieved to have some company. Terrence put his paws up on Hayden with approval, and Hayden laughed.

"This dog, it's like he *knows me,* man!"

Grace smiled. "I have always said Terrence is a great judge of character."

They began to walk toward the woods, leaving the empty platform with a crow perching on it.

Grace tried to make conversation as they walked.

"So, you just sort of showed up here in god, but you're not sure where you came from?"

Hayden turned to her, surprised. "Wait, showed up to *who?*"

"Not a who...a where, I guess. This is god. That's what the locals told me. I know, I'm confused about it, too."

Hayden just shook his head, perplexed.

"Strange... Yeah, I am not really sure about my past. It's all kind of a blur to be honest. I don't even know how I got here."

"I know what you mean. I'm not sure how I got here either, wherever *here* is."

"You know, when I was on that pole, at times I would get in this peaceful place and I'd get this happy thought and think maybe I could fly away. I'd love to ride the air currents, you know? I'd see those blue birds flying in the field and I'd think, 'Why can't I?' I think being free is what everyone wants."

Hayden looked downward, and Grace could tell he was deep in thought. "For a long time I have believed that true freedom came when you could control your mind, your thoughts. But lately I've begun to wonder..." Hayden's voice trailed off.

Then suddenly, as if he had snapped out of a trance, he turned to Grace, all smiles again.

"Wow, I am stoked to meet this Wizard dude!"

Grace smiled back. Hayden's childlike enthusiasm was very refreshing, and she was thankful not to be traveling alone anymore.

They walked toward the forest, continuing in conversation. Before long Grace's stomach began to growl, and her thoughts turned to how they were going to find food, much less a Wizard.

# CHAPTER 4
# THE FOREST

*"Not all who wander are lost."*

— J.R.R. TOLKIEN

Entering the forest felt like walking through a door into an expansive green cathedral. It was lush: dark-green ivy wrapped around clusters of knobby trees, and pale, spongy mushrooms, some the size of Terrence's head, sprung up from fallen logs.

The air was cool, giving off the fresh-dirt smell of decomposing leaves. It was quiet, besides the soft crunch of leaves beneath their feet and the faint sound of trickling water. Rays of light pierced through the canopy of trees, bathing the path in a golden hue.

Grace and Hayden walked for hours, with long periods of silence, both with an understanding of the mutual need for serenity. Terrence followed at their heels, occasionally stopping to sniff a mushroom or paw up some dirt beside a tree, as if digging for buried treasure.

Alongside the path there appeared a small stream. Hayden and Grace cupped their hands in the cool water to get a drink. Terrence waded in up to his neck, drinking deeply.

"Yum, this water is wonderful," said Grace. "The man who told me about The Wizard called this the land of a thousand springs."

"I think they are artesian springs," replied Hayden. "That means that the water table here is very close to the surface. That's crazy to think there is a huge reservoir of water just under us pressing against the surface rock, bursting out every place it finds a weakness."

"Mmmm. I'm so glad we have plenty to drink, even if we don't have food," Grace said in between sips.

Hayden continued, "Man, I love it here! This place feels almost...spiritual, you know? It feels alive! It makes me think of Thoreau's writing about how in the woods he sees only the essential facts of life."

"Yes, god is very beautiful. Sure beats the flat, dusty place where I come from."

"Sounds pretty boring. I don't know why you're in such a hurry to get back," Hayden teased her. "I mean, this is where it's at; just look at this place!" He spread his arms out, gesturing at the green stillness that surrounded them.

"That's easy for someone who doesn't even know where or who he is to say. But whether it's beautiful or not, home is home."

"Oooooh, well, you said you didn't know how you got here either! Are you *sure* that's where you are from? I mean, does anyone *really* know? How do you even know your home still exists? You said this place is called god, right? Maybe we are dead and in some alternative universe...or heaven."

"Whoa, this is getting a little too deep for me," said Grace. "There are a lot of things I don't understand. One thing's for sure, though, if we are dead then dying really makes you work up an appetite…'cause I'm, like, starving!"

The light coming through the trees was growing dimmer. Late afternoon was approaching, bringing with it the prospect of evening and a foreboding darkness. As they walked on the trees grew thicker, appearing more gnarled and less serene—a chaotic fractal of branches, trunks, and logs. The path was quickly narrowing. Hayden went in front of Grace and pushed back a tree branch, forgetting to hold it and letting it snap back in her face.

"Ow! Be careful!"

Hayden looked back.

"Sorry!"

As he apologized, he clumsily tripped over a small tree that had fallen onto the path. He landed on his knees, arms out to catch himself, tangling his hands in the branches.

"Owwww. I deserved that!"

Grace laughed out loud. He looked so awkward, all skinny legs and arms tangled up in the tree as if he were a part of it.

"Man, that fallen tree must be on your side!" he joked as Grace helped him to his feet.

*Fallen tree.*

Grace stood still; images were flashing before her eyes.

A storm.

A fallen tree.

The church.

The final scene before her "departure" was starting to come in clearly like a picture being adjusted on the TV.

"I got hit on the head," she said in a monotone voice.

"Yeah, I'm really sorry about that. I should have been watching out for you. You okay?" Hayden looked concerned as he brushed off his khaki pants, which were completely covered in dirt.

"No, I'm not talking about just now. Before. I remember... I think that's how I got here. There was a storm and a tree branch crashed into my room. I was hit on the head."

As they continued walking, Grace's head began to pound from anxiety. The shadows were shifting and growing longer.

Grace stopped and turned to Hayden.

"The further we walk, the path seems less like a path and more like a vague idea of a path."

Hayden looked around.

"Well, it looks like it goes to the right here, but it's really hard to tell. It could go this way too."

He crossed his arms, pointing to two semi-bare spots that were in the opposite direction.

"Okay, well, we have to decide which way to go."

"I don't know what to do," Grace confessed. "It doesn't look like we are going to make it out of this forest before it gets dark, and I really don't want to spend the night in here."

Hayden stared at her blankly, a grim frown stretching across his face. Then he snapped out of it and shook his head briskly like a dog drying off.

"I have an idea!"

He looked around, spotted a medium-sized tree with branches low to the ground, and began to climb.

Grace looked up at the roof-like canopy of tall trees.

"Hayden, you are not going to be able to see from that tree. It's not tall enough, and the forest is too thick."

Hayden kept climbing, with surprising monkey-like agility, until he found a wide branch about ten feet off the ground and perched on it.

"I am not trying to see over, at least not the way you think."

He gripped the trunk to keep balance and closed his eyes.

"What are you doing? It's getting dark, and we kind of need to decide what to do!"

He ignored her.

"Seriously, we don't have time for this. I'm starving and my head hurts. Are you planning to stay up there all night? Because I really don't feel comfortable sleeping in a tree."

Hayden opened one eye and looked down at her.

"Grace, please be quiet. I am asking for directions."

Grace turned away from him, rolling her eyes. She found a tree to sit beneath, leaning back on the tawny bark, and sulked. Her foot felt irritated, like she had something in her shoe.

What was she doing here? What if Hayden was right? What if she didn't even have a home anymore? What if she was destined to wander this crazy land forever?

Terrence put his small black-and-white head on her leg, whimpering softly.

"At least I have you, boy. We will stay together no matter what."

Terrence licked her knee in agreement.

Grace took her shoe off and found a small twig had somehow lodged itself into her shoe. She chucked it into the woods. Terrence ran after it, hoping she wanted to play fetch.

"I don't wanna play, boy, not now," she called out to where Terrence had disappeared, but then she noticed the brush had been pushed back. She got up, pushed her way through the foliage, and found Terrence chewing on the twig.

"Hayden, get down. I found it!"

"What, what did you say?" Hayden spoke as if waking up suddenly from a nap.

"I found, well, actually, Terrence found the path."

"Cool, I'll be right down. Dog finds path. Spacey."

Back together, the three made their way down the newly found path.

"I really hope we can find a house or something soon," Grace said.

Hayden sighed. "I was trying to find some answers, but apparently the universe decided to speak to a little dog instead, so maybe we should ask him?"

Grace chose to ignore his comment and picked up the pace. Her legs kept going, but her mind was telling her that they should find some shelter soon. The temperature was dropping, and dusk was about to make an appearance.

"Ow." Grace pushed aside some bushes with thorns on them. "Be careful."

Hayden stepped around them gingerly.

"Maybe we should try to make shelter before it gets dark," Hayden said with a tone of resignation.

Grace kept going, determined.

"How would we even do that? We don't have anything with us. Can you build a fort out of sticks?"

Hayden became excited at the idea. He went off the path, heading toward a large tree. He grabbed a long stick off the ground and leaned it against the trunk as if he was measuring. He then rested it against the tree and began looking around for another of the same size. When he couldn't find one, he took the branch leaning haphazardly against the tree trunk and threw it on the ground in disgust.

"Yeah, I don't even know how we'd do that. I wish I had my backpack with me. I had a tent in there and everything. Hmmmm..."

Hayden's voice trailed off. He looked down at his hands as if they belonged to someone else. Then he looked up at Grace.

"Backpack. I had a backpack. I was walking, somewhere. There wasn't much around. I was trying to get somewhere important... No! I was getting away from something or someone... Hmmmmm. It all seems so real all of a sudden."

Grace looked puzzled. "Are you remembering something from before you were meditating?"

Hayden nodded, his blue eyes wide. "Yeah, I am. It's pretty vague, but I know I was walking somewhere. I was in a hurry. Wow. This is all so trippy. Maybe we should keep going and try to find some shelter."

While they'd stopped to talk, Terrence had run ahead on the trail. He'd turned a corner and was now barking loudly at something.

"We should go see what he found," Grace said nervously.

They made their way to Terrence. In the twilight, they could see that the woods opened up into a small field. There were trees every few feet in neat rows that looked like they had been planted, contrasting sharply with the wild foliage of the forest. On the tree nearest to them were round, succulent-looking peaches.

"Whoa! Score!" Hayden exclaimed.

Grace smiled, feeling relieved. "What a find! Good job, boy!"

Terrence wagged his tail happily. They walked into the orchard, scouting it out. Grace grabbed a huge peach off the tree. It was so big that her hand hardly fit around it. She gently squeezed the peach, and it felt perfectly ripe. When she bit into it, a wave of sweet, syrupy juice rushed into her mouth. Her stomach grumbled in appreciation, and after a few bites, her headache began to melt away.

"Hey! This one has apples!"

Grace walked over to the tree Hayden was leaning against, a crisp red apple in his hand. He munched on it and closed his eyes.

"Oh my God. This is the best thing I have ever eaten in my entire life."

Grace just smiled and chucked her peach pit, grabbing a big red apple for herself. They walked around the orchard and found a tree that had purple plums, and another one had mangoes. With each delicious bite of juicy fruit, Grace felt more and more like herself. The haze that had been over her mind lifted, and she felt a deep peace even though the sky had turned dark. When they were full, Grace sat under the mango tree while Hayden explored the orchard. She noticed Terrence was eating a mango that had fallen from the tree but had not rotted.

"Wow, I didn't know you liked mangoes, boy! Come to think of it, I didn't know dogs ate fruit!"

The moon was coming out, almost full and casting a comforting light on everything in the orchard.

"Uh oh," Hayden said from behind a large peach tree.

"What?"

"There's a warning sign over here."

Grace got up and made her way toward Hayden.

She found him standing in front of a large wooden sign nailed to a tree on the edge of the orchard. She made out the words in the moonlight.

"Warning: It is unlawful to eat any food not sanctioned by the godverment."

"Great!" Grace exclaimed. "We just broke the law."

"Yeah, well, at least no one is around!" Hayden said. They went back to the mango tree.

"What now?" Grace said. "Do you think it's safe here? Hey, what's that?"

They listened. A faint whistling was coming from the woods.

It grew louder.

"What if it's the person in charge of the orchard?" Grace said. "Maybe we should hide."

They crept to the other side of the orchard, away from the sound, and got down behind a big apple tree. The whistling grew louder, and they could see a man emerge from the trees, carrying a large white sack. In the moonlight, they could only see his back. He looked around and then set the sack on the ground, continuing his happy tune. He pulled something from the sack that looked like a long white sheet and began tying it to a tree. He picked up another sheet and did the same thing. He walked around the orchard, as if strolling through a garden in the middle of the day. They watched the man pick a plum and bite into it.

"Mmmmmmm!"

Just then Terrence left their hiding spot from behind the tree and ran out to where the man was.

"Terrence, no!" Grace whispered loudly, but it was too late.

She watched her dog approach the man as if he knew him. The man turned around, not seeming surprised at all to see a dog in the middle of the orchard at night.

"Why, hello there, little fella." The man patted Terrence on the head.

"He seems friendly," Grace whispered to Hayden. "Maybe we should come out."

"Wait, hold on a minute. We can't be sure," Hayden whispered back.

The man stopped petting Terrence and looked directly at the apple tree. Grace could see his white teeth illuminated in the moonlight.

"Why are you hiding? You can come out," he said, amused.

Grace sheepishly came out from behind the tree, Hayden trailing behind her.

"Um, we're not in trouble?" Grace asked.

The man just smiled. He didn't seem angry at all.

"Please, eat. I planted these here for travelers like you. Someone else put up the sign."

Grace brightened. "Thank you!"

She liked the man immediately and felt a strong desire to give him a hug. She held back, though, embarrassed by the thought.

The man looked deeply into her eyes, smiling genuinely.

"My pleasure! I have more than enough. There are some delicious grapes also, growing on vines on the edge of the orchard. I recommend those for breakfast. My orchard is an excellent place to spend the night. Get some rest. I better go now. But if you need anything, I won't be far away."

"Thanks again!" Grace said as the man walked back into the forest, whistling.

"We never asked his name," she said to Hayden when the man was out of sight.

Hayden was checking out where the man had hung the cloths in the trees.

"Grace. They're hammocks! How sweet is this!"

He was already climbing into one of the hammocks that had been stretched on the low branches.

"Hey, remember what you said about sleeping in the trees? Not such a bad idea after all!" Hayden chuckled

"Sleeping in the trees, of course," Grace said, smiling. "Goodnight, Hayden."

She picked up Terrence and put him in the other hammock, climbing in after him. Once they were settled in, Grace looked up. Beyond the apple tree branches the moon hung large and bright. She could see the designs and shapes in it and tried to find a face. The stars twinkled in the black sky. Terrence snuggled close.

She could hear Hayden breathing deeply from the other hammock, either meditating or already asleep, exhausted from the long day of walking. Grace guessed the latter. She stroked Terrence's soft chin and rocked the hammock gently, inhaling the fragrant smell of fruit in the warm night air. She began to drift off under the bright moon, the happy tune the orchard man had been whistling still ringing in her ears.

Somewhere between consciousness and sleep, Grace imagined she could feel the massive underground aquifer, pounding, pressing against the earth, searching for weakness.

# CHAPTER 5

# UNDERCURRENTS

*"Only love can break your heart."*

— NEIL YOUNG

The sea surrounded her, empty and listless. The waves rocked her raft, an unstable thing made of scraps of material from the boat that had wrecked. Grace felt alone, her mouth parched, her fingers turning numb, her eyes dry from the wind. She looked down at her body and realized she was emaciated, nearly a skeleton. Her head throbbed in the heat and the glare from the sun.

She squinted in the bright sunlight and saw something coming over a wave. It was another floating platform, and it had people on it. As they drifted closer, she noticed the people were sitting happily, talking and laughing as if they were at a party, not floating in the middle of the ocean.

"Help!"

Her mind shouted but her mouth couldn't form the words; her vocal chords had shriveled up along with her body. Grace floated closer, within ten feet or so of the raft, but the group paid her no attention. She saw they were sitting in a circle, having a picnic. Grace recognized one woman as her fourth grade Sunday school teacher. She picked up a sandwich and took a bite.

Grace-—starving, dying of thirst, and frightened—tried her best to get their attention. She tried to wave her arms, but it was as if her body and mind were no longer connected and her limbs wouldn't obey. She struggled, panicking, as the floating picnickers continued to eat their lunch. Just then she realized they weren't eating sandwiches, but pieces of the raft. Or maybe the sandwiches had turned into wood as she was watching. Maybe it was all a mirage. Summoning her last bit of energy she rolled herself to the edge of the raft. Suddenly, she was falling, deep into a black ocean. She couldn't breathe, move, or scream. Blackness, emptiness, and fear surrounded her.

Grace woke up suddenly, startled, leaving her nightmare and coming to her senses. It was early morning, and Hayden was awake, looking at her from the other hammock, his hair disheveled and face covered in lines from sleeping face down on the cloth.

"You okay? I thought you were gonna fall out from all the tossing and turning."

"Yeah, I just had a bad dream." Grace looked down at herself, relieved to confirm her body size was back to normal, no longer a skeleton waiting to be rescued.

"It just felt so real. You ever have dreams like that?"

Hayden nodded. "I still wonder if we're living in one now."

Grace was not awake enough to get into a philosophical discussion. She stumbled awkwardly out of the hammock, still disturbed by how real the dream felt.

Terrence, who had jumped out of the hammock in the middle of the night to keep watch, approached Grace and sat down next to her, wagging his tail.

Her stomach growled, and she remembered what the mysterious Orchard Owner had said the night before about the grapes. She found them growing on the edge of the forest and picked several bunches.

"Hayden, I found the grapes!"

Hayden was already munching on an apple.

"Great, maybe we can bring some with us. I've got some apples."

He had stuffed his pockets with apples, which made his pants look lumpy.

Grace laughed, her mood lightening as she bit into the large red grapes, her teeth piercing taut skin, the sweetest juice with a tinge of tartness filling her mouth.

The early-morning sun streamed through the green leaves of the orchard trees, illuminating Grace's face. She sighed, feeling energized and ready to go.

"Let's go, the path is this way." She pointed to an opening in the grapevines where the sunlight was bathing the path with a golden glow.

They walked leisurely down the path, sharing grapes and apples.

Further down the path, they began to hear the faint sound of trickling water.

"It sounds like another stream. Let's find it. I'd love to wash up a little," Grace exclaimed.

Hayden dramatically sniffed towards her.

"Yeah, that's a good idea. Yuck! It must be rough being a sweaty girl. I don't need to bathe. I smell like fruit orchards and wildflowers!"

Grace pushed him jokingly.

"Yeah, you smell like fruit all right...rotting apples."

They walked off the path a few yards and came across a small brook. It looked fresh and clean, and Terrence immediately led the charge straight to it. Hayden and Grace followed, peeling off their shoes and wading into the cool water. Grace leaned over and splashed water on her face. Hayden took it a step further and took his hat off, dunked it in the water, and sloshed it back on his head.

"This is how I wash my hair."

"You look like a frog hiding under a lily pad," Grace retorted.

Hayden splashed her. Soon they were all soaked and refreshed, as the sun was now fully up and the day was looking to be a warm one. They walked a little ways upstream and found a spot where the water was flowing clean off the rocks, making a mini-waterfall. Hayden cupped his hand and drank deeply. Grace did the same. As she was sipping, she heard a strange noise coming from the woods on the other side of the stream.

"Ahhhhhhhhhh."

It was a low, desperate moaning noise. Whoever was making it sounded like they were in pain. Grace and Hayden looked at each other.

"Did you hear that?" Grace asked.

"Shhh. Listen, someone's over there."

"Ahhhhhh…"

This time the moan was followed by a sniffle.

They began walking cautiously in the direction of the noise. Making their way through a large thicket of bushes, they came upon a small clearing.

They saw a man sitting on a tree stump, hunched over, his face in his hands. He was dressed in khaki pants and a blue polo shirt. Grace could tell by his thin, graying brown hair that he was probably her uncle's age, maybe a little younger. Moved with compassion, she approached the stranger, Hayden and Terrence following close behind.

"Hello? Are you okay?" Terrence approached the man, sniffed, and sat down at his feet.

The man slowly lifted his head up from his hands. Grace stepped back, trying not to gasp. The man's eyes were puffy, bloodshot, and filled with a crusty gunk, so much so he could barely open them.

"Who are you? I can barely see you," he said, appearing startled.

"I'm Grace, and this is Hayden. What's your name?"

"Tim," the man pronounced. He looked unsettled and confused. He blinked his eyes repeatedly and put his hands over them again.

"Are you okay, man? Can we help you somehow?" Hayden asked.

Tim removed his hands from his eyes and squinted at them.

"I am sorry. I have this condition with my eyes. They get really bad if I don't put drops in them every few hours. I had them yesterday but now I can't find them. I've looked around but my eyes are so blurry."

"We'll find them for you, don't worry," Grace assured him.

She begin looking, walking around the circumference of the clearing and shuffling through fallen leaves.

Hayden joined in the hunt and within a few minutes, he found the bottle of eye drops hidden between the roots of a large tree.

He handed them to Tim, who smiled weakly.

"Thank you, thank you! I don't know what I would have done if you two hadn't come along."

He squeezed the drops into his eyes and blinked rapidly.

"Ahhhhhh! Much better."

Tim stood up slowly, bracing his back with his left hand and stretching out his legs, making his knees pop.

"Ow, I'm so stiff and creaky. I probably would have sat here forever if you hadn't found me."

"It's a good thing we followed the sound of water," Grace said. "Otherwise we would have kept walking on the path and would never have known you needed help."

Tim nodded, gently rubbing his right eye.

"It feels better already. I can actually see you two clearly. Why, hello!"

He leaned down to pet Terrence, who was looking up at him with beseeching eyes.

"Dogs are great creatures, so loyal."

"Yes, especially him. This is Terrence. So where are you from? How did you get here?"

Tim rubbed his eyes again and looked thoughtful.

"I'm not sure, but hopefully it will come back to me. I just remember being in this forest and not knowing where to go. Then I lost my eye drops and I just sat down on this stump and sort of gave up. Then you found me."

Hayden patted Tim's shoulder lightly.

"Tim, man, I understand. I was feeling kind of lost myself. Then Grace came along and things started looking up."

"Yes. It's hard to put into words. I wondered at first if this was some kind of punishment. But now that I'm not alone, I don't feel that way anymore," Tim said, smiling and looking gratefully at Hayden and Grace.

"You mentioned you were following a path. Where are you going?"

Grace cleared her throat and spoke. "Honestly, we are sort of lost and a bit confused ourselves. We are traveling to a place called the EC to find a man we believe can help us find our way. I hope he can tell me how to get home."

"I want to ask him the secret to wisdom," Hayden added.

Tim nodded slowly, looking confused.

Grace had a thought. "Hey, maybe he can help you with your eyes."

Tim shrugged. "My eyes are the least of my problems, really. I'll be okay now that I have my eye drops. Do you think he could help figure out what's wrong with me? It's like I have no idea where I belong. I feel sad a lot and have this empty feeling in my chest."

Hayden looked thoughtful. "Maybe he can, Tim. I mean, he holds all the secrets to this place, right, Grace? He should surely be wise enough to tell you what you need to know."

"Sure, I'll come. I have nothing to lose," said Tim. "Thanks for inviting me."

"Yeah, all right!" Hayden punched him in the arm lightly. Tim tried to crack an optimistic smile.

The odd trio began to make their way back to the path. As Hayden and Tim chatted, Grace thought about the hope she had given to her new friends and wondered why she had so much faith in The Wizard, someone she had never met.

# CHAPTER 6
# PLEASANT GROVE

*"God comes to the hungry in the form of food."*

— GANDHI

The forest eventually transitioned into a sparse landscape. Weeds grew in tufts, struggling to break out of dry ground. It wasn't quite a desert, more like a field where the grass had died. It was good to be out of the forest, but it wasn't very pleasant scenery. Even the atmosphere gave off a strange despair, or so Grace thought. Something didn't feel right, but she kept walking, determined to find the EC, and now driven by new motivation not to disappoint her traveling companions.

At one point, they stopped to rest on a large rock. The rock was long and flat and the perfect height to serve as a bench. They sat for a moment, Grace in the middle with Hayden and Tim on either side.

"Sometimes, it feels worse to stop because I realize how tired I am...and hungry," Grace admitted.

"Yeah, then it's that much harder to get up again and start moving. Man, I could use one of those giant apples right about now," Hayden said.

Tim sat there in silence. He had his hands over his eyes, once again. He jerked his head up suddenly as if waking from a nightmare. He pulled out his eye drops from his pocket and proceeded to squeeze them into his eyes,

"I was waiting for the music to start…"

"What?" asked Hayden.

"That's it. I was sitting down, feeling bad about myself, waiting for the music to start, anything to soothe my soul. I thought it would bring relief, but it was like throwing ice on a third-degree burn."

Grace looked at him, puzzled. "I don't understand."

He jerked to his left, looking at her, blinking rapidly.

"Before here… I remember."

Grace nodded. "That's good. Keep trying."

Tim stood up and paced back and forth in front of the rock.

"That's just it. Trying to remember doesn't work. It only makes me anxious and sadder." He started down the path.

Hayden and Grace got up and went after him, Terrence following behind.

The path led uphill and was lined with a handful of straggly trees, stripped of leaves and bark, making them look like skeletons.

"Something's not right about this place," Hayden said eerily, echoing Grace's feelings.

They could see a village at the bottom of the hill. It wasn't at all like the first village, neat and proper looking. It seemed more like a run-down camp. Scattered shelters pieced together with scraps of wood and tarps sat sporadically around the small valley. Buildings that had once lined the streets now lay in rubble, surrounded by mounds of trash. It looked like some disaster had hit the area.

People milled around, and some appeared to be hauling trash from one place to another. Smoke rose from several places, and it smelled like burning garbage.

"I don't like this," said Grace, a sudden fear gripping her. "It looks dangerous."

"Those poor people," said Tim, his voice cracking. He squeezed more drops in his eyes.

"Maybe they have food," said Hayden.

The path led directly through the encampment. They began to descend down the hill. As they approached the village, the sickening smell got stronger. The air was thick with the scent of rancid garbage and heavy smoke, which caused them to cough occasionally.

"What is this place?" Grace wondered.

As if to answer her question, they walked by an old, battered sign that read, "Welcome to Pleasant Grove."

"Doesn't look pleasant to me," Hayden remarked.

They noticed a woman walking in their direction. She was dirty and dressed in rags and was pulling an old three-legged chair behind her.

Grace approached the woman.

"Hi. We're traveling through. I was wondering. Um, is there anywhere to get food?"

The woman kept on walking, the remaining legs of the chair scraping lines in the dirt.

She didn't look up at Grace when she spoke.

"There's something like food, if you'll work for it."

She continued on her way.

The three companions looked at each other skeptically.

They passed a man carrying a very large lead pipe, with an angry look on his face. Grace eyed him cautiously, imagining multiple frightening scenarios in her mind, her heart racing.

"This place freaks me out," Grace said as the man disappeared behind a dilapidated shack crafted of boards and sheets of metal.

"What do you think happened here?" Tim asked curiously.

"Who knows?" said Grace.

There didn't seem to be any rhyme or reason to the work people did; they seemed to simply haul trash from one place to another.

An old sign that said "Diner" lay broken on the path. They walked around it.

They passed a couple of young boys sorting through piles of dirty ripped-up clothes that were scattered all over the streets. They were rail thin, almost brittle looking, and moved very slowly. The boys looked up at the group with empty eyes. Grace smiled, but they just turned back to their chore.

They passed a woman wearing a long blue dress, three sizes too big and hanging off her thin frame. Her hair was cut short, and she had a crying baby on her hip. She stared at them as they walked by her and didn't respond to any greetings.

"What is with this place?" Hayden asked.

"This is awful!" said Tim. "I can't believe people live like this! I wish there was a way we could help."

Just then a little girl came up from behind them and tugged on Grace's shirt. She turned around and, seeing the girl with dirty blonde hair and big blue eyes, kneeled to her level.

"Hi! What's your name?"

The little girl grabbed a stick lying nearby and began writing in the dirt. When she was finished she motioned for Grace to look. It took a bit of effort, but Grace deciphered the scribbling as RHODA.

"Hi, Rhoda. I'm Grace. Pleased to meet you."

Rhoda couldn't have been much older than five. She appeared somewhat frightened, but her curiosity won out over her fear.

Hayden kneeled down next to Grace.

"Hey, Rhoda, do you know if there is anywhere to get something to eat around here?"

The girl nodded rapidly and ran down the road.

"We should follow her," Grace decided. They picked up their stride and followed the girl.

They passed people huddling in groups talking in low voices. Others carried random objects such as windows or broken tables. The atmosphere was eerie and foreboding.

They followed the girl to what looked like the center of the camp, where big open tents were set up. Picnic tables sat scattered in between the tents. Lines of emaciated people waited to enter the tents. Seated at the tables were people dressed in uniforms, sorting and handing out papers. Tim approached an older man standing in line whose expression appeared a little softer than the rest.

"Excuse me, sir, can you tell me what's going on here?"

The man eyed Tim with slight suspicion.

"We're registering."

"For what?" Grace asked.

"So we can work and then…eat."

"Excuse me!" an irritated woman standing behind the man interrupted.

She was tall and very thin with long dark hair tied back by a dirty purple scarf. Her face looked weathered, and Grace noticed how calloused her hands were as she gestured behind her.

"You need to get in the back of the line. No cutting. I've been standing here for three hours." The three travelers looked at her, taken aback.

"Three hours, really? Is this the only place to get food?" Hayden was beginning to sound desperate.

The woman continued with a huff. "You've got to wait in line like the rest of us. Then register and you will be assigned a work duty. After you have completed your work you will be given a food voucher. Don't you know this? Where were you during orientation?"

Grace stared at her, ignoring her question. "You mean all these people hauling trash around are working for food?"

The woman put her hands on her bony hips. "It's what we do. Well, what they *make* us do. It's just the way things work here, since the storm blew through. But surely you know that. "

"Storm... A storm did all this damage? Grace asked

A middle-aged balding man standing impatiently behind the woman chimed in.

"I see what you're doing, the old 'chat and cut,' pretending to have a conversation and then sneaking your way into the line. Not going to work. I am watching you!"

The three backed away from the line.

"No worries, man, we'll get in the back," Hayden responded. As they walked away they could hear the man and woman talking in low voices to each other.

"Have you seen them before?"

"No. They look like strangers. I don't trust them. We should report them to security."

The travelers walked over to an empty picnic table and sat down.

Tim stared at the tent. "Maybe we should try to talk to someone in charge."

Hayden said, "I'd do anything for some food right now. Well, except haul around trash all day. I don't think I'd even have the energy for that."

"Yes, let's go talk to them," Grace agreed.

They got up and walked back toward the tent, passing the woman and men who had talked to them. The balding man spoke up.

"See! I told you they were trying to cut! You need to get in the back!"

They ignored him and continued to the front. The crowd in the line seemed irritated and gave them strange looks, but no one tried to stop them. The three marched right into the tent and up to the registration table. Two women sat at the table, dressed in green pants and green shirts. They each wore nametags—one said "Hester-Registration" and the other "Maud-Work Assignments." They both wore wire glasses and had their hair pulled back tightly in buns. Both women looked bored as they sorted papers into piles. A large neatly printed sign on the table read "godvernment Relief Program."

Hester looked up from her paperwork and peered over her glasses with a cold stare.

"Back of the line," she said evenly.

Grace leaned forward on the table.

"Please, we're not from here; we're just traveling through. We've been walking for, like, hours and need some food before we collapse. Is there any way you can make an exception?"

Hester shook her head. "You need to get to the back of the line. Then you will register, and there you will find an application to fill out." She picked up a stapled stack of papers as thick as a short novel and slammed it on the table in front of Grace.

"Then you will get back in line and hand your application to Maud and she will assign you a work duty. After you work your allotted time, you will go to tent B." She pointed to another tent on the other side of the picnic tables, with an equally long line,

"*There*, you will get your food voucher. *Then*, you will go to tent C." She pointed behind her.

"And wait in line for food. That's how it works. But if you had been paying attention during orientation you would have known that already. Next!"

She looked past them to the woman impatiently waiting in front of the table. The three stepped aside for a moment. Grace looked beseechingly at Maud, who had remained silent.

"Miss, please. We are exhausted. Isn't there any other way to get food?"

Maud shook her head. "This is the way it works. Everyone has to do his or her duty, and then we eat. Why do you keep questioning this? What part of this don't you understand, young lady?" She turned back to her paperwork.

Grace clenched her fists. Her legs and arms shook, but she couldn't tell if it was from anger or extreme hunger. Tim touched Grace's arm gently and spoke up.

"Wouldn't it make more sense to feed us *first*? *Then* we would have the energy to work. *Then* we might actually have the heart to work diligently. Starving people don't care about what they are doing. They are just going through the motions. Food is all they can think about."

Maud and Hester, with mouths wide open, stared at Tim in astonishment. They did not respond.

Tim smiled at the women and turned to Hayden and Grace. "Let's go. They simply don't get it. We'll have to figure something else out."

Shaking her head in frustration, Grace stomped back to the picnic table and sat down. Terrence lay at her feet, sniffing at an old, broken clock on the ground.

Hayden and Tim sat down on the other side of the table.

"Maybe we can go to Tent C and plead for food," Hayden suggested, rising to his feet. "Surely there is someone who is nice enough to give us something to eat."

"Okay, you go try that, Hayden. I'll just wait here," Grace said sharply.

Hayden sat back down.

"Some relief effort," Grace said sarcastically. "More like a labor camp."

Just then Rhoda appeared at the table. She looked up at Grace with wide blue eyes and climbed up on her lap. Grace couldn't help but smile. Terrence began to lick the little girl's dirty leg. She giggled softly.

"Hi, Rhoda. Where are your mom and dad?"

The little girl said nothing. She leaned her small head against Grace's chest in a moment of tenderness. Grace could tell by her matted hair that she hadn't bathed in a long time. A wave of compassion swept over Grace, causing her anger and frustration to fade. They were just passing through, while this child had to live in this hell day after day. She wondered about Rhoda's story, whether her parents were still around, and if her house had been destroyed by the storm.

*Storm.*

A strange, dark thought came over Grace. Could this be the same storm that brought her to this place? What if all this was somehow her fault? What if Rhoda and all these people were somehow trapped in Grace's nightmare?

Rhoda jumped off her lap as suddenly as she had climbed on, turned around and smiled. A gaping hole showed she had recently lost a front tooth. She started to walk away from the table, then turned back and smiled again.

"Where are you going?" Grace asked. The little girl pointed somewhere.

"I think she wants us to follow her," Hayden said.

Rhoda nodded rapidly, then turned and began to walk briskly. The three got up and followed her away from the center of the town. As they approached the big tent labeled "Tent C," more desperate-looking people could be seen waiting in line. Most of them stood in silence, exhausted. A putrid, fishy kind of odor drifted out of the tent and Grace put her hand over her nose.

"What is that horrible smell?" Hayden said, an expression of disgust on his face.

As they passed by they saw two men dressed in the same green uniforms as Hester and Maud, standing behind a table, handing out pieces of something jagged and dark brown to the people in line.

Tim noticed a few folks standing off to one side biting into the brown stuff. "Hey, that looks like jerky!" he said after getting a closer look.

They stood and watched for a minute or so. They noticed the people were working very hard as they tried to chew the jerky-like food, but they never saw anyone swallow. The awful smell was making it hard for them to remain there.

"Man, if that's dinner, I am glad we didn't wait in line," said Hayden, wrinkling his nose. Tim agreed.

They continued to follow Rhoda. She walked off the main path and into a narrow alley between rows of shanties made of cardboard boxes. They appeared to be mostly uninhabited, and Grace assumed their occupants were either waiting in line or dragging garbage around.

Rhoda stopped in front of a pile of wreckage that appeared to have once been a house. She gestured for them to follow her, and they did, carefully stepping around broken boards and bits of debris. It was then Grace who sniffed the air. She had been trying not to breathe any more than absolutely necessary because of the stench of burning trash and the disgusting, fishy-smelling jerky. But now a sweet smell filled her nostrils and she allowed it to go deep into her lungs. It smelled smoky, meaty, and intoxicatingly familiar.

"Barbecue!"

Hayden and Tim looked at her as if she were speaking a foreign language.

"Huh?" Hayden said.

Grace's face brightened. "I know that smell. It smells like… *home!*"

They followed Rhoda behind a partial brick wall and into a courtyard. It was as if they had entered another world. There were roughly ten or twelve people standing in line in front of a man who was cooking on two horizontal metal drum sections that had been fashioned into BBQ pits. Next to him was a table set up with plates and forks and a huge basket of rolls.

"Yeah! All right!" Hayden shouted.

As they approached the line, Grace stared at the man who was cooking. He had long metal tongs in his hand and was expertly turning chicken covered in a rich brown sauce slightly blackened by the heat. He moved to the other drum, grabbed a sweet potato with his tongs, and placed it on a large platter that was sitting on the table. He worked quickly and efficiently, all the time with a big smile on his face. He whistled a tune that sounded so familiar, and Grace instantly recognized him as the man from the orchard. He looked younger than she had remembered him, though. He had a thin face covered in brown scruff. His hair was short and slightly curly, and his eyes were a warm brown hue.

"Lunch is nearly ready!" he announced enthusiastically.

"That's music to my ears!" Tim responded.

"Sweet!" said Hayden. "That's the best news I've heard in a long, long time.

"What about registering?" Grace whispered cautiously to them. "I mean, maybe there's a reason only a few people are here."

Despite her misgivings, she followed Hayden and Tim to the back of the line and continued to watch the happy chef, who was busy flipping chicken and potatoes onto platters as if he were in a choreographed dance, all the while whistling his happy tune.

"Wow, this is great! It smells so good!" Hayden exclaimed.

Grace looked at the other people in line. They were filthy and dressed in rags. One guy hobbled on crutches, his foot wrapped in an unhygienic-looking cloth. A curvy, young woman in a stained and very short pink dress flirted with a man wearing overalls. Another man appeared and got in line behind them. He was smoking a cigarette and coughing after each drag. Grace couldn't help but notice his teeth, the ones that were still there, were stubby and yellow. His mouth was dried and cracked and she looked away in disgust. She turned to face Hayden and Tim.

"Look, I don't think we belong here. I don't know if it's right that we accept this food. Maybe we should go back and try to sign up for vouchers."

Hayden looked at her. "Are you crazy? That would take forever. Not to mention, that food looked terrible! We are hungry, this looks awesome, and no one is stopping us. As I always say, if providence smiles at you, smile back! "

"But what if we get in trouble? I don't feel right about this. Maybe they're not able to work. We aren't like them. They are all… poor and…helpless."

Tim spoke up, "But Grace, *we* are poor and helpless."

Grace gulped, and her stomach growled as if voicing its agreement with Tim's statement.

A group of men closer to the front of the line were having a heated discussion, and Grace eavesdropped for a moment.

"No, it happened because of all the immorality in this town," one man proclaimed, glaring at the girl in the pink dress. "We have been judged, found guilty, and now we are being punished."

"That's ridiculous," another countered. "Pleasant Grove is not any worse than any other town. As a matter of fact, we are better than most. It must be to teach us a lesson, you know, to help build our character."

"No, no," butted in a third man. "There is no rhyme or reason to pain and suffering. Stuff just happens."

The men caught Grace and her friends listening and shifted their attention to them. The third man eyed Grace.

"What do *you* think?"

By this time, the line had moved up and they were almost to the table. Grace looked up at the man from the orchard and saw he was looking directly at her. He smiled.

Grace looked back uncomfortably in the general direction of the men, feeling like she had been found out. Her thought from earlier returned, that she was somehow to blame for the storm. It didn't really make sense, but a part of her felt guilty.

"I don't know," she mumbled.

The first man scowled at her, and turned his attention back to the food line. It was now his turn, and he grabbed a plate of food from the Orchard Owner. He didn't say thank you; instead, he asked him the same question.

"What do *you* think caused this storm to come and destroy our town? It was because of all the immoral things happening behind closed doors, wasn't it?"

The second man shoved him forward and snatched the next plate.

"No, there's a plan behind everything; there's a purpose for this, right?"

The third man simply shook his head.

The Orchard Owner smiled and put hot rolls on each of their plates, then calmly spoke.

"I'd have to say D, none of the above. But why are you trying to answer such tough questions on empty stomachs?" He slapped an extra piece of chicken on each of their plates and grinned. "This is great sauce. I made it myself."

The three gave him strange looks and walked away abruptly and sat down at a picnic table. It was now Grace's turn in line.

"I know you. I remember you from the orchard."

She turned to Hayden. "Remember, Hayden?"

Hayden looked at the man, paused, and whispered discretely to Grace. "It was pretty dark. Are you sure that's the same guy?"

The man handed Grace a heaping plate of mouth-watering food and looked directly into her eyes.

"It's not your fault, you know," he said in a low voice.

"Wha…what?" Grace stammered, caught off guard.

"Enjoy the barbecue!" he said in a normal tone. "I made it just like home." He winked at her.

"Oh, and here is a plate made up especially for your puppy. All meat and no bones!"

Grace thanked the man sheepishly, took her plate, and walked away, feeling baffled.

Tim and Hayden accepted their plates of food with smiles and followed Grace. The only empty spots that remained at the tables were near the seductively dressed woman and her boyfriend. They sat down, with Grace managing a half smile in the direction of the woman.

As Grace picked up her fork, she realized for the first time that her hands were filthy. It occurred to her that she hadn't looked in a mirror in days and imagined she must be quite a spectacle. It was not like her to be so unmindful of her appearance.

She looked over and saw Hayden conversing with a man whose face was covered in barbecue sauce. Tim was lost in his meal, looking content.

Rhoda approached the table carrying her own plate, which held nearly as big a portion as the adults'. She grinned, and Grace scooted closer to Tim to make room. The little girl sat down, snuggled up to Grace, and took a big bite of chicken.

Grace smiled at Rhoda and then looked up to survey the strange picnic of the homeless and needy, dining happily in the midst of rubble. It was at that moment it hit her: she *was* just like them.

She picked up her own piece of chicken and took a big bite. Her taste buds immediately registered the juicy, meaty, sweet, tangy, and smoky flavors. She closed her eyes, her body receiving the protein in thanks. She experienced the pure, exquisite ecstasy that comes with being completely satisfied and content in the moment.

As she continued to dine, her spirit seemed to lighten with every bite. She looked around and noticed others were laughing and talking. The arguments had ceased and no unkind words were being spoken.

The three men who had been debating earlier were seated at a table directly behind Grace, and she overheard their discussion.

"Wow, it's really amazing how our whole town has come together in this disaster," one remarked.

"Yes, before the storm I kept to myself. I didn't even know the names of my neighbors, even though I've lived in the same house for twenty-seven years," the second remarked.

"This is the best chicken!" the third exclaimed, his words muffled, betraying a mouthful of food.

Hayden and Grace both looked up at the same time and their eyes met. Their faces covered in BBQ sauce, they laughed spontaneously.

Grace marveled at how the food was completely changing everyone, from the inside out.

# CHAPTER 7

# THE PAWN SHOP

*"I never thought much of the courage of a lion tamer.*
*Inside the cage he is at least safe from people."*

— GEORGE BERNARD SHAW

The talking and laughter around the tables reverberated off broken-down walls and heaps of wreckage. There was a palpable change in the atmosphere as the ragamuffin crew dined together. For a moment, things that had seemed so large before—differences, fears, prejudices, and selfishness—grew smaller with every bite. Like happy time travelers, they were transported to a better reality.

The Orchard Owner came by each table carrying pitchers of iced tea with clanking ice cubes and slices of lemons. He stopped at Grace's table and poured each of them a tall glass.

"There is plenty of food here," he announced. "Everyone make sure to have as much as you want!"

He smiled and patted Rhoda on the head. She looked up at him, beaming.

Just then a woman shuffled into the camp. Grace recognized her as the one dragging the chair earlier.

"What's this?" she asked, sounding surprised.

The chatter subsided. The Orchard Owner put the pitchers down and began dishing up a plate of food.

"My famous barbecue. It's been in my family forever."

He walked over to the lady, who looked nervous, and offered her the plate. The woman's eyes grew wide, and she looked panicked. She shoved the plate away, causing the plate of food to fall to the ground. Barbecue sauce splattered all over the Orchard Owner's feet. Terrence ran over, happy to help clean up the spilled food.

"This isn't right!" the woman began. "I've been working all day to earn my meal, and these people"—she pointed towards Grace's table—"they haven't lifted a finger! Don't you know it's dangerous to give away food? People are lazy and won't work if you give them something for nothing! Look at this group of lawbreakers! Don't you know who these people are?"

"I know exactly who they are," the Orchard Owner replied, his smile never wavering. "You look exhausted and hungry. Won't you sit down and have something to eat?"

The woman didn't calm down. "I'm not eating anything you're serving! The godverment has warned us about consuming unauthorized food. They've also warned us about rebels like you! How do I know this food isn't poisoned?"

Her face turning a darker shade of red, she continued her rant. "We trust the godverment to tell us what is safe. We trust the godvernment to feed us! Who are you to challenge the ways of god?" She paused, waiting for his response.

The Orchard Owner looked directly into the woman's eyes and asked, "Why work so hard for food that doesn't satisfy you?"

He smiled warmly, bent down, and began to clean up the mess.

Grace noticed the flirtatious woman in the short, stained dress quietly get up from the table and approach the scene. At first Grace thought she was going to confront the angry woman, but instead she did something completely unexpected.

She had picked up a napkin from the table. As she knelt to the ground, her short dress exposed too much and her breasts spilled out scandalously, but she didn't seem to notice. She began gently wiping the barbecue sauce from the Orchard Owner's feet.

The other woman was quiet for a moment, looking at the two of them suspiciously.

"I can see what kind of business you have going on here," she spat. "I know what kind of woman she is, and what that makes you. I am going to report you and all these criminals to the godvernment!" With that, she stormed off.

The woman on the ground stood up, adjusted her dress, and looked sheepishly downward. "I am sorry if I embarrassed you..." Her voice trailed off.

The Orchard Owner looked at her with compassionate eyes. "I am not embarrassed by you."

The woman looked up, questioningly. Her whole countenance began to change, and a broad smile lit up her face. "Thank you," she whispered as she quietly returned to her seat.

Many of the others seated at the tables began mumbling to each other. The "magic" of the meal had been overshadowed by the woman's accusations. An atmosphere of fear drifted into the picnic like a fog. The group of three men who had been arguing earlier, along with several others, got up and left quickly. Not one of them paused to thank their gracious host.

Hayden looked at Grace from across the table. "Maybe we should get going."

She turned to Tim, who was nodding his head. "Yeah, that lady seemed serious about informing the authorities. I don't think we want to be here if they come."

Rhoda, the woman in the short dress, her boyfriend, and a few others were continuing to enjoy what remained on their plates.

The three companions got up from the table and prepared to leave. Grace approached the Orchard Owner, who was now busy scrubbing the grill with a cleaning brush.

"Thank you for feeding us. It was delicious," she said shyly. "Um, please be careful not to get in trouble with the godvernment."

"You're welcome, glad you enjoyed it, and there's no need to worry. The godvernment sees lawbreakers and judges them. I see hungry people and feed them. Everything will work out fine, believe me."

With that, the strange, kindhearted man reached for a roll and tossed it to Grace. "Here's one for the road! Happy traveling." Grace stuffed the roll into the pocket of her jacket, thanked the man once again, and said good-bye.

As they made their way out of the town, the level of destruction decreased. Many houses were still intact, although most were covered in graffiti. Smashed windows showed jagged glass edges, and trash littered the sidewalks. A few people hid in the shadows between buildings, watching the ambling group pass by.

"This neighborhood doesn't feel safe," Tim said.

"Yeah, it definitely gives off weird vibes. If I was a criminal, I'd be lurking around here," observed Hayden.

As if on cue, a man with a scruffy mustache stepped out of the shadows and directly in front of Grace, blocking her path. He had a cold expression, and he was wearing a suit that was too big and torn at the sleeves.

"Hello there! You're not from around here, are you?" He glanced briefly at the guys then his eyes fell back on Grace and he grinned at her, exposing several missing teeth. Terrence jumped between Grace and the man and began to growl.

"Easy, mutt, I won't hurt the pretty girl, don't worry."

Grace looked to Tim and Hayden for help.

"Hey, man, we're just passing through," Hayden said peaceably.

The man looked at him, sizing him up, then at Tim, who was glaring and clenching his fists. The man ignored them both and turned his attention back to Grace.

"So, beautiful, if you find yourself in need of food vouchers, come find me. I can get you a real job in no time."

He winked and stepped out of her way, crossing the street and disappearing through the door of what looked to be a warehouse. Terrence stopped growling and rubbed against Grace's leg.

"That was... disturbing," Grace said.

Tim touched her arm gently. "Don't worry, if he would have tried anything, I would have cut him down to size." Grace cracked a smile.

Hayden giggled. "Whoa! Timmy's a fighter. Who knew!"

At what appeared to be the edge of town they approached a run-down building that stood alone. A sign that read "Pawn Shop," painted in messy handwriting, was displayed over the door. The windows were barred, but a light could be seen coming from inside.

"Maybe we should go in and ask how far it is to the EC," Grace suggested.

Tim nodded. "Sounds good! Let's see if anyone is home."

Grace pushed open the door, which was glass but covered in black paper, and walked in. Tim, Hayden, and Terrence followed. Inside it was dark and musty. Oversized bookshelves were crammed with outdated appliances, assorted knickknacks, and rows upon rows of bits and pieces that were once treasured possessions. There was an ugly purple couch that looked like it had been clawed by an angry cat. Stacks of records stood on the floor as high as Grace's waist. Behind a counter, a man stood polishing a bracelet with a cloth. He had a tired face and droopy skin around his eyes, with big fish lips that were cracked and pursed. He looked up at Grace momentarily but said nothing.

Drawing closer, Grace spoke up. "Excuse me, sir, I was wondering if you could tell us how far it is to the EC?"

Grace looked at the counter display. Underneath the glass there were pieces of vintage-looking jewelry. She saw a gold ring with a large emerald. The man noticed her gaze.

"You like?"

Ignoring her inquiry the man reached behind him and pulled a small key off a hook on the wall. Unlocking the case from behind, he pulled out the ring. Grace stared at it for a moment, lost in the depth of the green. Her trance was broken when suddenly the front door burst open and a short girl with wild black hair with caramel highlights stormed into the room.

"Frank, I couldn't find your damn sink part. What else do you want?" she demanded, addressing the man behind the counter and ignoring the others.

Frank chuckled and put the ring away.

"It's there, I know it is. You've gotta find it. It's the last thing on the list."

The girl brushed past Grace angrily.

"Come on, it's only one thing! Gimme those food vouchers, I need them!" she said, leaning over the counter, growling at the man.

Her oversized blue hoodie hung over skinny jeans and was rolled up at the sleeves; her outstretched arms revealed several tattoos. There were colorful tribal designs and markings, along with the words "Only God can judge me" inscribed on her right bicep.

Frank didn't seem fazed by the girl's aggressiveness. He grabbed her face with a chubby hand and squeezed it slightly.

"Go find me that part. If you can't, you will owe me big."

The girl went rigid and jerked the man's hand from her face.

She continued as if the others were not in the room.

"I told you I couldn't find it, Frank! Just pay me what you owe me, and don't try to screw me over or you'll be sorry!"

"Wait… You don't have to do anything for him," Grace announced. "I know where you can get food for free."

The girl turned and glared at Grace as if she was seeing her for the first time. She had the biggest dark-brown eyes Grace had ever seen.

"Are you talking to me? This is none of your business! Free food, are you crazy? Not in this filthy dump. Who are you anyway?"

Grace swallowed, attempting to remain unaffected by the girl's harsh words.

"I'm Grace. This is Hayden and Tim. We just ate at a place where a man was giving away really good food for free. I can tell you how to get there. We're on our way to the EC. Do you know how far it is?"

The girl looked even angrier. "EC? Never heard of it. But I'm not from this god-forsaken place."

"The EC. Good luck with that," said Dirty Frank, smirking at Grace. "The EC is very far away." He turned to the tattooed girl. "She's lying to you. There is no free food! Stick with me and I'll make sure you get fed."

Tim stepped forward. "Come with us," he spoke to the girl. "You don't belong here."

The girl softened slightly. With her short stature and tanned skin she looked almost like a child. Grace nodded, touching the girl's arm.

"Yes, come with us. We are going to see The Wizard to get help. I'm not from around here either, and I need The Wizard to help me get back to Texas.

"You, mingling with the beautiful people of the EC! Are you joking?! They don't accept your kind there. I bet they wouldn't even let you in!" Dirty Frank said, laughing, pointing at the girl.

The girl looked at Grace with wild, fearful eyes, and then she jerked her arm away and turned to face Frank.

"All right, Frank, I'm out. There ain't nothing wrong with me! You are the loser! And don't think I'm going to forget about the vouchers you owe me!"

The man clenched his fists behind the counter, his face turning red.

"I owe you nothing," he yelled. "Get the hell out of here, all of you! I got better things to do than waste my time with trash like you."

The girl lunged at Frank and threw a punch that narrowly missed his face.

Backing away from the corner, the man shouted, "Get out now! Last warning!"

The girl eyed Frank defiantly, slowly turned around, and flounced out the door. The pawnshop owner was spewing curses as the others followed, making a hasty exit, Terrence growling roughly.

Once outside, the girl began walking rapidly up the road in the same direction the three friends were traveling. They followed close behind, trying to keep up. Finally, they had almost caught up with the girl.

"Hey," Grace called. "Are you okay? If you are hungry, I can tell you where… "

The girl turned around, glaring at Grace. "Free food, yeah right, who are you trying to fool?" she said hotly. "Nothing in the world is free." She turned and began walking again.

Grace turned to Hayden and threw up her hands. Hayden shrugged and responded, "The more the merrier!"

The three companions walked briskly to catch up with the girl as the town faded in the distance. Her thick, frizzy hair stuck out like the mane of a lion.

"So, what's your name?" Hayden asked the girl.

"Leona," she responded tersely.

"Where are you from?" Grace asked.

"Don't remember. Feels like I've been here forever, but I think it's only been a short while. Everything is so blurry...screwed up royally. What a freakin' nightmare."

Grace nodded her understanding. She suddenly had a strange feeling like she had met Leona before, but she couldn't remember where.

They walked in silence for a good while as the path began to zigzag up foothills, the mountains looming in the distance. Grace sighed. It's going to be a long hike, she thought to herself. It had been hours since the chicken feast, and the sun was sinking down behind the mountains.

She watched Leona walk confidently ahead, as if charging forward ready to fight some unseen foe. Hayden ambled along, looking around and taking in the changing scenery, occasionally tripping on a rock or root. Tim walked behind them all, a slow and steady presence that made him seem like their guardian, despite his downward gaze. As always, Terrence trotted faithfully beside Grace, occasionally stopping to sniff something, then running to catch up.

"Come on!" Leona shouted impatiently from the top of the hill. How does she have so much energy? Grace pondered.

Tim smiled wearily. "What that girl lacks in size, she makes up for in spunk."

Hayden was already collapsing on a rock halfway up the hill. "Food," he groaned.

"Why don't you meditate and ask the universe to bring us some?" Tim joked.

He helped Hayden to his feet, and they continued up the hill. The terrain had gradually been changing from dry prairie to tropical lushness. The trees along the path were not like the evergreens of the previous forest, but massive trees with huge leaves

and dangling vines. Grace saw several colorful birds flitting between the trees. It was gorgeous scenery, but she was in no mood
for sightseeing, as the path was leading them straight into a moun-
tainous jungle, just in time for nightfall.

"Whoaaa! Did you see that?"

Hayden was looking upward at a bright yellow bird taking flight
above his head. Grace remembered his fascination with birds.

"Yes, Hayden," Grace replied, half-smiling at his childlike
enthusiasm.

They kept walking even as the last bit of light faded out of the
day. Luckily, the moon was full and shone bright enough through
the trees to enable them to make out the path. Grace was just
about to suggest they look for a place to camp when Tim stopped
suddenly.

"Hey, take a look through those trees," he said, pointing into
the jungle off the right side of the trail. "Do you see that flickering
light?"

Hayden disappeared into the forest in the direction Tim was
pointing. In a few seconds he called out, "Come on. It looks like a
campfire!"

The others followed, Leona recklessly tromping through the
underbrush, Tim following after at his methodical pace, and Grace
reaching down to scoop Terrence up into her arms, taking up the
rear, carefully watching her step.

When they arrived they saw Hayden standing in front of a blaz-
ing campfire positioned perfectly in front of a rock ledge, provid-
ing warmth and shelter. "Sweet!" he exclaimed. "Welcome to the
jungle! Awesome!"

"Hello? Is anyone there? Hello?" Grace called out a number of
times, but there was no reply.

They looked around thoroughly. Other than the fire, there
wasn't any sign that would indicate someone had been there. "No
bedding, no food, nothing," said Tim, who had also checked out

the perimeter of the clearing. "I don't see or hear anyone. It's like they disappeared."

"This is very strange," said Grace. "I mean, I don't know if we should stay."

"Yeah, this ain't right," Leona agreed.

"Well, whoever built this fire is bound to be back soon," Tim said. "I say we wait and see who shows up. In the meantime, Hayden, let's you and I gather up some firewood. Maybe whoever it is will allow us to camp out here tonight. It's too dark to go on any further."

Grace joined the guys in gathering up wood from around the perimeter of the campsite. Leona stayed near the fire, standing watch in case the mysterious camper returned, her ears attuned to the symphony of jungle noises.

After a few minutes Grace returned with her arms loaded down with firewood. Hayden followed shortly carrying a load so large he could barely see over the top of it. After dropping his haul onto Grace's pile, he picked up a few limbs and added them to the fire.

Tim emerged soon after carrying a stack of limbs with something odd piled on top.

"Dinner!" he exclaimed, adding his wood to the pile and holding up a small stalk of bananas. "Not too many here, but beggars can't be choosers. Looks to be one apiece. Everyone grab one."

Leona lunged toward Tim and snatched the largest one off the stalk. She immediately sat down beside the fire, peeled the banana, and almost without chewing, devoured hers in seconds.

"What are you looking at?" Leona said when she noticed the others staring at her. They all looked away quickly.

"Thanks, Tim." Hayden walked over, snapped two bananas off, and handed one to Grace. They sat down and began eating, thankful for even a small bit of food.

Hayden and Grace had almost finished theirs when Tim broke off the last banana. He hesitated for a moment, then walked over to Leona and placed it in her lap. "Here, you can have mine. I had a big lunch."

Leona grabbed the fruit and tried handing it back to Tim as he walked away. "I'm not taking this! What's your game, man?"

A light rain began to fall.

"No game. I'm just not really hungry."

"Suit yourself," Leona said defensively, then peeled the banana and took a big bite. Tim smiled and sat down alongside the others.

The light rain quickly became a steady downpour, and the four companions huddled under the rock ledge, warming themselves by the fire. No one spoke for some time, as they all appeared mesmerized by the sound of the falling rain. Grace did notice Leona occasionally glancing in Tim's direction.

"I'm thirsty," Hayden announced suddenly, standing up. "I will show you all how to quench your thirst in the jungle." He walked out from underneath the ledge and stood in the pouring rain, with his head tilted back and his mouth wide open.

Grace and Tim chuckled. "Have a drink for me, my friend!" Tim called out.

"I know a better way," Leona said as she stood up and walked toward Hayden. "Come with me, Tarzan, and I'll show you how it's done." She grabbed hold of his shirt and led him to a grove of large plants on the other side of the campsite. The leaves of the plants were huge and formed in such a way that rainwater collected in them like a bowl.

"Watch." Leona bent down and sipped water from one of the leaves.

Hayden observed and quickly did the same. He stood up, smiling. "Groovy!" He leaned over to have another drink. Tim and Grace followed suit as the rainfall had now decreased to a light shower. Grace helped Terrence get a drink as well.

After receiving the much-needed hydration, they returned and sat underneath the natural awning, drying themselves by the fire.

"I wonder what happened to whoever started this," Grace said. Hayden shrugged his shoulders. By this time everyone was having trouble staying awake. They agreed to sleep in shifts, taking turns keeping watch and stoking the fire.

Tim volunteered to take the first shift. Hayden drifted off instantly, and Grace was nearly asleep when she heard Tim and Leona talking quietly.

"I hadn't eaten in a long time," Leona said, a sad bitterness in her voice. "I couldn't even swallow what the godvernment was calling food. I had decided it would be better to starve."

"I understand," Tim replied.

"You guys are all right," Leona said sleepily.

"You're not bad yourself. Now get some rest."

Grace opened her eyes a bit and saw Tim staring at the flames with a look of pure contentment on his face. Grace was thankful for peace and allowed sleep to overtake her, body and soul.

# CHAPTER 8
# OUT OF THE JUNGLE

*"We may have all come on different ships, but we're in the same boat now."*

— Martin Luther King, Jr.

Morning came early with the shrill sound of birds chattering. Grace woke up, stretched, and saw Leona poking the few remaining embers with a stick. The sun was rising, and through the canopy of trees it appeared to be a clear day.

"We were just about to wake you, sleepyhead," Hayden said cheerfully. "Okay, Tim, she's awake, let's get this fire put out." The two guys began scooping up dirt with their hands and throwing it onto the embers.

"Good morning, Leona," Grace said as she stood up, brushing herself off.

"Yeah, okay. We need to get going if we are going to try and make it to the EC today," Leona replied.

Grace ignored Leona's lack of morning decorum and chatted with Tim and Hayden as they finished their chore. In a few minutes the campfire was completely extinguished, and the quirky quartet and the little pooch hit the trail once more.

The path wound up a small green mountain, zig-zagging back and forth. Luckily, the switchbacks made for a gradual incline that wasn't too tiring.

Turning down the path at one of the switchbacks, they could hear the sound of water flowing. The group agreed they all needed a drink and to clean up a bit.

Rounding the corner, they saw a small waterfall a few yards off the path, flowing over a rock ledge into a small pool surrounded by trees. Grace shouted in delight. It looked so inviting, the group immediately took off their shoes, rolled up their pants, and waded in.

The water was shockingly cold and invigorating. Everyone ended up getting wetter than expected, so afterwards they all sat on a rock to dry out in the sunshine.

Hayden gazed at the waterfall, deep in thought.

"Man, being out here, you really get down to your basic needs, you know?"

"I know what you mean," Grace said. "You really only need food and water to survive. And sleep, of course."

"People are trapped by need," Hayden continued. "We believe we need things that didn't even exist a hundred years ago. And the more we have, the less and less content we become."

"Yep. No matter what we have, it's never enough," said Tim. "People are never going to stop being fueled by selfish desires. And fear. We're driven by fear."

Something that was said seemed to hit a nerve in Leona.

"Is that such a bad thing? I mean, going after what you need to survive? You gotta do what you gotta do." She stood up, leaned against a tall tree, and began picking off the bark with her small hands. She seemed irritated.

"Leona, what do you want to ask The Wizard?" Grace asked kindly.

"I don't need to ask him anything. Besides, I know you only invited me to come along because you felt sorry for me. Well, guess what? I don't need your pity. I was fine by myself!"

Grace was shocked by Leona's abruptness and looked down sheepishly. The others looked uncomfortable as well.

Leona noticed the effect of her sharpness and, after a short but awkward silence, spoke up.

"But it's cool, I'll tag along for a while. Nothing better to do anyway," she said with a little grin and began putting her socks back on.

One by one the others followed suit, and once everyone was dressed and ready, the four travelers and dog made their way back to the path to continue their journey to the EC.

Hours later, they finally made it down the other side of the small mountain. The path was now winding through a valley, the lush jungle vegetation thinning out. The sun was only intermittently peeking through the tall canopy of trees. The humidity was increasing, and exotic insects buzzed around their heads.

Grace noticed some bright blue birds in the trees above. She found herself humming the tune that the Orchard Owner had been whistling. Her anticipation grew with the hope of reaching her destination. She looked at her companions, hopeful that they too would find what they were looking for.

As the path reached the edge of the jungle, it opened up, revealing a massive lake. It spanned what appeared to be many miles and ran along the whole edge of the jungle. In the far distance, a city skyline was visible.

"That must be it!" shouted Grace.

"So close, yet so far away," lamented Hayden.

"There's got to be a way to get around this," said Leona.

Tim shaded his eyes with his hand to avoid the sun reflecting off the lake. "The path ends at the shore of the lake."

They all walked ahead to see. He was right, the path stopped at the shoreline where water lapped against a grass-covered bank. Tim noticed an old wooden rowboat nestled in some tall reeds.

"I'll take a look at it." Tim took off his shoes and waded into the shallow water through the reeds, pulling the boat by a fraying rope that was tied to a rock on the shore.

"I don't feel right about using it without permission," Grace said, looking around nervously.

"It looks like it's about to fall apart," scoffed Leona. "It's obviously been abandoned."

"It's going to take a very long time to walk around this lake. Let's just see if it can hold us, then we can decide whether or not we should try to go across," decided Grace.

"I'm not getting in that thing," said Leona. "It's tiny! It may not even hold our weight."

"We could go across two at a time," suggested Hayden.

"Then one will have to come back and get the others. I think we can all fit. Let's just try it," Tim said, applying his eye drops.

Leona grumbled, "Fine, but if you guys sink me, I won't be happy." She kicked at the water with the toe of her shoe.

Hayden, Grace, and Leona piled into the small boat, Grace holding Terrence carefully on her lap. Tim pushed the boat off the shore and jumped in, rocking it and splashing water on them.

"We're gonna sink," Hayden said as the water splashed into the boat and wet their feet.

"Nahhhh, we'll be fine," said Grace, trying hard to believe it. .

With the weight of four people in the boat, the sides were only a few inches from the waterline. It creaked as Tim grabbed the oars that were resting in the middle.

"I'll start rowing," he offered.

Grace shifted carefully, trying to keep the weight evenly distributed. Tim awkwardly lifted up the oars and started rowing out toward the middle of the lake.

"You're splashing me!" complained Leona, who sat in the front.

Hayden sat in the back, shaking his head. "I wish I had something to bail with."

Tim kept rowing. Grace looked at the shoreline growing farther away and wondered if they had made the right decision.

"*Ow!*" Tim cried out suddenly as he let go of the oar and grabbed his shoulder. The oar slipped out of the holder and splashed into the water. The boat rocked.

Hayden grabbed for the oar but it was too late. The old oar disappeared into the deep.

"Are you okay?" he asked Tim.

"I think I pulled something. I dropped the oar." Tim looked dejectedly toward that side of the boat.

"I knew this was a bad idea," snapped Leona.

"Leona," Grace snapped back, "Tim just hurt himself. I don't see *you* doing anything to help!"

Leona looked at her angrily and then stood up.

"Don't! You're gonna tip the boat," Grace warned sharply.

Leona ignored her. "Move, Tim, let me do it." She shuffled toward the middle, and Tim, still holding his shoulder, crawled to the front.

"Let me do it," Hayden said. "There's only one oar now, it's going to be hard."

"Don't tell me what I can't do!" said Leona defiantly.

She sat down, grabbed the remaining oar, and began to row. The boat started to move slightly, but at an angle as she was only rowing on the one side.

"You need to even it out," said Hayden. "Try pulling it out of its holder and switching it back and forth."

Leona yanked on the oar, and the holder gave way like the other one, snapping with a crack. The momentum caused Leona to fall back onto the bench, and the oar fell into the water, where it sank slowly out of sight.

"Wonderful," said Grace sarcastically, looking at the broken oar holder.

Leona looked at her angrily. "Whose idea was this to cross in a broken boat anyway? I suggested walking around."

"Yes, because walking miles off the path, through the jungle, would have been easier," Grace retorted.

"Better than drowning out here!" said Leona hotly. "I knew I should have gone by myself."

"Well, I'm sorry I invited you!" burst out Grace. She immediately regretted saying it and knew she couldn't take it back, but tried anyway.

"I didn't mean it, Leona. Look, I'm sorry."

"Whatever, being sorry doesn't change the fact that we're stuck out here."

"This is my fault," said Tim, putting his head in his hands. "I suggested it. I thought I could keep you guys safe." His voice trailed off as he grabbed for his bottle of eye drops.

"Guys, come on! Let's not fight, let's use our heads! We can get out of here," Hayden said.

"Okay, what's your big idea? Are you going to turn into a bird so you can fly us over the lake?" Grace asked.

Hayden pondered for a moment. "Hey, not a bad idea…. Do we have any food left? We can coax some birds to come, then use our clothing to tie them to the boat and they'll pull us, like in that kid's book about the huge peach. Mmmm, I wish I had a peach right now."

"Are you serious?" said Leona. "Birds? Why don't you jump in the water and pull us to the other side? Now that's a plan!"

"At least he's trying to think of something instead of just being negative," Grace said, defending Hayden.

"All my fault," moaned Tim. "It would have been better if you had just left me alone in the woods."

"Yeah, I should have stayed at that apple orchard, just chillin' in the hammock eating fruit," Hayden said.

"I was better off scavenging for Dirty Frank than being stuck on a boat," said Leona, crossing her arms.

Silence filled the boat.

They floated in the middle of the lake. The air was still; there wasn't even the slightest breeze.

Grace's stomach growled. That sparked a memory. She reached in her jacket pocket and found the extra roll from the barbeque.

She felt trapped. She was starving and she didn't have enough bread for her, much less to share. *Great*, she thought, *stuck floating in the middle of a listless lake without a paddle.* Terrence whimpered, and she looked down, realizing she was petting his fur backwards.

She absent-mindedly tore off a small piece from the roll and nibbled on it. As she swallowed, she remembered how the bread was a gift and thought about the needy people in Pleasant Grove. She thought about the kindness of the Orchard Owner and how he loved feeding the hungry.

Squeezing the roll tightly in her hand, she looked around the boat at the crew, miserable and silent, staring out at the lake. Tim looked so broken hearted. Hayden looked confused and lost, like he was trying to concentrate on something but couldn't. Leona looked angry, but there was something else just beneath the surface. Grace realized it with sudden clarity as she looked into her wide, brown eyes. She was afraid.

Swallowing hard and taking a deep breath, Grace offered the roll to Leona.

"Here. It's not a lot, but have some."

Leona looked up at her suspiciously.

"I'm fine," she said. Just as she said it her stomach growled.

"Please," Grace said. "Have some. I want you to have it."

Leona stared directly at Grace with a look of childlike confusion. "Why are you doing this?"

"Because you are hungry." Grace smiled and put the roll in Leona's hand.

Leona looked down at the bread and mumbled thank you. She tore a chunk off the roll and then passed it on to Tim.

Tim shook his head. "No, I don't deserve any. It's my fault we're out here. You all eat it."

Leona shook her head. "It's not your fault. Eat." As Grace heard those words she remembered them being spoken to her by someone else.

Tim looked up at Leona, surprised.

"It's not your fault," Grace repeated earnestly. Tim took the roll out of Leona's hand, tore off a bit of it, and stuffed it in his mouth, chewing slowly.

He continued the circle by passing it on to Hayden.

"Man, no, I'm okay. I'll be fine, I've fasted for days at a time. I can…"

All three of them interrupted him. "Eat!"

Hayden smiled and grabbed a chunk and handed it back to Grace, who expected it to be nearly gone.

She gave a piece to Terrence, who gobbled it up, tail wagging. "Um, you guys can have more. There is still plenty."

They passed it around again, this time each taking bigger pieces.

"How is this possible?" Tim spoke what they were all thinking.

The roll was not shrinking in size. It stayed the same no matter how much they took. They passed it around again, almost ceremonially. Each person was able to eat as much as they wanted. Terrence ate his fill as well.

"Just when I thought I'd seen it all," remarked Hayden, laughing and shaking his head.

They all laughed along with Hayden. The bread had changed everyone's mood, and they chatted excitedly about the day's events.

"You know," began Tim, looking seriously at each person, "even though we have only been together a short time, I feel a connection to all of you."

Grace nodded. Looking from person to person, seeing the afternoon light on their faces, she was filled with gratitude that she wasn't alone.

"We're all in the same boat," she said softly.

"Pun intended!" Hayden joked.

Leona didn't say anything, but looked peaceful.

"Look!"

Tim broke the stillness, pointing into the water. Arising from the depths of the lake there appeared dozens, then hundreds, and then seemingly thousands of strange luminescent objects.

"Jellyfish!" Hayden shouted.

"Jellyfish? That's impossible!" said Grace. "They only live in the ocean. Right?"

They all watched in wonderment as the jellyfish moved in unison, like dancers in a choreographed routine. Reaching the surface they rubbed their bodies against the bottom of the boat and swam in the direction of the shoreline, so strongly that the boat began to move. The water appeared fully illuminated with the stunning underwater light show. No one spoke a word.

Ever so slightly, then steadily and surely, the boat began to drift in the same direction as the jellyfish.

The temperature began to cool and a breeze arose, tussling Grace's hair, tickling her face.

Hayden closed his eyes, feeling the rush of wind. "Whoa," he said, smiling.

Tim and Leona stared at each other for a few moments, not knowing what to say.

The breeze propelled them along even faster now, as it was blowing serendipitously in the same direction as the jellyfish, straight toward their destination.

Terrence wiggled from Grace's lap and put his paws on the edge of the boat, barking loudly as if to say, "Land ho!"

# CHAPTER 9

# THE CARNIVAL

*"It is difficult to see the picture when you are inside the frame."*

— R. S. Trapp

The boat softly scraped against the mucky bottom. All four humans and the dog jumped into the shallow water and headed to shore as Tim pulled the boat onto the bank.

For a few moments they all stood quietly on the shoreline and gazed at the lake. The jellyfish were nowhere in sight, and the wind had begun to die down. Within a few minutes the air was still once again.

Tim broke the silence. "I'm beginning to realize that life itself is a miracle, and I like that a lot!" He smiled at the others.

"So true," said Hayden softly.

Grace was too stunned to speak. She smoothed down her tousled hair. Leona looked like she wanted to say something but then caught herself before the words escaped her lips.

Gradually, they turned their attention away from the lake and onto the path that lay before them.

Hayden surveyed the situation. "Man, it's still like a day's walk, I bet."

"Yes, but at least we're getting closer," said Grace positively. She wondered how long it would take to get back to Texas from here, once The Wizard helped her figure out how.

The four companions and one little dog marched down the path.

"Do you smell something?" Hayden was sniffing the air, looking like Terrence.

By now, they had been walking for hours. The path led them up hills and down into small valleys, only to go back up again like a roller coaster. From hilltops they could see the faint outline of a cityscape, which they presumed to be the EC. They were walking up yet another hillside when Hayden sniffed the air again.

"I'm sure I smell food!" Hayden said.

Reaching the top of the hill they saw something none of them were expecting. In the valley below, there was a display of colorful tents, small buildings, booths, and a Ferris wheel. They could see people milling around and heard the faint sound of music and shouting.

"It looks like some kind of carnival," Grace said.

Tim leaned forward, trying to get a better look. "What in the world?"

"Food!" Hayden said.

Leona was ecstatic. "Finally, civilization!"

Terrence stared down the hill and began growling softly.

"What is it, boy?" asked Grace.

He looked at her and then back toward the carnival, growling again.

"It's okay, boy, they'll have food," she said, reaching down and patting his head. Terrence continued growling but loyally followed Grace down the hill along with the others.

As they neared the carnival, the smell of food vanished and was replaced by a sickeningly sweet smell mixed with a rotting stench. Grace crinkled her noise in disgust.

"What's that awful smell?"

"Yeah, that is quite a distinct odor," Tim answered.

Hayden was not concerned. "It's the smell of fun and freedom!"

"Smells like a party!" Leona agreed.

Slightly crooked pillars holding up a huge red banner marked the entrance to the carnival. On the banner in giant yellow block letters were the words:

"GAME LAND"

Underneath in smaller letters:

"Leave your worries behind"

"Yeah, that's what I am talking about! No worries, man!" Hayden looked like a little kid, bouncing as he walked.

They walked under the banner and into the fairgrounds. They passed a building painted with cartoon characters on the front under a large sign that read "Fun House". Booths were lined up in rows with men standing in front, shouting to draw attention.

"Be whoever you want to be! Live out your fantasies!"

"Win the best prize here for your lovely lady!"

"You think you're smart? Come this way and prove it to the world!" Hayden stopped when he heard this one, his curiosity piqued. He walked over to the booth under a bright neon sign with blinking lights that read "Tower of Intelligence."

"Hayden, come on, let's not get distracted. We need to find food," pleaded Grace.

But Hayden ignored her. He was captivated by the carny's pitch.

Grace turned back around to ask the others for help with Hayden, but they were gone. Looking around she noticed Leona further down the row talking with a man at another booth.

"Tim!" Grace shouted.

He was walking toward the funhouse, where a fire breather was setting up for a show. She turned back to Hayden, but by now he was sitting on a stool in front of a tall video screen. On the screen appeared to be some kind of ultra-reality video game.

"Hayden, come on. Everyone has wandered off on their own! We must stay together! Besides, we don't have any money to pay for games!"

Overhearing Grace, the man running the games spoke up. "Don't worry, pretty little lady, we don't want your money. We only want *you*...to be happy, you know." He took a drag from his large cigar, blew out a big cloud of smoke, and then smiled devilishly, revealing two gold front teeth.

"See, Grace, lighten up! Stop stressing about everything and go have some fun. It'll be good for you!" Hayden said without turning away from his game.

"Fine, have your 'fun.' I am going to find the others."

She turned away in frustration, leaving Hayden to his game. The crowd was thick, and the atmosphere was vibrant with all the bright lights, colors, and noise. She looked down at Terrence, who was thankfully right by her side. High, thick clouds and a low-hanging mist veiled the sun.

"Stay close to me, boy," she said nervously.

She continued walking down the main path, overwhelmed by all the sights, sounds, and odors. No one made eye contact, and they all walked slowly, in a trance-like state, heads down, yet somehow moving in sync, in the same direction, like a herd of sheep. Others stood at booths or sat on stools staring at screens, expressionless, mesmerized as if they were drugged.

Grace pondered how strange it was that the only food that appeared to be available was cotton candy, with vendors set up every few feet.

The only people who appeared to notice Grace were the men who ran the booths, as they all fought for her attention.

"You with the beautiful eyes, you look like you're having a bad day! Let us lighten your load!"

"Hey, gorgeous, you can be queen of the universe. You're guaranteed to win!"

"Step right up, little lady. I have games that will make you forget all your troubles! Numbness is pleasure. Lose yourself in the game!"

Grace tried her best to ignore them and walked briskly until she came upon a large red-and-white-striped tent. At the entrance was a black board that had a single word written sloppily in chalk.

"Concessions."

She breathed a sigh of relief, looked around to see if anyone was going to stop her, and then pushed her way through the fabric door and into the tent.

There were not any stands selling food in the tent like Grace had expected. Instead, she found herself next to a stage set up in front of a large audience, all seated in wooden fold-up chairs. Most of audience was made up of men, and they all looked captivated.

On stage there was a woman dressed in a thin, sparkling gold dress that barely covered her curvy body. Her long brown hair shimmered down her back as she moved her ample hips back and forth. Music started playing from the loudspeakers. It was upbeat and exotic, and Grace found herself immediately entranced by this woman. Her presence filled the entire tent with sensual electricity.

She sang along with the music in a sweet yet sultry voice, commanding attention with every note.

Grace stood still, unable to move. No one had noticed her, even though she was standing right next to the stage. The woman turned around in her dance, and Grace saw her face for the first time. Grace covered her mouth, suppressing a gasp. The woman's dark-brown eyes, thin nose, and facial features resembled her own. She was an older, curvier, sexier, more confident version of herself.

The woman locked eyes with Grace but never missed a note or a dance step. The lyrics to the song she was singing seemed directly aimed at her!

*"I am everything you want to be. Hey, hey, come to me and be free."*

She sang with passion as she slowly turned her back to the audience of men who caressed her with their eyes.

Grace was hit with a wave of jealous resolve. She knew she wasn't anything like this woman, but she wanted to be. She was sick of being ignored, of having to be the practical one. She remembered what Hayden had said about stressing over everything. She wanted the confidence and "I don't give a crap what you think" attitude that Leona had. She lusted for the sheer feminine power, sensuality, and sex appeal that this woman possessed.

Grace slowly began to sway along with the sultry music. The swaying soon turned to dancing, and she found herself drawn toward the stage. She was now dancing alongside the woman in perfect unison. The men hooted their approval, and Grace drank it in, deeply.

It was so wonderful to be adored and to have such power over the men. She had so longed for a man to tell her she was pretty. She wasn't a boring and shy girl anymore, but a strong woman, and a free spirit like her mother.

Her mother!

*RING!*

*Grace awoke to the sound of the phone ringing in the middle of the night. She pulled her small nine-year-old body out of bed, despite the fear lodged in her throat. She listened, ear pressed to her bedroom door, and by the panic in her Aunt Emily's voice, she knew something was terribly wrong.*

*Sobbing. The phone was hung up.*

*"She's gone, Harry."*

*"Oh, Emily, I am so sorry."*

*More sobbing.*

*"I have to tell Grace," her aunt managed.*

*"It can wait until morning. Let her have one more night of childhood."*

*Grace crawled back into bed stiffly, pulled the comforter over her face, put her fingers in her ears, closed her eyes, opened her mouth wide, and screamed, silently.*

Immediately, all the emotion came flooding back. She panicked and ran out of the tent, with Terrence on her heels, barking.

Grace was running with nowhere to go. The grief was fresh and as real as if it had happened yesterday. She stopped and fell to her knees off to the side of a tent. Her head was spinning, and she felt as if she was being sucked into a vortex of conflicting thoughts, desires, and emotions. Raw, fresh despair exploded from her in a fountain of tears. She couldn't stop crying. The pain was so deep, her heart felt like it was being squeezed tighter and tighter, and would soon explode…

*Oh, God…help!*

Suddenly, her thoughts turned back to her friends. Where were they? She had to find them. She got up and started to push her way through the crowd. She suddenly felt lost and vulnerable without the others. She took a few moments to catch her breath and rub away the tears from her cheeks as best she could before setting off to try to find her companions.

Grace found her way back to the main path. The men at the booths were shouting, and Terrence growled at each one, showing his teeth. She walked by a teenage boy standing in front of a large painted box and staring aimlessly into it. Lines of people stood behind him, waiting to see whatever was in the box.

"When is it going to be my turn?" someone whined.

"Man, you've been there for hours!"

Grace approached an older lady standing in line.

"Excuse me, do you know which way the entrance is?"

The woman didn't look at Grace. Instead, she stared straight ahead, teeth clenched.

"Ma'am?"

"Why would you want the entrance?" the woman finally replied, still not making eye contact. "The entrance is for coming in. Once you're in, you have everything you need."

Grace looked at her curiously.

"You have everything you need," the woman repeated robotically to herself.

Grace frowned and turned away. She approached several other people, but they ignored her. Obviously, she wasn't going to get any help from these *zombies*.

She kept walking until she spotted Leona at a booth off to the side. She was standing in front of a large dollhouse, a toy mansion that was almost as tall as she was. Grace approached from behind, trying not to startle her.

Each room of the dollhouse was meticulously decorated and furnished. The figurines, representing a family, looked particularly lifelike.

"What in the world?!" Grace said, shocked. Taking a closer look she realized the people in the dollhouse were moving!

Leona didn't look up. She was busy moving a joystick back and forth, apparently maneuvering one of the small people in the house.

Grace blinked her eyes several times. It looked so real.

"Leona, hey, what are you doing?" she asked her gently.

Leona's eyes remained fixed on the dollhouse. She spoke in a soft, gentle tone, which was unlike her.

"Setting the table. Company is coming over soon, a very important man and his wife. I need to make sure the wine is poured in the wine glasses. Everything has to be perfect."

Grace gazed at her quizzically.

"Leona, that's really nice, but this is just a game. Maybe we should go now, round up the guys and find some *real* food."

But as she spoke, Grace noticed the tiny person in the dining room of the dollhouse was indeed carrying a tiny bottle of wine to the tiny table. The person was small, even for a doll figure, and had curly frizzy hair. *Leona.* It looked exactly like her, only curvier. Grace rubbed her eyes in disbelief. Faint shivers ran down her spine.

"Wow, that's so realistic," Grace said, staring. Terrence began to bark loudly.

"Shhhh, Terrence. Hold on." Grace watched in awe as Leona maneuvered tiny Leona with the joystick, setting lace placemats on the table.

"He should be home soon. My husband." She smiled without turning her eyes from the game. "Everything is perfect."

Terrence barked again loudly.

A short man wearing a greasy baseball hat approached them.

"Is there a problem?" he asked Grace.

"No, not at all," said Grace quickly.

Terrence bared his teeth at the man.

"I am going to have to ask you to leave."

He turned to Leona. "You too."

Leona ignored him. "The guests are coming over soon. I need to finish. I need to impress the guests so I can win that teapot."

Grace noticed the row of cheap-looking metal teapots hanging from the tent above the dollhouse.

"Sorry, out of time. You lose," the man said, ripping Leona away from the controller by her shoulder. She look stunned at first, then shook her head, as if coming back to reality, and stared at the man. Grace wasn't sure if she was going to punch him. Surprisingly, she didn't, but simply turned and walked away sadly.

"What was that?!" asked Grace, catching up to her.

Leona was silent before responding. "For just a moment, everything was perfect."

They continued walking. This was no ordinary carnival, Grace realized, and she wished they were far away from it. Anxiety and a deepening fear gnawed at her stomach. All she wanted to do was find Hayden and Tim and leave as soon as possible. Before she could say anything, Leona spotted something that grabbed her attention.

"Oooooh! Cotton candy!" Leona squealed like a little girl.

Grace was bemused to see this side of Leona, and she followed her to the stand where an elderly man was spinning the silky, pink, and sugary strands into a cocoon on a paper stick.

He handed one to Leona.

"Here you are, honey. Enjoy. Would you like one?" he asked Grace.

"No, thanks," Grace responded. The thought of it was revolting.

Leona devoured her cotton candy like a wild beast, leaving a sticky pink ring around her mouth.

"Tastes kinda different and leaves a funny aftertaste, but it's so fun to eat! How can you resist?"

"Um, trust me. It isn't hard. Now come on, we have to find the guys!"

They slowly made their way back toward the carnival entrance. Grace had to continually pull Leona along, as she was often tempted by the games.

They found Hayden at the same place where Grace had left him.

A small crowd was squeezed around the booth, watching Hayden. Grace pushed her way forward while Leona hung back. Grace was about to tell him to stop playing the game and come with them when her eyes locked on the screen. It was split in two, vertically. On one side, Hayden was maneuvering a digital version of himself, picking up giant puzzle pieces that fit into each other and slowly building a tall tower on the screen.

On the other side of the screen, another digital character was building another tower, like they were racing. His hair was graying, but Grace noticed he had the same blue eyes and nose as Hayden. Grace couldn't see anyone maneuvering the man, so she assumed Hayden was playing against the computer. The computer was winning as far as she could tell.

Hayden was mesmerized, his eyes hardly blinking, his tongue poked out of the corner of his mouth in concentration.

"I am gonna beat you this time, Dad," he mumbled.

Graced stared closer at the screen.

"Hayden. Please, can we go?" She put her hand on his shoulder. He ignored her.

"Just watch. You never thought I was smart enough. I'll show you."

Grace watched his character choose a piece to assemble onto the tower. A red light went on, and the whole tower crumbled to the ground.

The words "GAME OVER" shot across the screen.

"No!" Hayden yelped, pounding his fists on the screen.

Then he noticed Grace.

"He beat me! You...you distracted me!"

"He?" Grace said skeptically. "Hayden...it was just the computer..."

The man running the game came over and ushered Grace and Hayden out.

"You lose. Better luck next time." He motioned for the next guy in line to step up.

Hayden followed Grace to where Leona stood waiting, his head hung low, mumbling to himself.

"It was just a game," Grace began.

"No," he interrupted sharply. "You don't understand! *He* was there. I failed him. *Again."* He added in a choking voice.

"Who are you talking about?" asked Leona. But Hayden didn't answer. His mind was trapped in another world.

After a short walk, they approached the entrance to the fun-house. "I have a feeling Tim is in there," Grace said, trying to be practical. "This is where I saw him last. We've got to go in." She pointed to the entrance.

The face of a creepy-looking clown was painted on the wall, and the entrance door was in the middle of his mouth. There were no carnival workers around and no customers lined up.

"I guess we just go in," Grace said, gulping. She didn't want to admit it, but she had always been afraid of clowns.

"Let me go first," said Leona, stepping forward bravely. Grace silently agreed and followed her into the mouth of the clown. Hayden trailed behind them. They walked into a dark tunnel lined with strips of lights going down both sides.

"This is weird," Grace said, feeling uneasy. "Let's just stick together."

They continued walking down the tunnel.

"Tim?" Grace called out.

No response, only an eerie silence. They continued to the end of the tunnel where a door stood. Leona twisted the doorknob and opened the door, and they walked through slowly into a room covered wall-to-wall with mirrors.

Grace immediately looked at herself, seeing the reflection within the reflection, an endless mind-bending mirage that stretched into infinity.

As she watched, her image in the mirror began to change. She saw the woman from the tent, the dancer. She locked eyes with Grace, smiling that enchanting smile and beckoning with her hands. Fear and longing surged through Grace's body, and she began to tremble. Terrence barked fiercely, causing Grace to snap out of the trance. She looked down at her little furry protector. When she looked back at her reflection it was normal again.

"Whaaaaaaaat!!" Hayden shouted in alarm at the mirror, and then he turned to look at Grace with fear in his eyes. "Dad."

Leona cursed loudly, sounding frightened as well. "What the hell is going on in this place?

A small notch where one of the mirrors didn't quite line up together caught Grace's eye. She walked over and pushed on it, and a door opened. "Let's go," she said to the others, her heart thumping violently in her chest. She desperately wanted to find Tim. Now.

They walked into a similar room, only this one was longer and wider, and the mirrors seemed endless.

Tim stood in the middle.

He didn't notice them. He was moving strangely, as if his limbs had strings attached to them and some unseen puppeteer was jerking them.

He spoke in an odd off-key voice that didn't sound like him.

"Honey, I got a promotion…"

He turned, staring at another reflection.

"Everything is good, my eyes are much better!"

He turned again, like a robot.

"Here's your early Christmas present. Yes, it's that car you wanted!"

Then Tim spun around, facing his three companions, making all of them jump. He didn't speak, but as if looking through them, he kept his eyes focused on the mirrors.

He smiled sweetly and then spoke in a different voice, deeper and breathier.

"Come sit close to me, honey, and I'll write you a love song that will make you forget all about your husband."

Grace had heard enough and decided it was time to intervene. Without thinking she ran to Tim, took him by the shoulders, and shook him repeatedly.

"Tim! Snap out of it!"

Tim's body became rigid, and he stared straight ahead with eyes as big as saucers. After a few moments, he relaxed his shoulders and looked at Grace.

"We need to leave," he said in a melancholy tone.

Grace took his hand and led him toward the door they had last walked through.

"Don't stop. Keep your eyes on the person in front of you. Don't look at the mirrors, just follow me."

Almost running, they eventually found their way through the maze of mirrors and burst through the mouth of the clown.

Safely outside, they all stopped, and Tim reached into his pocket to get his eye drops. Blinking as tears ran down his cheeks, he looked longingly toward the funhouse entrance.

Grace felt panicked, realizing this place was even more dangerous than she had thought. She was filled with an urgency to get out as soon as possible.

"Come on," she said firmly. "It's going to be dark soon. We need to find the way out."

"Yeah, seriously, let's get out of here," said Leona, back to her normal self.

Hayden nodded, his eyes beginning to focus as if coming out of a nightmare. Tim still stared into space.

They pushed through the crowds. Every once in a while, Tim would get distracted and veer off the path toward one of the games. Grace would herd him back. After a short time, he seemed normal again, as if he was coming off of a drug. They managed to get past the booths, ignoring the cries of the carnies, and slipped out a back entrance.

Making their way back to the path, they passed by a large tent that stood outside of the carnival perimeter. A few people were milling around the entrance, and smoke rose up from a pipe coming out from the center.

"Eww, what's that smell?" Leona was the first to notice it, but soon all four were holding their noses, along with their breath, as much as possible.

That sickeningly sweet smell mixed with the rotting stench was almost overwhelming.

"I wonder if it is coming from that tent," Tim said, choking on his words.

"I don't care where it's coming from, let's just get away from this stench! I feel like I'm going to hurl!" Leona said, speeding up, leading the others to follow her pace.

Once they were halfway up a hill and safely away from the carnival, Grace sank on the ground with exhaustion.

The others followed suit. They sat in a row on the hill facing the carnival as the sun was setting behind the EC in the distance.

"What the hell was that about?" Leona said, speaking for all of them.

"Shattered hopes and dreams," Tim mumbled.

"Huh?" asked Grace.

"The mirrors. They projected the man I longed to be. The man...*she* wanted me to be."

"I could have been trapped in there," said Hayden. "It was so real; I could have kept playing that game forever."

Leona said nothing, but stared off into the fading light.

Grace took a deep breath and shook off the grief of her past. She pushed it to one side of her mind and left it there, for the moment.

"Let's get out of here. We have to try to make it to the EC before it becomes too dark to see."

# CHAPTER 10

# A RESTING PLACE

*"In a world of fugitives, the person taking the opposite direction will appear to run away."*

— T.S. ELIOT

"Maybe we should think about finding somewhere to spend the night. It isn't looking like we will make it to the EC tonight," Grace said as she stopped walking.

The sky was streaked with orange and pink. The air had suddenly become chilly as the sun descended out of sight behind the hills.

Leona was not a happy camper. "Another night sleeping outside on the ground in the middle of nowhere! We should have stayed at the carnival and found someplace there. Maybe we should go back?"

Grace disagreed. "I'd rather sleep with wild animals and bugs than the walking dead! Besides, we've gone too far. There is no going back now. Let's just keep walking on the path and hope for the best."

"Okay, okay," grumbled Leona.

The group continued on in silence.

Grace thought about her aunt and uncle back home. She wondered if they were worried about her, if they had noticed she was gone.

"We're going to have to stop soon," said Tim after a few more minutes of walking. "It's hard to see, and it's getting colder by the minute."

The sun had fully set, and the night had started to settle in.

"Ow!" Hayden cried out as he stumbled over a rock and fell heavily to his hands and knees.

"Hayden has proven my point," said Tim, helping him up.

"This is ridiculous. Let's go back to the carnival. We're walking into the wilderness!" said Leona. Her voice had an edge of fear in it.

"I wish I had some matches," Tim interjected. "We could find a spot to set up camp for the night and make a fire."

"We may have to do that, with or without a fire," said Hayden.

"Let's keep walking. I'm sure we will find *something!*" Grace exclaimed. But they didn't move from the spot where Hayden had tripped. They couldn't go any further in the dark, and Grace knew it.

"Maybe we can all huddle together to keep warm. It's getting a little chilly here," said Hayden.

"That's it!" snapped Leona. "I can't believe I let you talk me into this craziness. We can't even see the pa...ooooh. What was that?"

A small light blinked off and on. It hovered in front of the group at eye level.

"It's a firefly!" exclaimed Tim.

Grace spotted another one to their left as it flew over and joined the first. Within seconds a third appeared, and then a fourth.

"Where are they all coming from?" asked Hayden. No one answered. They just stood there and watched as several more tiny lights appeared and joined the group of blinking bugs.

Grace watched, her eyes wide, adjusting to the darkness, fixated on the lights.

A warm breeze began to blow into the valley, and dozens more fireflies rode it like a wave into the presence of the stunned travelers.

Instead of flying separately, the bugs swarmed together, looking like one dazzling, twinkling yellow orb. The orb grew larger and larger as fireflies flew in from every direction, many sparks adding to one giant flame.

They hovered in front of the group in perfect synchronization, like a school of fish.

"Wow," said Leona, her fear now replaced with wonder.

"Crazy!" said Hayden.

Tim started to reach for his eye drops but stopped, raised his arms in the air, and exclaimed, "Magical!"

Terrence didn't bark, but wagged his tail while his eyes darted back and forth into the night sky.

The mass of lightning bugs began slowly moving away from the group, their glow now illuminating the path ahead.

"Let's follow them," Grace said.

Without debate, everyone began following the swarm of lightning bugs, Terrence now yipping with excitement. He occasionally jumped up to try to catch one, but they were just out of his reach.

"It's like they are traveling the same path as us!" Hayden said, almost laughing. "But flying insects don't follow paths." He scratched his head repeatedly as if trying to entice the explanation to come out of his brain through his scalp.

After a few minutes, his head tilted back and he began sniffing the air. "Hey, do you guys smell what I smell?"

Grace thought she had caught a whiff of something in the air.

"Yeah, smells like food cooking! Where is it coming from?" asked Leona.

The main path narrowed and veered off across a field. In the darkness under the stars, they could make out a small cottage with smoke rising from the chimney. Faint light shone through windows in the front.

The fireflies hovered over the point where the tiny path began, then suddenly scattered, like sparks escaping from a fire.

"They're gone," whispered Tim.

They stood in the dark, taking it all in.

"Let's see who's home," said Grace.

Grace, Hayden, and Tim followed Terrence toward the house. Leona stayed back a moment.

"I don't know about this. We have no idea who lives there."

"But the fireflies!" said Hayden, not understanding Leona's reservations.

"Yeah, so what? You're just gonna follow any bug you see?" Her tone was sarcastic, but everyone knew she was simply afraid.

"Come on. It'll be safe. I feel good about this," Tim said, motioning for her to join them.

Leona relented. "Fine."

It was a small wooden cabin nestled in a grove of young trees. Grace walked up to the front door boldly and knocked.

They could hear footsteps inside. Then the door cracked open and an eye appeared through the crack.

"Hello?" said the eye.

"Hi," began Grace. "We are traveling to the EC and need to find a place to stay the night. We are, um, not from around here."

Grace wasn't sure why she said the last part, but she did.

The door opened wider. A small woman with mousy hair and kind eyes greeted them. She wore a simple yellow dress.

A tall pudgy man with a beard appeared, towering over her.

"Madeline, who is it?" He looked at Grace and her friends and immediately broke into a wide grin.

"Come in, come in! Welcome!"

Madeline opened the door for the guests. They walked into the cabin, thanking her. It was a cozy place: a large room with a wood stove in the middle, a small kitchen in one corner, and a closed door in another. A ladder led to an upstairs loft, and floral-print curtains were draped over the entrance. In the center, in front of the wood stove, was a large, fluffy cream-colored rug surrounded by a plaid couch and several chairs.

"Sit down, please," the man insisted. Grace sank into a black leather chair.

The man thrust his large hairy hand toward Grace. "Hi, I'm Cal, and this is my beautiful wife, Madeline."

They each shook hands and introduced themselves, then they took seats around the wood stove. The fire warmed them.

"Are you all hungry?" Madeline asked shyly. "I made a huge pot of stew. Cal was just complaining that he'd be eating it for weeks." She smiled brightly. She was a very pretty woman.

"Yes, please, thank you!" they all responded.

Madeline got up and went to the kitchen and began ladling steaming meaty stew into simple brown ceramic bowls. It smelled fabulous. She returned with the bowls, two at a time.

"Please, eat. We've already had ours."

The four companions devoured the thick stew, continually commenting on how wonderful it was. Madeline even dipped a small bowl for Terrence, which he gobbled up in seconds.

"This must be what heaven tastes like," Hayden sighed.

Cal took a seat in a wooden rocking chair. Terrence surprised Grace by walking over to him and jumping onto his lap. Cal laughed and stroked the small dog, immediately his friend.

"Where are you folks headed this evening?"

"We are on our way to the EC," said Grace, placing her empty bowl on a side table.

"Yeah, we are going to go see The Wizard," said Hayden excitedly.

Cal slowly nodded his head. Grace noticed Madeline making eye contact with her husband.

"Why do you want to see him?"

His question surprised Grace, but she answered.

"We…err, *I* was told that he has special wisdom and powers. You see, I'm lost, I mean, I don't know how I got here or how to find my way home. Honestly, home is kind of a fuzzy memory. A tree branch hit me on the head." Grace stopped abruptly, aware she was rambling on.

"I am hoping he'll tell me how to tap into the secret knowledge of the universe!" exclaimed Hayden after an awkward silence. "I want to be able to figure things out, make sense of everything."

"What about you, Tim?" Hayden said, passing the baton to his friend.

"I am hoping maybe he can help me not feel so sad all the time," said Tim sheepishly.

Cal nodded in understanding.

They looked at Leona, wondering how she would answer.

"I'm just along for the ride, mister," she said, flashing a fake smile.

"What makes you think he can help you?" Cal asked, not directing his query to anyone in particular.

Grace was again surprised by his question. "Well, someone came to me on my first night here, and he insisted that The

Wizard would be the one to help. But what do *you* know about The Wizard?"

Madeline gave her husband a strange look. Cal didn't seem put off. He smiled.

"If your hearts are set on something, you should go after it. If you look close enough, you'll find what you are looking for."

Madeline got up abruptly "Who wants more stew?" she asked, changing the subject.

Everyone had a second helping. They continued chatting around the fireplace.

Tim spoke up. "I don't mean to pry, but how come you live out here in the middle of nowhere? Do you enjoy the seclusion?"

Cal smiled at his wife, his eyes twinkling.

"Madeline and I used to live in the EC, a long time ago."

"Why'd you move out here?" asked Hayden.

"The EC became a little overcrowded for us. We love the peace and quiet. Besides, we are a great rest stop for weary travelers." He grinned at his wife.

Madeline put her hand on her husband's shoulder. "It gets lonely out here at times, but we have each other, and we know it's where we need to be."

She stood up and took their empty bowls.

"You must be exhausted. You can spend the night here. We have a small shower in the bathroom through that door if you want to clean up. I can make up some beds for you down here by the stove. I know it's not much, but you're welcome to it."

"If it's not too much trouble," said Grace, overwhelmed by their hospitality.

"No, no trouble at all," said Cal, smiling and rising from his rocking chair. "We'll have breakfast in the morning, and you'll be all rested and fed for your journey. You're going to need it. The EC is an interesting place." He chuckled. "Especially if you plan on seeing The Wizard."

The morning came with the smell and sound of sausages frying in a pan. Grace sat up, rubbing her eyes. She and Terrence were curled up in a chair beside the wood stove. Leona was sprawled out on the couch, stirring a little. Tim and Hayden slept on pallets made of layered blankets and pillows.

Grace heard the cheerful sound of whistling, and the door opened. Cal walked in and, seeing Grace was awake, smiled.

"Coffee?" he mouthed, as not to wake the others. Her eyes got wide, and she nodded. She got out of the chair and went to the bathroom. She looked in the mirror and saw her thick hair was sticking up all over the place. She figured that's what she got for sleeping on wet hair. It had felt so luxurious to take a shower, though. She smiled at herself, determined to make the most of the day. Today they were off to see The Wizard.

As she emerged from the bathroom the others were slowly waking to the smell of coffee and breakfast cooking.

"I thought I was dreaming," mumbled Hayden. Leona was up, heading for the restroom.

Tim sat up, slugging Hayden in the arm lightly. "Next time, don't try to cuddle with me."

"No way! I moved away from you!"

Grace giggled. She moved to the kitchen, where Madeline was preparing breakfast and Cal was pouring coffee. He handed her a steaming mug.

"Go sit down, dear. We don't have room for a table, but we prefer to eat in the comfy chairs anyway."

Grace sat down on the couch and sipped the hot coffee. It was as delicious as it smelled.

The couple served the food to Grace and the guys. Leona joined them, and they all sat around eating and drinking.

Madeline had gone all out, making sausage, scrambled eggs, and fried potatoes. Thick pieces of toast smothered in a home-made berry jam put the meal over the top.

"This is delicious!" said Hayden between mouthfuls.

"Love this coffee!" Even Leona was in a good mood.

"Cal," Grace began curiously, "I was just wondering. You don't live in the EC...are you under the godvernment?"

"We are not," Cal said, shaking his head, half smiling.

"I didn't think so," Grace responded. "We've had a hard time finding food because it seems like they control it all. So where do you get your food?"

"That's a legitimate question, Grace," said Cal, sipping his coffee. "I could tell you, but I am not quite sure you'd understand."

Grace looked at him, confused.

"When you come out from under a system, it's frightening at first. You've grown accustomed to the way things are done and to being told what to do to be accepted. But soon you begin to see you were never meant to live that way, and that everything you need is right in front of you. Everything has been provided for as a gift, and you have been accepted from the beginning."

Madeline smiled at him and, as if to confirm what he was saying, took his plate to the kitchen to dish him up another serving of potatoes.

Grace nodded, but as Cal had predicted, she did not understand.

When everyone had all they could eat, they all pitched in to clean up and wash the dishes. Soon it was time to go, and they stood on the porch saying good-byes.

Grace had the urge to hug Cal and she did so, surprising herself. She hugged Madeline's small frame as well, and the woman kissed her gently on the cheek.

"You be safe now, sweetie. Remember, the proof is in the pudding," she whispered. Grace looked at her quizzically. Before she could ask her what she was referring to, Madeline whispered one last line: "Fame is a fickle food upon a shifting plate."

She hugged her tighter and then released her, leaving Grace wondering what exactly she meant.

"Why do you think Cal was so vague when you asked him about The Wizard?" Leona asked as they walked down the path, which had begun to wind through a valley. The skyline of the EC was now clearly visible in the distance, and it appeared to be surrounded by an extremely high wall.

Grace shrugged her shoulders. "I don't know. Maybe he just doesn't know very much, since they haven't lived there for some time."

Leona frowned. "So all *you* know about The Wizard is what you heard from some stranger? What if you have come all this way for nothing?"

Grace hesitated for a moment, stung by Leona's words. "It isn't for nothing," she said finally, trying to convince herself.

"Cal said we'd find what we are looking for. We've just got to believe."

"That's strange," remarked Tim. "I wonder why they put a wall around the city. I hope they let us in."

No one responded to Tim, but they all kept walking down the path that was in front of them.

By early afternoon, the city walls were drawing near. The path had broadened and turned from dirt to gravel to pavement. Giant billboards stood beside the path.

*You are now within the city limits of the EC. Welcome!*

"We're really here!" Grace said. Hayden jumped up in the air in excitement. Leona picked up her speed, and Tim smiled widely. Even Terrence barked in anticipation.

They came to a large green billboard. Plastered on it was a large face of a very good-looking, smiling man. He had a chiseled face with a strong jawline, and perfect white teeth. His dirty-blond hair was short and well kept, and his green eyes were large and expressive. The caption read:

"Gray skies are going to clear up, put on a happy face!" – The Wizard

"Wait, *what*? *That* is The Wizard?!" exclaimed Grace. "I was picturing an old man. This guy can't be that much older than thirty! Maybe younger!"

"Maybe he was a child prodigy," said Hayden

"He looks sort of plastic to me," Leona replied with a smirk.

"I guess it's what's inside that counts," said Tim.

Grace just stood and stared at the face on the billboard.

"Wow."

Leona noticed Grace staring at the billboard and laughed.

"You think he's gorgeous, don't you? Not *my* type."

Grace ignored her.

They came upon another billboard a little farther down the road. It was another picture of The Wizard. He was sitting on a stool dressed in fitted jeans and a dress shirt with rolled-up sleeves that showed off his muscular arms. He was grinning again, and the caption under him read:

"Take off that gloomy mask of tragedy; it's not your style!"

"You got to be kidding me," chuckled Leona. "We came all this way to see this guy?"

"What's the problem?" Hayden spoke up. "Sounds like good advice to me!"

They continued walking, and they soon approached still another billboard. The Wizard was standing in front of a group of immaculately groomed children seated in a semicircle.

"If you're feeling sad and bitter, don't sit and whine. Just follow the Thirteen Secrets and you'll be fine!"

"Thirteen Secrets?" Hayden said.

"The EC looks like it will be nice," Tim remarked. "The people on the billboards seem genuinely happy, unlike other places we've been."

Leona shook her head.

The closer they got to the city, the closer together the billboards became. More pictures of The Wizard in different poses, always dressed nicely, spouting pearls of wisdom.

As they were the only ones on the road, they continued to walk in the center, only stopping to read the messages.

"The Wizard seems like a cool guy! I'm digging his quotes," Hayden remarked.

Grace agreed. The more billboards she saw, the more her anticipation grew.

"I can't wait to meet him," she said.

Finally, they approached what appeared to be the last sign. The Wizard pointed straight ahead and the picture made it appear that he was pointing at each person individually.

"YOU don't have to be sad or angry any longer. Think positively and follow my Secrets to be Happy, Healthy, and Wholesome."

"Think that one is obviously a special message for you," Hayden said to Leona, who scowled.

"No comment," she muttered under her breath.

The path soon ended in front of a large gate. The gate stood in the middle of a giant concrete wall that was painted pure white and was as high as a four-story building. The gate was metal and modern looking, and built beside it was a guardhouse made of the same sturdy concrete. It resembled a security complex or a prison.

"Oh, gosh, I hope we don't have to have ID or something to get in," Grace worried.

They approached the guardhouse, and Tim rang the large green buzzer that was outside the door. It made a hollow ringing sound as he pressed it.

A man opened the door and stood staring at them. He was dressed casually, wearing jeans and a tucked-in green polo shirt. He was thin and looked a little bit younger than Tim. He had a short haircut, similar to The Wizard's. He smiled widely.

Terrence stood by Grace's side and growled.

"Hello, weary travelers. Welcome to our magnificent city! I have to ask, who are you and what are you doing here?"

"Funny you should ask, we were hoping The Wizard could tell us," joked Hayden.

The guard kept smiling.

Leona pushed her way to the front and spoke for the group.

"Let us in. We need to see The Wizard!"

The guard looked surprised by her demand. He walked back into the guardhouse and returned with a small stack of papers.

"Well! Obviously you are not from around here. I have some reading material for you to familiarize yourself with the EC."

He handed fliers to each of them.

Grace looked down at hers. On the cover was a collage of several good-looking, model-thin smiling people with a caption that read:

"Familiarizing Yourself with the EC."

"We would like to see The Wizard, please," Grace tried politely. "We've come a long way."

The guard wrinkled his forehead and placed his index finger on his temple.

"I'll be right back." He walked into the guard booth. They could hear his muffled voice inside, followed by a click. As he walked back out to them, Grace held her breath.

"All right. First you need to complete the EC Membership Class. There you will learn about the vision of the EC."

"We didn't come here to take a class!" interrupted Leona.

"Yes, we've come such a long way. Can't we just see The Wizard?" pleaded Grace

The man ignored her. "It won't take very long, and the next one starts"—he looked at his watch—"in about thirty minutes, so you are just in time."

"Well, I guess if it's our only option," said Tim.

Leona looked suspicious. "We don't need to take a class! Can't we just talk to this guy? Do we need an appointment or something?"

"He's a celebrity, Leona," said Hayden. "They don't just let anyone in. Obviously he's the guy with the power, so we've got to play by his rules. Right, Grace?"

Grace looked perplexed. "I mean, I guess if that's the only way…"

"It is," replied the guard, a fixed smile on his face.

"Now, in order to prepare you for the EC, I am going to ask that you wear what I'm about to give you. Just temporarily, only until your facial muscles become accustomed to being happy."

"Facial muscles? Accustomed to what?" asked Leona.

The man walked over to her, hooked his fingers in the corners of her mouth, and pulled them upward, so that it appeared as if she was grinning wildly.

"Exactly. Turn that frown upside down, sister!"

Leona shoved his hand away from her mouth. "Watch your hands, creep!!"

The man didn't seem put off. He walked back into his guard booth and came back out with a small light-green cardboard box.

"Here we go, these should fit!" He pulled out what looked like the bottom half of a plastic mask, just enough to cover one's mouth. On it was a pair of large, plastic red lips that formed a huge clown smile. He handed one to each, and took one for himself for demonstration. The four friends looked at one another in shock and bemusement.

"Now, the back of this is adjustable for comfort." He adjusted the strap that went around the back of his head. "Until you are accustomed to our way of life here, this will help you fit in quite nicely."

Hayden stifled a laugh. Tim stared at his mask.

"I'm not gonna wear this! Are you insane?" Leona asked.

The man, who had put the mask over his mouth, making him look ridiculous, spoke with some seriousness in spite of his smile.

"Think of these as training wheels!"

Grace was already putting her fake smile on and adjusting the straps in the back. "Well, it's not going to hurt anything. It's kind of strange, but whatever it takes."

Hayden had his on and was bugging his eyes out toward Leona. He looked more like a clown than ever. Grace bit her lip to keep from laughing.

Tim already had his on. "Why not?" he said. "I've been faking a smile for years."

Leona sighed, aggravated. "This is crazy! I can't believe you are all agreeing to wear these!"

The others just stared at Leona and *smiled*. Even though she was angry she had to fight to keep from bursting into laughter.

"Well, I guess I will play along if I have to." She put her mask on awkwardly and crossed her arms.

The guard laughed eerily from behind his mask. "You all look great! So happy!"

A door that was within the gate suddenly opened, and a woman stepped through. She was tall with long blonde hair. Her smile was natural, without the help of a mask, and she wore dress slacks with an emerald green silk blouse. Her teeth were immaculate, brilliant white and perfectly straight. It reminded Grace of the toothpaste advertisements on TV. Her eyes were deep, kind looking, and were a brilliant emerald green. In fact there was an air of unreality about her.

She had a nametag that read "Greta: Greeter."

The guard took off his mask and motioned to Greta.

"This is the lovely Greta. She will be your tour guide. If you have any further questions, please direct them to her. So wonderful to meet you, I hope your stay here is most pleasant."

They all turned and looked at Greta, who was reading from a clipboard she held with both hands.

"Welcome to our wonderful city," she began in a bubbly, game show announcer voice, "We hope you have a lovely visit here. Please follow me and I will show you everything there is to see... Wait. What is that?" Greta stopped her presentation and pointed to Terrence. Her smile remained frozen on her face.

"My dog," said Grace.

"I am not sure about our policy on *dogs*." Greta looked appealingly at the guard for help, still smiling.

"Hold on." The guard went into his booth and came out again holding a long rope, which he handed to Grace.

"We can't have him running around disturbing the peace."

Grace begrudgingly tied the rope onto Terrence's collar. He looked up at Grace sadly, as he was used to being free.

Leona moved her smile mask around her mouth. "How long do we have to wear these...smiles?" she asked.

"Hmmm, well, let's see," said Greta consulting her clipboard. "Ah! Until you have graduated the New Members class. I trust you have been informed about it already."

Leona looked angry and began to say something sarcastic. As she did her words became muffled inside the mask and came out sounding like undecipherable mumbling.

Her eyes grew wide, and she put her hand over her fake mouth.

Greta grinned.

"As long as we can take this off long enough to eat, I'm cool with it," said Hayden.

Greta just laughed. "That's one thing you definitely won't have to worry about. Now follow me."

"I've got a feeling this journey is about to get even more interesting," said Tim.

Single file, wearing big fake smiles, the four friends followed Greta through the gate, still clutching their pamphlets.

# CHAPTER 11

# THE CITY

*"In the antiseptic world we try to purge ourselves of difficult things. Don't dwell on it, switch off the light and go home. But this is home."*

— JEANETTE WINTERSON

The EC was unlike anything any of them had ever seen. It was gorgeous, majestic, and everything was absolutely pristine. The city appeared to run like a well-oiled machine: a sanitized, glistening, white machine.

Grace felt out of place in her clothes, which showed much wear and tear from her journey, despite the fact she wore a new apple-green jacket Madeline had kindly given her. The roads were immaculate, as if someone swept them hourly. It helped, of course, that everyone was on foot.

It was a grand city. Tall buildings seemed to scrape the sky. It hurt Grace's neck to look up. The group followed Greta, speechless. It was a surreal experience, after being in the country for so long. Even though they all were experiencing some culture shock, it was a relief to be back in civilization. People they passed walking down the street were smartly dressed without a hair out of place. They all wore big smiles, as if today was the best day of their lives.

Grace didn't notice anyone wearing the fake smiles like they were. There was very little noise, only the soft padding of feet and low murmur of voices at times. In many ways, it was the perfect city. Nothing was out of place, and everyone was happy. Serious looking, but happy.

Some people ignored the odd-looking group; others casually acknowledged them, nodding toward them and saying hello. Occasionally, someone would stop and shake their hands. No one ever introduced themselves but would always say, "Hi, how are you?" then smile and walk away without waiting for a response.

Everywhere, on sides of buildings, on signs, and posters were images of The Wizard, always smiling and looking handsome.

They passed in front of an enormous bright-white building with many stairs leading up to a large entrance with pillars. Above the pillars was an inscription across the whole building entrance:

"Help Yourself to Success." – The Wizard

"Sweet!" remarked Hayden.

"This," began Greta, looking at her notes, "is the EC Library. You can find anything you're looking for here. Well, anything that's *true.*" She emphasized the last word and smiled like they knew what she meant.

"Follow me, please. We're almost there."

They passed the steps and continued down the street. Hayden approached Grace, looking as goofy as ever in his fake smile mask.

"Can you believe this place? It is everything I hoped it would be. These people have definitely reached enlightenment!" He swung his arms around, excited like a child seeing the world for the first time.

They passed a restaurant with a silver sign hanging outside of it that said "Café EC." As they passed, Grace noticed several tables of people browsing through menus. She walked to the front of the group to speak with Greta.

"Greta, can we get something to eat? My friends and I have been walking a long time, and it's been hours since breakfast."

Greta smiled. "Dear, don't worry about a thing now. Just do what you're told and everything will fall into place."

But Grace's curiosity was growing. "I heard that the EC is separate from the rest of the land of god. Is that true? How did that happen?"

Greta continued walking, thinking for a moment. She turned to her clipboard and leafed through some pages.

"Well, it's funny you asked that because I was just about to show you this. Aha!" The group stopped abruptly in front of a statue surrounded by a small garden. The statue was clearly The Wizard, posing heroically.

"Here he is," said Greta, smiling.

Tim read the gold engraving on the bottom of the statue. "Erected here in honor of our great and powerful Wizard, who gave us The Formula to happiness and freedom."

Greta stood in front of the statue, reading from her clipboard.

"Long ago, the evil godvernment ruled over all the land of god. Their regulations were oppressive and unbearable. They treated god's people like slaves, and sought to control every part of their lives. They outlawed pleasure, fun, and happiness, and fed their followers dry, leathery food they could hardly chew, swallow, or digest. And so, there was an uprising. Many of us decided to abandon *their* rules and make our own...way. The land of god was divided.

"But we were lacking a true leader. The Wizard rose up from among us. He shared Secrets that changed the way we *do life*. He is our hero, our example, and our guide.

"We have created a place where happiness isn't simply allowed, it is mandated! We are required to be Happy, Healthy, and Wholesome!

"This is how the EC was born!"

The group listened, intrigued by the tale.

"Well, when do we get to meet The Wizard?" asked Leona.

Greta smiled condescendingly. "I would strongly suggest patience, my dear."

Leona's nostrils flared, and her eyebrows sloped inwards. Her mouth let loose a string of obscenities, but what came out through her fake smile was more mumbling.

Leona's eyebrows lifted, and her eyes looked like they might bulge out of the sockets.

"All good things will come in time, Leona," Greta said, winking. "First, we are off to the Training Center!" She walked away from the statue, her chest thrust out and her head held high. The four new students followed behind, with plastic smiles on their faces and pamphlets in their hands.

"Wow, this place has some wonderful architecture!" Tim gushed as they passed a glass office building. They could see through to the neat and modern spacious cubicles. People sat talking on phones and staring at glowing computer screens.

"Oh, that's the ROTGC building," Greta said happily. "The building is glass on purpose. We have nothing to hide here, even behind closed doors! The ROTGC sends out trained volunteers to other parts of god to bring happiness and to invite them to be a part of what we are doing here in the EC."

"What does ROTGC stand for?" Hayden asked.

"Reach Out To god's Citizens," replied Greta, as if it were common knowledge.

Grace watched the people hard at work. They all looked so happy and fulfilled, like they were really making a difference with their jobs.

They turned a corner and came upon an impressive-looking white stone building. It looked older than the other buildings. They stood in a landscaped courtyard admiring the building. On a tree in the courtyard a plaque hung that read:

"Come As You Are"

And in smaller inscription beneath it:

"Leave Happy, Healthy, and Wholesome"

The four weary travelers and one little dog followed Greta up the stairs. She stopped at the top, looking around proudly. This time, she didn't consult her clipboard.

"Welcome to the EC New Members Training Facility! Here you will learn firsthand what it means to be part of this *amazing* community. This is where you become educated about the EC culture. Any questions?"

"Yes," said Leona, sounding irritated but carefully choosing her words. "How long is it going to take? And when do we see the MRNMMFFFF...great and powerful Wizard?"

Greta kept her smile, but Grace could tell she was annoyed with Leona.

"Oh, you'll be in and out of there in no time. And don't worry, it won't be boring. It's a very enriching experience. The *last thing* we are into here at the EC is *boring*."

She said it like it was a dirty word.

"Follow me."

They followed her through the front doors into a large lobby with high ceilings. Across from the door was a tall wooden desk, where a young woman wearing plastic-rimmed glasses sat. Next to the desk was another large door. Plastered all over the lobby were giant posters of happy people with quotes next to them. Grace read one on a poster of a girl with red hair who looked about her age:

"Before I came to the EC, I was lost. Overworked and underfed by the godverment and needing a fresh start. Thanks to The

Wizard and the amazing staff here, I found a new beginning and a family."

Grace noticed Leona staring at the poster after the others had moved on to look at others.

Greta was talking to the woman at the desk.

"Yes, thank you, Fran. I'll finish up quickly before class begins." She motioned for the group to join her.

"Okay, I need to get a little background information," Greta said, attaching a new sheet of paper to her clipboard. She hurriedly took down names, ages, and birth dates for all four, and then continued.

"Now, since we are pressed for time, someone fill me in briefly about how you came to be here at the fabulous EC."

The group looked at each other for a few moments, not knowing what to do. Finally, Hayden spoke up. "Grace, why don't you tell Greta our story? After all, if it weren't for you the rest of us wouldn't be here."

Grace felt uncomfortable but, sensing Greta's impatience, spoke up quickly.

"I'm lost. I mean, I'm not from here, and I'm trying to find my way back home. Someone I met told me that The Wizard could help me, so I started walking. Along the way I met these three new...well, friends and...well, they were kind of lost too, so I invited them to come along. We have walked a very long way, and it's been hard. We really need The Wizard's help. Er... thanks."

Greta's forehead wrinkled, and she touched her index finger to her lips.

"Let me get this straight. You were lost and set out to find The Wizard. Along the way you convinced these others to follow you on a long journey to ask him for help, based solely on the advice of a stranger? You must be a *very* trusting *and* persuasive person! Very good, yes, very good," Greta said, quickly scribbling on her clipboard. "Yes, the leadership will be very interested in hearing about this, for sure."

Grace looked at Hayden, puzzled by Greta's response. Hayden shrugged his shoulders.

Lights above the large door began to flicker on and off. After a few seconds the door opened automatically.

"Looks like my timing is perfect *as always*. Orientation is about to start. Right this way!" Greta motioned for the group to follow her.

"Excuse me!" Fran, the receptionist, called out. Greta turned around.

"Yes?"

"I am afraid they can't bring that *animal* in there. It's against policy."

Grace scooped Terrence up defensively.

She chose her words carefully, realizing it would do no good to argue.

"Ma'am, I was hoping you could make an exception. Terrence is a special dog. I need him. He won't be any trouble, please."

Fran looked at Grace and Terrence, then back to Greta. Greta shrugged her shoulders.

"All right, I suppose, but if he causes any trouble, he's out."

She held her dog closer. He sniffed her plastic smile, confused.

"I'll make sure he behaves," she said. They followed Greta through the door.

They walked down a long, narrow hall to a door at the end. A sign hanging on the door read "ORIENTATION." Greta glanced at her little group, smiled, and pushed open the door.

"Right this way. Come in and take a seat."

They entered a medium-sized classroom. There was a large white screen on the front wall and beside it stood a small platform with a podium and microphone. Chairs were positioned in a friendly semicircle facing the podium.

Several people were already seated. They were not wearing masks, and they looked slightly bored. Grace overheard one young girl with dark skin and black hair whisper "newbies" to a girl seated next to her. Grace nodded at them politely and continued walking. She felt self-conscious in her mask now that the girls were looking at her. She held Terrence close and sat down in one of the chairs in the front. Hayden introduced himself to the two girls, but they didn't reciprocate. Tim sat next to Grace and Leona next to Tim.

After a few minutes, Greta left the room and in walked a handsome man with a goatee and brown shaggy hair. He looked like he was in his mid-thirties. The young girls applauded enthusiastically and smiled flirtatiously at the man. He smiled back.

"Hello, everyone, please take your seats." He gestured at Hayden, who had stood to applaud as well. "We are about to begin." Hayden sat down. Leona was staring at him and shaking her head in disbelief.

"Welcome, welcome, everyone." The man stepped onto the platform and stood behind the podium. He tapped the microphone, realizing it wasn't on.

"Well, I don't need this anyway. Looks like a small group today! Welcome, newcomers." He pointed toward Grace and her comrades. "And welcome to those who are here for a re-dedication. I am Jared. And this is the EC New Members Orientation."

He stepped back from the podium, reached behind it, and pulled out a box.

"I am going to pass these out to enhance your viewing experience. Please wait for instructions before you put them on."

Jared walked around the room passing out black plastic glasses.

"What are these for?" asked Leona suspiciously as he handed her a pair.

"To help you *see* into your *future*." He flashed a grin at her.

"Thank you," Grace said when he handed her the glasses.

"What next? Are they going to give us fake noses?" Leona grumbled under her breath.

Hayden already had his glasses on.

"Whoaaa. Everything looks...trippy."

Jared stepped back onto the podium.

"All right, put on your glasses." The lights dimmed in the room. Grace put on her glasses, and a man appeared on the screen. Grace knew it was only an image, but he looked so real. He stepped forward until it looked like he was standing directly in front of her. It was The Wizard in 3D!

He was wearing grey slacks and a nice black dress shirt. He bent his right leg at the knee and began to sit, and instantly a stool appeared underneath him. He sat causally with his right foot on a rung and left leg on the floor.

"Hello, my friends." His voice was rich and smooth. "Welcome to our beautiful city. We hope you are beginning to feel comfortable and happy here. I'm The Wizard, and I am so excited to talk to *you* today about our vision here at the EC."

As he said "you" he pointed, and Grace flinched, because it looked like his finger was going to poke her in the chest. He looked so real Grace was taken aback. *This* was not how she had envisioned meeting The Wizard.

Still, Grace felt strangely drawn to the man and his words. It almost didn't matter what he was saying; his voice was so comforting, she felt as if she could listen to him *forever.*

"Here at the EC, we have created a society free from the bondage of godvernment's oppressive rules." Grace sat back in her chair and listened.

"The godvernment has always been stuck in the old traditional ways, but here at the EC we are always on the cutting edge of everything that's modern and relevant. The godvernment is always trying to get you to *do* something you don't like, or keep you from the things you desire. At the EC, your happiness and fulfillment are our primary concerns. We believe if people *feel* good, they will *be* good." He flashed a smile so warm and inviting Grace swooned. A collective sigh echoed across the room.

On the screen behind him, images of smiling people flashed by. Some were working, shaking hands firmly with each other, while others simply strolled hand-in-hand on pristine streets and in courtyards. Grace recognized a few spots they had walked by, including the ROTGC building.

"Here, we are about *relationships* and helping people fulfill their destiny. We are all united under one idea, one common goal: to help you have the most totally awesome life ever! We are seeking the special ones, the elite, the brightest, most zealous and loyal to join us! Why wouldn't you want to be a part of the best god has to offer?"

A video clip of people wearing ridiculous-looking smile masks appeared on the screen. The Wizard continued.

"You may have noticed these training smiles, or maybe you are wearing one yourself. We initiated this fun practice to help new-comers get accustomed to our way of life. We understand it takes time for some to get the hang of being happy all the time...no matter what! Pretty soon continuous smiling will be second nature, and the mask will, as we like to say, *become you!*"

Hayden looked perplexed, and Leona rolled her eyes.

"Now get ready to learn some fun facts about what the EC can do for *you*." He pointed again, and Grace jumped slightly. "Trust me! You'll love it."

"Please welcome back my dear friend *and* your awesome coach, Jared!" Sporadic, awkward applause followed as Jared made his way back to the platform.

"Jared is going to share a few *Secrets* that help keep the EC Happy, Healthy, and Wholesome. Thanks for watching and see you soon!"

With that, The Wizard disappeared and the house lights came on.

Jared looked out at the audience, smiling from ear to ear. "You can take off your glasses now." The group complied, except for Leona, who was slumped down in her seat. "He's awesome, isn't he? It's such an honor to work for a man of god like that. All right, as you heard, I am your coach and will now be sharing some wonderful *Secrets* with you. Here we go!"

The lights dimmed a little. Words appeared on the white screen with a rainbow in the background.

*The Thirteen Secrets to a Happy, Healthy, and Wholesome Life*

*Well, who wouldn't want that?* thought Grace.

The points came up one at a time. For some, Jared elaborated briefly.

1. Don't give up! Just try harder!
2. Eliminate all negative godverment terminology from your vocabulary.
3. Keep everything sparkling clean.
4. Remember! Smiling people are happy people! So smile and be happy!
5. Avoid deep conversations about depressing subjects,
6. Greet everyone with "Hi, how are you," and always answer "Great," or repeat the question.
7. Avoid the carnival, and don't accept ANY unauthorized food from strangers.
8. Always be relevant, hip, and *never* boring—strive to make a good impression on visitors.
9. You can't be too thin, or too happy. Think Good, Look Good, Feel Good!
10. Keep to a well groomed and professional dress code.
11. No sad or depressing music, only happy songs!
12. If you don't have anything nice to say, just smile and nod approvingly!
13. If you feel weak, remember the Formula.

Jared stepped off the platform and began passing out paper and pens to everyone in the classroom. Grace looked at the paper and saw that it contained the same *Thirteen Secrets.*

Jared explained. "On the bottom is a place for your signature. Please sign on the dotted line, committing to uphold our *Thirteen Secrets* to ensure love, life, liberty, health, wealth, and so on. After you do that, you are free to take off your training smiles!

"Thank you for attending this training class, and we will see you at the meeting tonight at seven. If I were you, I would get there early to grab a good seat."

Grace looked around at her friends. Leona was sitting up straighter, but Grace noticed her neck muscles were tight and her veins were visible.

"Sign me up!" said Hayden as he signed his form.

Tim shrugged his shoulders, saying to Grace under his breath, "May as well do what they say, so we can meet The Wizard in person, right?"

Grace signed her name in a flourish, not thinking about it too much.

"I sure hope so."

# CHAPTER 12
# CAFÉS

*"Every poet and musician and artist, but for Grace, is drawn away from love of the thing he tells, to love of the telling..."*

— C.S. Lewis

Very soon after signing her name, Grace started experiencing an uneasy feeling in the pit of her stomach. She looked down at her feet, which felt like they were tingling strangely.

Jared walked around the room picking up their signed commitment forms. He instructed them to place their 3D glasses in a box that was being passed around.

The other students got up and left the room quickly, but the four of them lingered. Grace tucked Terrence under her arm and approached Jared, who was organizing the papers on the podium.

"Excuse me?"

Jared looked down at her. "Yes, what can I do to help you?"

"Um…when will we be able to meet The Wizard? The video was great, but we really need to talk to him."

The others stood beside her.

"Yes, please tell us where we can find him," said Tim politely.

Jared looked at his gold wristwatch. "Well, unfortunately, it is not as simple as just telling you where he is. He's a very busy man with a lot of important responsibilities…"

Leona interrupted, "Listen, we were led to believe we would get to see him after we took this stup…this *class*. Now, let's see him!"

Hayden agreed. "Seriously, dude, we gotta talk to him!"

Jared considered it for a moment.

"Well, he will be making an appearance at the meeting tonight at seven p.m."

"Where?" asked Grace excitedly.

"In the Great Hall. Ask any citizen where it is. You can't miss it."

"Thank you," said Grace. "So what do we do now?" She looked around, realizing the room was empty.

"There's plenty to explore in the EC. Why don't you have a look around, and you'll discover why this is the best place in god!"

"Is there anywhere we can stay the night?" asked Grace.

"Talk to Fran in the lobby," Jared responded, already back to his papers. "She will show you to our guest accommodations."

From the lobby, Fran led them down another corridor to some simple, clean guestrooms equipped with beds, dressers, and bathrooms. The group freshened up and met back in the lobby to discuss what to do next.

"We should try to find something to eat," said Grace. The suggestion was sounding all too familiar.

"There was a café we passed on our way here," said Tim.

Grace shook her head. "We don't have any vouchers. How are we going to get anything to eat?"

"Madeline's beef stew would taste so good right about now," Tim replied with a hint of sadness in his voice.

Leona shuffled uncomfortably then spoke up.

"Let's just go to the café. I can cover it. I've got some food vouchers."

They all turned and looked at her.

"You have food vouchers?" Grace was surprised. "How did you get them?"

"It doesn't matter, okay? I offered to buy you guys dinner, so just accept it. God!" Leona stomped out the door.

"Well, okay!" said Hayden, brightening.

They followed her out the front door. Grace put Terrence down, and he immediately started running in circles around her, happy to be back outside and free of the rope.

They walked down the spotless streets. A couple walked by and smiled. They were tall and thin, with perfect hair and straight white teeth. They could have been models.

"Have you noticed there hasn't been one single person here who isn't thin and good looking?" Grace pointed out.

"Uh huh. A land full of models!" Hayden said, turning his head to check out a cute red-haired girl strolling by.

Grace felt out of place. She looked at Leona whose coffee-colored skin was flawless, and her long dark eyelashes framed her beautiful brown eyes. Grace felt a twinge of jealously.

They neared the café they had passed earlier. People were seated in small groups around glass tables on the patio, talking and smiling.

"Let's go in here," decided Leona. No one argued.

They pushed open the gate.

A teenaged hostess came up to them. She was wearing a green tunic and apron with a small green cap on her head. As she sized each one up, a scowl slowly emerged on her face. This was something new to Grace, in this city where everyone smiled.

"Can I help you?" she asked.

"Four for lunch," responded Tim.

She looked down at Terrence, who was hiding stealthily behind Grace's legs.

"I'm sorry, you can't bring…that thing in here."

"Please," pleaded Grace. "I don't have anywhere else to put him. He won't be any trouble."

"Sorry, he's going to have to stay on the other side of the fence. You can tie him to that bench over there," she said, pointing.

Grace reluctantly went back through the gate and tied him up as she was instructed.

"Sorry, boy. You just stay here for a bit. I'll bring you out a doggy bag."

Terrence whimpered but then obediently curled up under the bench.

"At least we can see him from here," she said to the group as she joined them at a large round table under a green umbrella.

The hostess handed them each a menu. "Enjoy." She turned around abruptly and walked off.

The morale of the group instantly increased at the thought of a good meal. It was late in the afternoon, and Madeline's breakfast seemed like a distant memory.

Tim suggested they take off their masks before the food arrived and agreed to hold onto them. This made everyone feel even better.

Hayden read from the menu out loud. "Never, ever give up…. Huh?"

Grace opened hers and read the first thing her eyes landed on.

"Smiling people are happy people…. What is this?"

"This isn't a menu," said Leona angrily. "It's more propaganda!"

"Maybe it's just the reading material they pass out *before* they give us the real menus," suggested Tim hopefully.

"It's those *Secrets* again," Hayden said, reading further.

"Two. Eliminate godvernment terminology from…"

"That's it!" Leona interrupted irritably. She pushed her chair out and stood up.

"Excuse me!" She waved at a waitress who was chatting with another table across the patio.

"*Excuse me!*"

Grace sunk down in her seat, embarrassed, as everyone stared at them.

A waitress came over, smiling but looking irritated. "Yes?"

"Can you give us your actual menus?" Leona demanded.

"Please," added Grace, smiling.

The girl looked confused. "Those *are* the menus."

"Um. No," retorted Leona. "Food menus! "We need *food*, not a to-do List!"

Grace looked around, aware people were staring at them. She noticed the other patrons didn't any have food. Several had drinks that looked like milkshakes. "Maybe we came to the wrong place?" she said.

"It says café on the sign," said Hayden.

"What do you have to eat?" Tim asked the confused waitress kindly.

The girl looked upset. "Uhh. I'll be right back."

She walked off quickly into the indoor part of the café.

"What kind of weird restaurant is this?" Hayden asked.

The waitress returned with an older man with slicked-back hair, presumably the manager.

"Hello," he said to the table. "What seems to be the problem?"

"The problem *seems*," began Leona, "to be that we want to order some food! When I told *her* that"—she gestured toward the poor teenage girl, who was standing behind the manager, looking scared—"she looked at me like I said I wanted to eat *her.*"

The man nodded. He looked at the waitress. "Go bring them the special."

The girl stalked off, relieved to get away.

The manager turned to the table. "You're not from around here, are you?"

"No," responded Grace. "But we have vouchers, and we really need to eat…"

The man laughed.

"Vouchers? We don't accept godvernment vouchers here. This is a free society. I am sure you will enjoy our special. It's on the house." He walked off.

"Okay, so they are bringing us food, they must just not have it on the menu," said Grace, relieved.

"It had better be good," Leona grumbled.

A minute later, the waitress came back with a tray. On it were four very tall glasses filled with a foamy light-brown liquid.

She set them down on the table. "Bon appetit!"

"Uhh, what is this?" asked Leona.

"The special…er, you requested," the waitress replied then walked away quickly, before they could ask any more questions.

Hayden sniffed his. "Must be a milkshake or something?"

"It looks like what the other people here are drinking," commented Grace. "At least it will fill us up, hopefully. It looks pretty thick."

Leona wasn't convinced. "This is a bunch of…"

"Maybe it's like a smoothie?" suggested Tim.

"Okay, guys, on the count of three, let's all take a sip." Hayden had his glass ready at his mouth. The others did the same.

"One…two…three!"

Grace took a mouthful then spit it back in her cup, trying not to gag.

"*Sick!*" Leona spit hers out immediately as well, spewing it onto the floor.

Hayden swallowed and then looked like he was about to vomit.

Tim held his in his mouth; his cheeks puffed up like a chipmunk, not wanting to swallow.

"Dude, don't do it, man, it's not worth it. Spit it out!"

Tim turned his head and spit the liquid back into his cup.

The others in the café were staring and pointing. A couple at the table near them got up and walked out, huffing and mumbling.

Grace desperately wanted something to get the nasty taste from her mouth. "Gross!" she exclaimed.

"Ew! Ew! *Ewwwwwww!*" Leona shouted.

She picked up the tall glass with what remained in it and flung it across the table. She hadn't aimed to hit anybody, but it struck a passing waitress on the shoulder, covering her face and neck with the milky slime. The woman stood in shock. The glass lay shattered on the stone floor.

One woman gasped, while another fanned herself vigorously with her menu. Everyone else froze.

The manager came charging to their table, red faced and waving his arms. "No, no, no, we can't have this here! I am going to have to ask you to leave."

Leona was livid. "We want *solid* food! Surely you people eat! What is the problem?"

The manager didn't seem fazed by her anger.

"This is what we serve. *We* don't have a problem. No one else is complaining. *You* are the problem."

Leona glared at the manager. "You people are messed up." She scowled. "Come on, guys."

She got up and walked out the gate, slamming it behind her. The others got up out and sheepishly followed.

The manager yelled after Leona, "Somebody needs to put their training smile back on!" Then he turned back to the mess in the restaurant.

Grace's head was aching from hunger and anxiety. She sat on the bench and untied Terrence. The others sat down as well, trying to process what had just taken place.

Two couples that had been inside the café came out, chatting.

"Mmmm, that was so satisfying," one of the women remarked.

"Yes," the other said, "that's my favorite café. I like it much better than any of the others in the city."

Their male companions were talking as they helped the ladies with their coats. "Number seven does the trick for me," one said passionately.

"Well, you haven't devoured the *Secrets* like I have," the other man replied condescendingly. "Yes, sir, the EC would be a better place if more people *really* digested number four."

The two couples continued their discussion as they walked away.

"What the hell is wrong with these people?" muttered Leona. "Has everyone gone crazy?"

Hayden's stomach let out a loud growl. "That's the freakiest café I have ever been to. Must be a hangout for intellectuals. So, what are we going to do now?"

Leona stood up suddenly.

"Well, there's no point in sitting here. Let's go."

"Where are we going?" asked Grace.

Leona was already a pace ahead of them. She turned back, her big eyes flashing and a slight smile on her face.

"To find some food!"

Grace's mind wandered as they walked along. The city that had seemed so open and welcoming before now seemed unfriendly and overwhelming. They were lost and stuck out like sore thumbs in this bright, clean city. Hayden looked like an unmade bed. Tim had dark circles under his eyes, which were bloodshot, leaving him looking like a desperate animal. Leona's hair was as untamed as ever, and she had a continual sour look on her face. Grace walked with her head down, tired and hungry.

They walked through what appeared to be a residential area. High-rise apartments lined the road on either side of them. There were balconies, each with two identical chairs, a small table, and one tall plant in the corner.

At the end of the row of apartments there was a high wall covered by a large mural. It wasn't like the outer walls surrounding the city; it was thinner and made of wood, like a backdrop to a play. On it were pictures of the shops and apartments they had passed before, all neatly in rows. It was two stories high and stretched as far as they could see.

"That's odd," remarked Grace. It looked so lifelike even though it was about half of the normal scale. She touched it.

"Why do you think they did this?" asked Hayden.

"I wonder…" said Tim.

Hayden walked up to the mural and pounded on a door on one of the painted buildings. "Hey, anybody home?" he called out with a mischievous grin on his face. "We are just poor, wayfaring strangers!"

The fake door cracked open slightly.

"*Ahhhh*!" Hayden jumped back, surprised.

It opened wider, and a man emerged from the facade. He didn't look like anyone else in the EC. He was large, bald, and had a thin scar running from his lip down to his chin. He wore dirty sweatpants and a ripped T-shirt.

"Hello," he said to the group with a slightly raised eyebrow.

"Hi?" said Hayden, still staring in awe at the wall that had just opened up. "We come in peace."

The man cracked a smile. It was a real smile, not forced like the others. He looked both ways down the street. "Come in quick while no one is looking."

Hayden and Leona were already stepping through. Tim went in next and looked back at Grace, who hesitated. "Come on, Grace. It's okay," Tim said, motioning for her.

Grace raised her eyebrows and shook her head back and forth. "I don't want to go in there." The man walked through the entrance and met Grace on the other side. She took a step back, recoiling at his appearance.

He smiled, looked directly into her eyes, and spoke softly. "I understand. The decision to step behind the façade is often the most terrifying part of the journey."

He walked back to the door, put one foot on the other side, and held out his hand. "It's your choice, young lady."

Grace decided to take the risk and walked through the door, Terrence on her heels.

What they saw on the other side was no longer the shining, clean streets of the EC, but pot-holed, half-ripped-up pavement with trash scattered all over. There were buildings made of old brick, some of them abandoned with smashed windows. Others were boarded up.

"Why did they build a wall around this place?" asked Grace curiously. The man turned to her.

"Well, it is natural to try to hide what you are ashamed of, I guess."

Grace pressed him. "Why paint a mural on the wall?"

He chuckled to himself.

"A façade is a powerful thing, young lady. Stare at it long enough and the illusion becomes the reality."

Leona was discussing something with Tim quietly.

"You really think we can trust this guy? He could be bringing us anywhere."

"I think it's okay," said Tim. "Something about it feels right."

Grace wanted to find out for herself. She approached the man again as they continued to walk.

"So, um, who are you and why do you live here and not on the other side?"

The man considered her question.

"I'm Charlie, and I prefer it here. I don't exactly fit in with the beautiful people."

Grace looked at him suspiciously. "Are you, like, a criminal?"

The man looked amused.

"Some might call me by that name. Others might say heretic, or maybe revolutionary. I prefer *ragamuffin* myself."

Leona joined the conversation.

"Okay, man, how can we know you're not leading us into some kind of trap? Why should we trust you?"

The man just smiled at her.

"Maybe your question should be, 'How can you trust those the people out there?'" He jerked his thumb toward the wall. "Relax, we're almost there."

Grace caught a whiff of something delicious. Her stomach groaned in anticipation.

Charlie stopped at a brick building with boarded-up windows and opened a door for them.

"In here," he said, motioning. Leona took the leap and went first, the others following. They walked into a large room where a few long tables were set up, surrounded by mismatched chairs. Several people were sitting down. It smelled incredible! The scent was familiar, like bread baking, mixing with another spicy scent.

They followed Charlie's motions to sit down, their hunger overcoming any fears they had.

The others seated at the tables looked like the rejects of society. Some were overweight, most wore ragged clothes, and some were just plain scary looking. This was not the same scene they had witnessed earlier, with "perfect" people in the fancy café.

Grace noticed some ladies seated at a table in the corner. They were dressed very casually and looked to be thin, and pretty. They all wore dark glasses and were hunched over their plates. They looked out of place with the rest of the crowd.

Just then, Charlie reappeared from a back room carrying a large round tray filled with a steaming-hot pizza. A man followed behind him carrying two trays. He had a black chef's apron on that was covered in flour, as was his face.

"You!" Grace shouted suddenly, to her own embarrassment.

The man approached their table, setting down a large pizza in the center.

It was the Orchard Owner.

"Hi there, friends. I hope everyone is hungry!"

"You keep showing up!" exclaimed Grace. "I mean, I am a little concerned you are following us."

The man smiled that warm smile of his. "Actually, *you* keep showing up wherever *I am*, yet I'm not concerned." The Orchard Owner laughed out loud, grabbed a slice from the tray, and bent down to give it to an eagerly waiting Terrence.

"Well, what are you doing *here*?" asked Grace. "And who *are* you?"

The man smiled brightly at her then turned to Charlie, who was serving another table.

"Charlie, who do *you* say I am?"

Charlie turned to Grace and her friends.

"The best damn baker in the EC, that's who!" They grinned at each other like old friends.

"But, what...who...how?" Grace couldn't get her mind around it. The others didn't seem to notice anything strange.

"Hayden!" Grace said in a loud whisper. "This is the guy...the Orchard...the barbecue man! Don't you recognize him?"

Hayden was preoccupied with devouring his slice. "Huh? Who? The guy covered in flour?"

Grace turned to Tim. "He fed us barbecue, remember?"

"Yeah, maybe...but remember, my eyesight isn't so good," Tim murmured, enraptured by the flavor of the hot pizza.

Grace couldn't take her eyes off of the Orchard Owner as he moved from table to table, greeting his guests. Coming back around, he picked out a large piece of pizza covered in sausage, peppers, mushrooms, onions, and olives, and plopped it on Grace's plate.

"Grace, you are worried about so much. But right now, there is only one thing that's important. Please eat before this gets cold. It's brick-oven-baked crust, the best kind!"

He walked away, serving the other people. Grace noticed how he touched people's shoulders gently and talked and laughed with them.

She couldn't understand how this man kept showing up in the same places they were. Who was he really and what were his motives? Was he with the godvernment or the EC? Just then, she remembered one of the Secrets warned, "Don't accept food from strangers!" What if this was some kind of trap?

"Hey, guys, I don't know if this is such a good idea," Grace whispered to the others. "We may get into trouble."

Tim was staring at his pizza. "We're hungry, and he is feeding us. I don't understand how this could be a bad thing." He closed his eyes, took a big bite, and smiled rapturously.

"Right on, Tim, my man." Hayden was giddy as he reached for his third slice. Holding it up, he began to sing, "If loving you is wrong, I don't wanna be right."

But Grace was now very worried that their decision to ignore the *Secrets* could somehow prohibit them from seeing The Wizard. She didn't want to be a revolutionary or a ragamuffin. She just wanted to go home.

Leona, who had not touched her food, got up and approached the Orchard Owner, who was chatting with Charlie.

"Look," she began, "I don't know who you are, or who any of these people are, but I'm able to pay my own way. Charity is for losers! I've got some vouchers here..." She scrounged in her pocket until she pulled out a few pieces of paper.

The baker shook his head gently. "I'm sorry. This food isn't for sale."

Leona reached out and thrust the vouchers in his face.

"Don't give me that line! Everything is for sale in this world! Everybody has an angle and everybody wants something! What do you want from us?"

"I want you to eat. It's impossible to see things clearly when you are empty. Eat, and everything will be fine, I promise."

Suddenly looking very weak and small, Leona shoved the vouchers back in her pocket and sat back in her seat. She glanced back up at the Orchard Owner, and without thinking about it, she grabbed a slice of pizza and took a big bite. It wasn't long before she had finished and was reaching for another piece.

Hayden did the same, munching with his mouth open. "Yummm!"

Tim's eyes were closed, and he had the most contented, grateful expression on his face as he savored every morsel.

Terrence was busy, visiting tables and snacking on handouts.

Grace stared at the food directly in front of her.

"Grace."

She felt a hand on her shoulder.

Something in his voice made her trust him.

Without hesitating, she took a big bite. The savory goodness exploded in her mouth. A feeling of peace, like slipping into a warm bath on a chilly night, began to course through her body.

# CHAPTER 13

# THE SHOW

*"Man is least himself when he talks in his own person.*
*Give him a mask, and he will tell you the truth."*

— OSCAR WILDE

The Orchard Owner passed out cups of fresh-squeezed lemonade. Charlie helped him.

Stomach full and feeling like a new person, Grace took a sip of the faintly sour yet refreshing drink. Looking around, she noticed one of the women in the sunglasses staring hard at her. Or at least it looked like she was staring, as it was hard to tell with the sunglasses.

Grace gulped. What if this woman was a spy from the EC? What if the Orchard Owner was some sort of revolutionary or criminal? Her heart began to race, and she felt flushed. She had a sudden urge to get up and run away from the pizza feast.

She leaned in toward Hayden. "Maybe we should hurry up and get out of here. We need to make sure we get to the meeting on time."

Hayden helped himself to another slice. "Yeah, okay, I guess you're right," he said half-heartedly.

Grace turned to Leona, thinking she'd be in agreement. "Maybe we should leave soon."

Leona looked up from her pizza. "Yeah, sure. We need to get out of here," she said, taking another bite.

Tim looked over at the Orchard Owner, who was serving another table. "He looks familiar but I can't place him."

"Tim," said Grace, "we just saw him! That's what I said earlier. He fed us barbeque chicken, remember?"

Tim squinted at the Orchard Owner. "I don't know, Grace. Are you sure that's the same guy?"

"Of course I am! How can you not recognize him?"

"Whoever he is," began Leona, "nobody just gives away food for free." She took the crumpled vouchers, straightened them delicately, and put them back in her pocket.

The Orchard Owner approached them, and everyone stopped talking.

"Mind if I have a seat?" he asked.

"Go ahead, man," said Hayden.

The Orchard Owner sat down at the table. He still had flour on his face. Grace felt ashamed. She hoped he hadn't overheard them.

Leona broke the silence with her usual bluntness. "So...what's going on here? Why are you hiding out? Are you a godvernment spy? What's the catch?"

The Orchard Owner laughed out loud. "No catch, Leona. Hungry people come to me, and I feed them."

Leona looked confused, and then she blurted out, "Hey, how do you know my name?"

He cracked a half-smile but didn't answer. Instead of pressing him further, Leona fell silent.

Hayden nodded his head. "I get it, man. It's good karma. Do for others what you want them to do for you, and all that. Very cool, thanks. We'll be sure to return the favor down the road and keep the good vibes going."

"Yes, thank you," said Tim, pulling his eye drops out of his pocket. He squeezed drops into each of his eyes.

"My pleasure," said the Orchard Owner, smiling warmly.

Tim blinked his eyes several times, and the drops formed like tears, running down his face. He blinked again and looked at the man with the flour on his face. "You...you gave us chicken before..."

Before he could respond, Leona got up from the table. "We should probably head out. We don't want to be late for our *important meeting.*"

Her tone was slightly bitter. Grace was relieved they had an excuse to leave.

"Thanks again," she mumbled toward the Orchard Owner.

The baker looked at her like he could read her thoughts. For some reason, she didn't want him to know she would rather be on the other side of the mural. Once again she felt compelled to warn him. "I believe those women over there are part of the EC. Better be careful," Grace whispered.

"I'll see you around," he said. "I'm glad you came. And, Grace, I never worry about other people's opinions, and neither should you. It always spoils your dinner."

Hayden reached out his hand, and the Orchard Owner shook it. "Sorry to eat and run, but we've got to go to a meeting. Thanks for the awesome pizza!"

"Any time," said the Orchard Owner. "Was a pleasure being with you again."

Hayden looked at him curiously then turned and joined the rest of the group.

They walked out of the building and made their way back down the road, toward the secret door. Arriving, they opened it and stepped back outside into another world.

Grace looked around, making sure no one saw them come through the hidden door. Not seeing anyone, she breathed a sigh of relief. "It's good to be back in civilization."

She fastened the leash back onto Terrence's collar. The dog squirmed but obediently let her do it.

"It's getting late," said Tim.

"To the meeting!" said Hayden.

Grace was really excited about the meeting, although the thought of talking to The Wizard made her nervous, in a thrilling kind of way.

"Does anyone have a clue which way to go?" Tim interrupted her thoughts. The four stood looking at the high-rise apartments.

"We should just go back the way we came," Grace assured him. "Jared said everyone knows where the Great Hall is, so we won't be able to miss it. Does anybody know what time it is?"

"Sorry, I left my princess watch with my stupid fake smile," said Leona.

"We could ask someone," suggested Tim.

But the streets were strangely barren.

"It's gotta be close to seven o'clock." Hayden squinted up at the sky. "If the buildings weren't so tall I could try to tell by the position of the sun."

"No doubt, nature boy," Leona quipped.

The group picked up the pace and continued toward the center square. They noticed a few people gathering on the steps. Grace decided to approach them.

"Hey, do you know where the Great Hall is?"

A woman with enormous lips and big green eyes answered her.

"Of course! See that big round building? You can just see the top of it behind the training center."

Grace looked and saw a large, round building that looked like an enclosed stadium.

"Yes," responded Grace excitedly. "Do you know what time it is?"

"You have about thirty minutes," replied the woman. "You better hurry if you want good seats."

"Thank you!"

Grace approached her friends. "Let's go. We need to get good seats."

"Good seats?" Leona said sarcastically. "I thought we came here to meet with this dude in person!"

"It's in that big building; that's the Great Hall," Grace pointed out, ignoring Leona's comment.

"Sweet!" said Hayden.

Tim handed out the smile masks, and everyone, albeit reluctantly, put theirs back on.

As they approached the building, they saw a mass of people zigzagging in a large, partitioned line. Men dressed in suits, wearing earpiece walkie-talkies and sunglasses, guarded large doors.

"Seriously?" said Leona. "Is this for real?"

Tim shrugged. "I guess we should get in line."

They took their place at the back of the line and stood with the others. People were chattering politely, excitedly, waiting to get in. Everyone looked slim, gorgeous, and content, albeit some looked a bit too thin. Not one looked depressed, angry, or frustrated.

Leona was getting impatient. "How long is this going to take? Can't we cut the line?"

"With all these people, I am a little worried we won't get a chance to talk to The Wizard," Tim remarked.

"Tim's right. Let's blow off this meeting," scoffed Leona.

"Guys, come on, this is our only option. We'll figure out a way to see him." Grace was slightly annoyed.

"Yeah, I've got to talk to him! Even if I have to jump up on stage and tackle him!" said Hayden.

A woman standing in line in front of the group was obviously eavesdropping on their conversation. She turned to her friend standing next to her and whispered. They both smirked.

"Hayden, *shut up,*" Grace urged.

"What?" said Hayden.

The line started moving forward. Grace craned her neck around the crowd and saw the doors had been opened. She picked up Terrence so he wouldn't get lost in the swell of moving people.

"Here we go, Terrence! We're off to see The Wizard!"

They crisscrossed through the line, occasionally nodding at someone in the passing aisle. Finally, passing through the large double doors, they entered the concourse of the large arena. A giant screen hung on the wall. A video was showing scenes of the EC and clips of The Wizard talking. It reminded Grace of the video they watched in orientation. Upbeat music played over loudspeakers. They followed the crowd to the nearest door and walked out into an enormous arena.

The four of them looked around at the tall ceilings held up by thick rafters. Spotlights shone on a massive stage on one end of the arena. Several giant screens hung from the ceiling.

"Whoaaaa!" said Hayden, holding out his arms in amazement. "This is impressive."

Grace urged the others to hurry down the stairs to try to get as close as they could to the stage. They were about halfway down when a security guard stopped them.

"I am sorry, this section is reserved for new members and special invited guests only," he said tersely.

"What if we are?" challenged Leona.

The man look amused. "You're not."

"It's okay, let's just sit over here." Grace pointed to some empty seats a couple rows up.

They sat down and got comfortable. The seats were soft and padded. Grace held Terrence close. No one seemed to mind or even notice he was there.

The music was loud, a sort of repetitive, rhythmic beat that was irritating, yet hypnotic. The arena quickly filled up with people.

Grace felt a building anticipation. She whispered to Hayden, knowing he would understand.

"Do you ever feel like you are just in the right place at the right time, like maybe all of your life has built up to this one moment?"

Hayden nodded slowly. "Like destiny?"

"Something like that," she whispered back.

Leona and Tim were having their own conversation. "This is crazy. He's like a major celebrity. Are those security guards by the stage?"

Tim wasn't put off by her questions or harsh tone. He was even-keeled, as always.

"Don't let it bother you, Leona. This is why we are here, to meet this guy. Relax and enjoy the music."

"I'm relaxed!" Leona huffed. Surprisingly, she listened to Tim and leaned back in her chair, taking a deep breath.

The audience was mostly seated when the lights dimmed and a lone spotlight shone brightly on center stage. A man appeared from behind the curtain and walked out into the light.

"Jared," Grace said, disappointed.

"Man, this guy gets around," Hayden whispered to Grace.

"Shoulda known," added Leona.

"Welcome, everyone!" Jared began. "It's my pleasure to be your host for tonight's meeting. In just a little while, we'll hear from *the man* himself. But to start things off I'd like to crank up a little something for all the newcomers here today. Watch and enjoy!"

A video started to play on the giant white screen.

"Everyone's welcome at the EC!" said the voiceover. The video played footage of citizens looking casual while chatting in cafés and throwing Frisbees in a park.

The video showed people laughing, reading menus, and sitting in classrooms, raising their hands while the voiceover continued, explaining how the Formula and the *Secrets* kept them happy, healthy, and wholesome.

When the video was over, the spotlights came up on the stage. A full band and a large group of singers rose up from beneath the stage on a platform, and they began to play. The whole thing was playing on the giant screens, which made it seem larger than life.

Words began scrolling across the screen as the singers sang,

*"O, when we live by the Secrets,*
*We can give all the Secrets.*
*For we give and we live*
*O, the Secrets are the way of life."*

The music was building, and some people in the crowd stood up and clapped along to the beat. Grace felt moved by the words and shot up from her seat to join in. The rest of the group looked at her strangely, but she didn't care.

A beautiful, thin, dark-skinned woman got up and led the audience in another song. Her voice was high and clear.

*"The chains of bondage are broken*
*We no longer play by their rules*
*We make our own reality*
*And The Wizard gives us the tools"*

The woman sang it with such passion and bravado that Grace felt every note. The lights flashed, and the energy in the room was palpable. She felt her body swaying to the rhythm, her whole being feeling alive in the moment. The song finished, and everybody clapped ecstatically.

Jared came back on stage, smiling. "Wasn't that amazing? Please be seated, everyone. And now, I am going to ask you to put on the viewing-enhancement glasses located in the seat-back pocket directly in front of you."

Grace fished for the glasses, finding them next to some pamphlets and a pen that had "The EC" engraved on it.

Jared continued, "And now it is my privilege, my honor, and my greatest pleasure to introduce to you the one, the only, *The Wizard!*"

The crowd went wild. Grace quickly put the glasses on, and like a magician, The Wizard appeared out of thin air. Grace jerked back in her seat, startled. He looked so near, so real, but she knew once again it was only an image.

"Hello!" The Wizard began in his usual sugary voice. He was so close Grace could see the hazel flecks in his green eyes. She felt an impulse to reach out and touch his face and see if he was really there, but she didn't want to look stupid. A part of her feared she would feel flesh instead of empty air.

"Welcome!" Once again he sat on a stool, smiling, dressed in black slacks and a grey button-up shirt that complimented his sculpted arms.

"You are indeed very fortunate people to be here tonight. I have some absolutely awesome things to share with you all!"

He looked around the room then his eyes went right back toward the center. It looked like he was talking directly to Grace, as if no one else was in the room.

"Isn't it wonderful to be here? What a fabulous city we've made. I just *love* it here! Don't you? It's so beautiful, the best place in god. You guys look amazing out there, as usual. Special welcome to all our newcomers! I hope you already feel like a part of this community. Hey, listen closely now, we are about to hear a true story of how one EC citizen's life has been transformed from awful to awesome! You may now take your glasses off, temporarily."

The video stopped, and one woman sat on a stool in the center of the stage.

"When I first came to the EC, I was afraid," she said. "I didn't know how to live apart from the stern godverment rules. But as soon as I graduated from the New Member's class and began to apply the *Thirteen Secrets,* my life began to change! And the Formula has kept me going strong!"

Grace glanced at her friends to see what they thought. Hayden was leaning forward in his seat, looking excited and focused. Tim looked relaxed, leaning back. Leona had her arms crossed and still had her glasses on.

"Now I am Happy, Healthy, and Wholesome! I can't say enough great things about The Wizard, and the EC!" I am so grateful! Thank you all so much! I love you, Wiz!" She began to choke up as she rose from the stool and walked off the stage.

The audience clapped. Grace clapped, too.

"That was so scripted," she could hear Leona say to Tim in a cynical tone.

The lights cut out again as music started.

Jared was center stage again, and he spoke into the microphone.

"Now turn to your neighbor and whisper in their ear: 'I've got a Secret!'"

The group felt awkward but pretended to comply, mumbling in each other's ears.

All except Leona. "I'll tell you a secret, these people are smoking something. Strong!"

Jared continued, "Hey, don't go around looking all lame and needy! Get with the program! It's worked for countless others. Don't be left out of the party!"

The lights dimmed.

*BOOM!*

Grace jumped as the sound of an explosion came from the stage. There was a flash of light, and she realized flames were coming from either side of the stage.

Dancers dressed in tight, sparkly dresses began to run onstage from all directions, weaving around each other, waving flags and banners that had the *Secrets* written on them in gold lettering.

The choreography was superb and precise. The costumes, banners, and flags were all perfect. The lights flashed, and flames shot up once again. The audience oohed, aahed, and clapped in appreciation of the professionally choreographed dancing and pyrotechnic display.

The presentation went on for several minutes, and then the dancers left the stage, the music and lights faded, and once again the video came on.

"Please put on your viewing-enhancement glasses once again," a voice announced over the speakers.

Just like that The Wizard was once again directly in front of Grace. It gave her a little thrill.

"Wasn't that a wonderful story earlier? And how about a big round of applause for the EC dancers! And as always, please give it up for the most awesome act in the land, the one and only EC Band!" The audience erupted into loud applause.

"Speaking of stories, now I am going to tell you one about myself."

The audience cheered. Grace found herself cheering, too. There was something about him that attracted her, but she couldn't put her finger on it.

He launched into a story about being a child, growing up in a poor home under the godvernment rule and how their family never had enough.

"But then I realized, I was okay!" he said passionately. "And then I realized, *you* were okay, too! I knew the people of god needed a new way, a better way, our own way!"

Everyone cheered.

The Wizard lowered his voice to a whisper for effect. "And then, friends, I went up to the top of a high hill, sat down, and thought... and thought and thought. And when night fell, I thought and thought some more. When the sun rose I was still thinking.

"I was thinking that the people of god were ready for a change... no, a revolution! We were ready to be free! We could do this! We could become awesome people of god without all the rules that were just making us miserable and uptight. I asked myself, 'What does everyone really want in life?' The answer came down from the sky and hit me like a lightning bolt: to be Happy, Healthy, and Wholesome! Then a second lightning bolt hit, and I realized *how easy* this all could be accomplished: just give people what they want! Now, how easy is that!

"I closed my eyes and fell into a deep sleep on that hill. In my dream, a voice whispered in my ear, 'god helps those who help themselves.' Again the voice spoke, 'god helps those who help themselves.' 'But the godvernment controls the food supply!' I said.

"The voice in my dream spoke again. 'There is a formula, there is The Formula.'

"Friends, I won't ramble on with the details about what happened next, but suffice it to say when I woke up, I had the *Secrets* to success and the Formula for living. I came down form the mountaintop and told a few friends, and they told others, and soon there was an uprising, of positive energy.

"Hey, if that's too heavy for you, don't worry! All you need to remember is found in *Secret* number four. Smiling people are happy people! So smiling *must* be the secret to happiness! Now how simple is that?"

Loud cheers erupted across the stadium.

"We are so laid back, we bend over backwards to make people feel welcome here! The godvernment is so rigid! We don't want to act like them, and we sure don't want to look like them, do we?" He gave a broad wink to the crowd.

"*No!*" everyone shouted in unison.

The Wizard continued, "Newcomers, join us! Citizens, keep up the good work. Be one of the chosen ones, one of the beautiful people. Be a dreamer, a world changer, a true man or woman of god! I want *you.*" He pointed his finger, and once again Grace flinched as she fully expected to feel his touch.

Then, just as quickly as he appeared, he disappeared again. *BOOM!* Flames shot up from all sides of the stage.

The spotlight on the stage came on, and Jared appeared.

"What a great message!" Jared said enthusiastically. "You can put your glasses away, and stand up as we sing one last song! Please be sure to join us for refreshments in the concourse afterwards. And don't forget, the New Members meeting continues tomorrow morning at nine."

Jared went off stage as the platform holding the band and singers rose up once again. They were already jumping into a song with an upbeat tempo.

It was repetitive, so this time Grace found it easy to sing along. A video of colors and shapes and pictures came on. Along with the lights and sound, it created a hypnotic effect, making Grace's head spin.

The flames came up again with one last blast, and the song ended with a burst of color and noise.

The house lights came on, and the people started filing out.

Hayden, Tim, and Leona sat staring at Grace. Terrence was resting under her chair, undisturbed by the loud special effects.

"Wow, that was something." Grace turned toward her friends. "When he said, 'I want you,' it was like he was talking just to me."

Hayden smiled. "Yeah, it was pretty cool. I'm diggin' this guy. He really seems to know what he is talking about. Power to the people and the energy of positive thoughts, right on!"

"That was complete and utter crap," said Leona flatly.

Tim wiped his eyes. "That woman seemed so happy." He sniffed.

"Yeah, she did," said Grace, still too in awe of the whole experience to listen to Leona's negativity.

They followed the crowd out of the arena and back out to the concourse.

People all around were shaking hands, smiling, and saying to one another, "How are you?" Some answered "Great," while others didn't respond but simply repeated the question. The friends found it odd at first but quickly began to participate in the shallow greeting ritual. All except for Leona, of course, who was scowling with her hands stuffed in her pants pockets.

"Jared said something about refreshments," said Hayden, looking around.

They noticed a large group of people gathering in a corner.

"Maybe over there?" suggested Grace. They walked over, curious.

A line was forming under a sign that said "Refreshments". They got in line, moving with the rest of the crowd. Grace noticed people leaving the line carrying cups of various sizes. A few people had giant cups that could have held a half-gallon of liquid each. They looked slightly embarrassed. Others had tiny shot glasses that they downed quickly, throwing the empty paper cups in a garbage can, walking away looking satisfied.

"Maybe this is a coffee bar," said Tim.

They made it to the front of the line. Several men behind the counter were pulling levers attached to huge barrels.

A foamy tan substance could be seen flowing through the spouts.

"Oh God, not that stuff again." Leona wrinkled her nose.

The man behind the counter smiled and said, "Welcome, new-comers! Be right with you."

The man reached up on a shelf, grabbing four giant half-gal-lon-sized cups.

He filled each one with the liquid and handed them to the group.

"Fresh Formula," he said matter-of-factly. "Extra, extra large for you." He winked at Leona.

They queasy quartet grabbed the cups and walked away from the counter.

"What is it with these people?" complained Leona. "Where's the real food?"

"Are you sure it's the same stuff? I am gonna try it. Maybe it's not so bad," Grace said. She was feeling thirsty and was hoping she was right.

She sipped hers gingerly. The same warm, sour taste filled her mouth. She swallowed.

"Maybe it's an acquired taste?"

Hayden shrugged his shoulders. "It wasn't that bad…"

He started chugging his.

Leona looked away. "Ewww. I can't watch you, I'm going to gag."

The group walked out of the arena. It was late at night now, and the city was lit up in a soft glow. They headed back toward the New Members building.

"It's going to be so good to crash in that bed," said Tim, yawning.

Leona walked off the main road, found a nice flowered bush, and quickly dumped her Formula out. "Sorry, bush, I hope this shit doesn't kill you." She threw the cup behind the bush.

Terrence sniffed at the ground then turned and ran away quickly. Grace ignored Leona, hoping no one would see. She was really getting sick of Leona's pessimistic attitude.

Hayden was still sipping his drink occasionally. "It's not *that* bad." He made a face as he said it. Tim and Grace carried their giant cups, not sure what to do with them. Terrence followed, his leash wrapped around Grace's wrist.

They walked back inside the lobby of the New Members building.

"Well, I am going to crash. Good night. See you all in the morning," Grace said. The others said good night and went to their separate rooms. Entering her room, Grace immediately removed Terrence's leash. He looked grateful. She set her cup of Formula on her nightstand, still not sure what to do with it.

Laid out on her bed was a pair of soft blue pajamas with a note attached: "Please put dirty clothing outside the door. They will be washed and returned by the morning."

"How thoughtful!" she said to Terrence. After washing up and brushing her teeth with the complimentary EC toothbrush, she put on the pajamas, placed her filthy clothes outside the door, and crawled under the covers of her simple bed. Terrence jumped up after her, snuggling at her feet.

"Goodnight, boy," she said.

As she lay in bed, she pictured The Wizard's kind, strong face. She tried to imagine what she would say when she finally met him, and rehearsed it to herself until she drifted off to sleep.

# CHAPTER 14
# THE PARADE

*"You can fool the whole world down the pathway of years,
and get pats on the back when you pass, but your final
reward will be heartache and tears if you've cheated the
guy in the glass."*

— DALE WIMBROW

G race woke up to her alarm clock. She yawned, not wanting to get up after a comfortable night's sleep on a real bed. Her stomach growled. Terrence was stretched out at the foot of her bed.

Grace sniffed the air. "Ew, what *is* that?"

She realized the foul smell was coming from her cup of Formula. She rolled out of bed, picked up the cup, and began dumping the foul-smelling liquid down the bathroom sink. She noticed small chunks of something in the mix, causing her to gag. She quickly rinsed out the cup and sink, making sure she didn't leave a single drop.

After showering and putting on the fresh clothes that had been left outside her door, she put on Terrence's leash and walked out into the lobby, where Hayden and Tim were waiting. They greeted each other good morning.

"Where's Leona?" Grace asked.

Hayden shrugged his shoulders. "Running late I guess. *Women!* Want me to go pound on her door?"

"I'd like to see what happens if you tried that," Leona responded, walking out into the lobby to join them. She had a slight smile on her face.

"Sleep well?" asked Tim.

"Yeah, besides some creepy nightmares about having to sit through meetings all day and listen to a guy you can only see by wearing 3D glasses. Oh, wait..."

They headed back to the classroom they had met in the day before, entered the room, and sat down.

"That Wizard had better show up this time," Leona remarked.

The room filled up pretty quickly, with more people than the day before. The door opened behind them. Grace turned excitedly, hoping it was The Wizard. It was only Jared. She tried to hide her disappointment.

He walked up to the front of the room.

"Good morning, ladies and gentlemen!" He looked around the room, smiling.

"Good to see, no, *great* to see so many of you have chosen to take the narrow road and join our ranks here at the EC. Today you are going to have the special privilege of hearing more from The Wizard himself. If there is time, we will also have a question-and-answer session at the end."

Grace's eyes lit up. She turned to her friends seated in the row with her.

"See!" she mouthed to them. Hayden grinned, and Tim smiled at her. Even Leona looked a little less annoyed.

This is what they had all been waiting for. Leona raised her hand.

Jared glanced at her. "I am sorry, questions will have to wait until the end. Now, it's time to hear from the great Wizard."

Grace leaned forward in her seat, expectant. He could be walking through the door at any moment. Jared walked to the back of the room and fiddled with a computer sitting on a desk.

Suddenly, a grinning face appeared on the screen in front of them. The Wizard was back, but this time no glasses were required.

"Hello, everyone! Welcome to day two of New Members orientation!" he said enthusiastically.

"They can't be serious," whispered Leona loudly. Grace elbowed her in the ribs. Leona elbowed her back, harder.

"Hey, pal!" Jared addressed the screen from behind them.

"Jared! Good to see you!" said The Wizard.

Grace was excited to see that this was going to be interactive, instead of simply another video presentation.

"Always great to see you," Jared said from the back.

The Wizard on the screen looked around the room.

"We have quite the group here today. It's so wonderful to see you all. I am very pleased that you have decided to take the next step of commitment in becoming a member of our family here at the EC."

As he said the last part, Grace could swear he was gazing directly at her. His smile grew wider, and she melted into her chair.

Hayden looked at her, his face crumpling up like he was stifling a laugh.

"I have so much I want to tell you, so much I want to show you," continued The Wizard on the screen. This time he was looking directly at Tim.

"I want you to know I understand where you are coming from, my friends. I understand the *emptiness* you feel inside."

Tim averted his eyes.

"But know this, my whole reason for being here is *you!*" He pointed directly at Grace and her friends.

"I want *you* to be the best person you can be. I want to help you reach your full potential, to learn the Secrets to a successful life. In short, I am here to help you to become Happy, Healthy, and Wholesome."

His gaze shifted to Leona. She had a sullen scowl on her face and shifted in her seat uncomfortably.

"You are all here because you are searching for something. You have been searching for a long time but have failed to find it, haven't you?" He paused and nodded his head.

"Perhaps what you seek eludes you *because* you seek it. Maybe if you stop searching, what you seek will find *you!*"

"*Wow!*" Hayden whispered, his eyes and mouth wide open.

"You spend your days gazing into a mirror," The Wizard continued, "and wonder why all you can see is yourself. *So...*" The tone of his voice changed from a concerned fatherly one to that of a salesman making a pitch.

"I am going to ask you to do something for me, for the EC, for god. This is the first step on your journey towards your destiny."

The Wizard disappeared, and a video played on the screen. It showed a dull landscape, a shantytown, filled with dilapidated shacks and desperate-looking people dressed in rags. They looked miserable. The voice of The Wizard continued.

"These people live just around the corner from you, but they live in ruins. Burdened and enslaved by the harsh, evil laws of the godverment, they have lost everything."

The video showed people carting around heaps of trash. It reminded Grace of the town devastated by the storm, only worse. Her heart immediately went out to them.

"The city is in chaos, but the rebellion has begun. Revolution is at hand! The people are breaking out from under the old system, and that opens a window of opportunity to show them something better. They need *you*. They need you to come and rescue them from terrible pointless lives and invite them to live in this beautiful city. After they get cleaned up, of course!"

The images disappeared, and The Wizard came back on and continued speaking.

"Once you have done this, you will have proven that you have what it takes to be a citizen of the EC."

He looked right at Grace and held her gaze for a while. She had trouble breathing.

"You will be seen as confident, purposeful, as someone who is making a difference."

Leona mumbled and coughed into her hand. Tim squeezed drops into his eyes.

The Wizard kept his eyes on the row they were sitting in. "A few of you have been chosen for a special mission."

Grace hoped more than anything she was one of them. Maybe he saw something in her no one else did. She always knew she was meant for something greater. Somewhere beyond the bland scope of her own reality, there lay a deeper purpose for her life. She just hadn't discovered it yet.

"Right now we are going to go over some important training information. Jared, are you ready?"

"Yes, sir." Jared passed out some colored pamphlets. He gave each of them a small stack.

Grace took a pamphlet in her hand. It had a picture of a happy family on the front, all dressed sharply and smiling. Grace recognized it as the same photo from the billboard.

"This flier will help explain to these poor broken people what the EC is all about. It will answer some basic questions, and give a few hints about the *Secrets*. Make sure you don't actually *give* them the *Secrets*. That comes later, in due time. We don't want to overwhelm these poor souls. Just a taste will be enough."

The image of The Wizard remained on the screen while Jared went through the pamphlet for about twenty minutes, describing what to tell people about each page. Grace listened as closely as possible.

"You can make a difference!" The Wizard announced with great passion. "It's all about *you!* These people need *you* to make a difference in their lives."

Slow and reflective music was starting to play, along with more footage of the impoverished people. It touched Grace to the very heart. The longer the slow, sad tune played along with the images of weary and joyless faces, the more desperate she felt to make a difference.

"Okay, the time has come! If you are ready to go on the front-lines, help god become a better place, and in the process transform yourselves, I am going to ask you to stand up. Don't worry about that person sitting next you or what they may think. Make the decision today!"

Grace remembered Rhoda, the little girl they had met, and how she wandered the streets barefoot. Her heart began to beat faster, and her palms were sweaty. She knew she was meant to help these people. She knew this was her destiny.

She was the first to stand up. "I'll go!" she blurted out passionately. Normally, drawing attention to herself like this would have mortified her, but she was captivated by The Wizard.

The Wizard looked at her and grinned. "Here we have a true believer! What is your name?"

"Grace," she said shyly.

"Grace..." He mulled over it for a moment. "Grace, yes...I can tell you are a special one. A true leader!"

Grace beamed and felt weak in the knees.

"Now, is there anyone else who wants to join Grace?"

Awkwardly, slowly, the others in the room stood up, everyone except Leona.

The Wizard looked at Leona but didn't speak. After a number of seconds that felt like minutes, she ambled to her feet. Grace knew she only stood because she wanted to stay with their group.

"Looks like it's unanimous after all," said The Wizard excitedly. "So great to see everyone has caught the EC spirit!"

Leona simply could not hold back anymore. She ripped off her mask, dropped it on the ground, and spoke in a loud and penetrating voice. "Hey, dude! My friends and I didn't come here to 'catch a spirit,' to be *members*, or to go on an errand for you. We came a long way because we heard that you help people that are in trouble or lost. We came here to see *you*. I know the people in that town are in rough shape. I came from a place like that. But my friends are *needy* too. How about helping *us* first!"

Grace turned a bright shade of red, her cheeks burning with embarrassment.

The Wizard spoke. "I am trying to help you, miss, uh..." Everyone in the room turned around to look at the little group.

"Leona"

"Leona. Right. You seem a little angry and sad. Maybe you should have worn the smile-helper a little longer."

"I know your game," retorted Leona hotly. "*They* may not be able to see through you, but I can." Everyone gasped.

The Wizard laughed. "Jared, be sure to write '*great energy*' on Miss Leona's chart." Then he addressed her again.

"Leona, I am so happy and proud that you and your friends have faith in me. I *can* help, and that is just what I am going to do!"

They all looked at each other.

"Really?" asked Leona somewhat skeptically.

"Of course! Helping people is my *passion*. But first, I need you to do something for me. Go on this journey. Spread the news about our fabulous EC! Help me reach these people, and I will help you."

"Can you really help us all?" Grace asked eagerly.

The Wizard flashed his most perfect smile. "Of course I can! Granting wishes is what I do!"

Grace and the others looked at each other and nodded their heads.

"I guess there's no choice," Leona grunted as she sat back in her seat.

The class went on for another thirty minutes. They learned all the proper responses to the questions the people might ask. They learned how to deal with godvernment representatives if confronted by them while on the mission. They learned how to survive in the harsh conditions and were strongly urged not to accept "food" offered to them by outsiders.

The meeting ended abruptly with The Wizard saying good-bye and good luck and suddenly disappearing. Jared announced that, unfortunately, due to the interruptions, there would be no time for questions and answers.

"Congratulations," Jared continued. "You have completed the first step of the membership process. You can now remove your masks and pass them to the front. Just remember to keep smiling!"

Everyone gladly complied, and he dismissed the class.

As everyone was beginning to file out, Jared called out.

"Hold on. Grace, you stay." Grace looked at the others and nodded.

"I'll be okay."

"We'll wait for you in the lobby," said Tim.

Leona leaned in toward her.

"If he tries anything…"

Grace gave her a reassuring smile. "I'll be okay."

"Right," said Hayden. "We'll catch up when you're done."

When everyone else had left the classroom, Jared turned to Grace.

"The Wizard has had his eye on you! He sees something very special in you, Grace. You have great passion, enthusiasm, and you don't allow the negativity of others to undermine your beliefs. You project innocence, purity, and honesty. These are the traits that lead people to trust and to want to follow. The Wizard is always on the lookout for leaders like you! Of course, being a very, very pretty young woman doesn't hurt either."

Grace blushed

*"You* like it here, don't you?"

"Oh yes!" Grace replied enthusiastically.

"The Wizard believes your destiny lies here in the EC. You know what you want, you just need to believe more in yourself."

Grace looked down, embarrassed

"Now, at some point on this mission, you will be given the opportunity to speak. You will do fine—just study the pamphlet. We have designed this system so that people like you can present our message without having any firsthand knowledge. The script is written. All you have to do is memorize a few lines."

That didn't sound too hard. "Um, okay...I guess I could do that."

"Wonderful!" Jared continued, "Secondly, there is a man, a man called Zay. He was an important man, until he went, well... kind of crazy."

Grace looked at him wide-eyed. "Is he dangerous?"

"No, no. Not in the least. He is a little strange, but not dangerous. He is not important anyway, but what he has is very important. He has a book, and I need you to get that book and bring it back to The Wizard."

"What makes you think I can get it from him? There must be people better qualified to do this?"

Jared smiled. "Well, The Wizard believes you are the perfect person for the job. He believes you are the perfect person to confront Zay. We need you to do this, Grace, for The

Wizard, for the EC, for god. The Wizard is counting on you! Your friends are counting on you! Are you up for this *very* important mission?"

Grace looked down at Terrence, who was sprawled out on the classroom floor. He looked up at her and wagged his little tail. She thought for a moment. She wanted to prove to The Wizard he was right about her, that she was special. She had no idea how she'd complete the mission, but she had to try.

"Yes, I'll do it."

"Good!" said Jared. "I'll brief you further once we arrive."

"Okay," said Grace nervously.

"You can leave now. Gather your belongings before we meet out front for the big send-off."

Grace smiled wryly to herself at the word "belongings." She had nothing. "All right. Thank you, Jared, for, uh…giving me this opportunity."

"My pleasure, Grace."

Grace began to walk out of the room, Terrence following.

"Oh, and Grace…" She stopped and turned around, facing Jared.

"Yeah?"

"Don't tell your friends about the book, okay? Just tell them I asked you to speak."

"Okay," replied Grace. She was curious about the need for secrecy but didn't want to ask any more questions.

She walked out to the lobby, where Hayden was pacing.

"So what'd he want?" Hayden immediately asked her.

"He wants me to give some speeches when we get there."

"Cool!" said Hayden.

They pushed open the big lobby doors, walking outside to gather by some benches.

"So…they want *you* to speak?" Leona started. "You *are* brainwashed. This guy just wants us to work for him. It's the same old manipulation game. I've been there before. I know a scam when I see one. I doubt he's ever gonna help us!"

Grace was indignant. "Leona, maybe if you stopped being so suspicious and negative about everyone and everything, you may actually be happy for once!"

"You've forgotten why you came here in the first place!" Leona fumed. "I thought you were trying to go home."

"You say I am brainwashed, but at least I believe in something!" Grace yelled, not acknowledging Leona's last comment. "You don't believe in *anything*! By the way, no one is *forcing* you to do any of this. You didn't have to come to the class. What do you *want*, Leona? Why did you come with us?"

Leona was looking down. She looked a little hurt. The air was filled with awkward silence before Leona answered coldly.

"I know what I want, and it doesn't have anything to do with any of the garbage Mr. Wiz-bang was dishing out. Admit it. There is more happening here than *citizenship classes*. You like this Wizard dude. I mean you *really* like him! You've actually got a crush on him!"

Grace's cheeks were flushed, and her eyes stared downward. Hayden and Tim stood silently, watching the conversation play out. Once the girls had stopped talking, Hayden spoke up.

"Okay then! So, I thought that class was pretty interesting. I wanna know more about what this guy has to say! This is why we are here, right?"

Tim agreed. "Those poor people. We need to do something to help them." He looked gently at Leona. "You still have some time to decide if you want to go or not. If you decide not to go, I will stay here with you. I won't leave you here alone."

Leona looked up at Tim. "No, I won't keep you from going. You guys won't survive very long without me, anyway. I know what kind of place you are heading into…all too well."

"I thought you believed The Wizard was a con artist," mumbled Grace under her breath.

Hayden gave her a look. "Let's all try to get along," he suggested. "We've made it this far, *together.*"

Grace looked away, wondering how long their little group would last. It wasn't like she wanted them to leave, at least not Tim and Hayden. She still wanted them to find what they were looking for.

She glanced over at Leona, looking so small on the bench with her thin arms crossed. The tattoo, written in cursive, running down her coffee-colored forearm:

*Only God Can Judge Me.*

Ironic, considering where they were. Grace sighed. Deep down, she didn't want Leona to leave. She just wanted her to see what she saw: the brilliance of The Wizard and the EC. If she would just clean up her act a little, lose some of her attitude, and stop mouthing off, Leona could fit in.

People began assembling outside of the arena. The crowd was growing larger by the minute. They lined both sides of the street leading down toward the town hall. Grace's excitement grew, and she couldn't wait to see what would happen next. She recognized a few others from the New Members class.

Jared came strutting toward them. "Please gather around, everyone," he said.

The group formed a circle. Grace noticed not everyone from the class had come. *Some of them must have wimped out,* she thought.

"Is The Wizard coming?" she asked him.

Jared ignored her. "All right, guys, it's almost time for the commissioning parade to begin. Here come the batons."

Two guards came carrying boxes. They put them down on the ground next to Jared. He picked out gold batons and passed them out. He lingered for a moment when he came to Leona.

"I'm sure this trip will be life changing for you."

"Yes. I am sure it will be," Leona responded without batting an eye.

A marching band arrived and began to play. They were wearing sharp green uniforms with funny-looking green hats brimmed with yellow tassels. Grace giggled out loud as she saw crowds of people lining up all the way down the street as far as she could see.

"This is a big deal!" she said to Tim excitedly.

He nodded, smiled nervously, and reached for his eye drops.

Terrence stayed very close to Grace, growling occasionally.

A large cart pulled by two beautiful white horses approached. There was seating on the cart along with a large television screen streaming live video of the event.

"Here's your ride," said Jared, grinning.

The group climbed up a short ladder into the back of the platform and stood around the large double-sided video screen. The crowd noise was increasing as the anticipation grew. A group of guards and people dressed in fancy costumes formed a procession behind the float. Grace noticed their tour guide from earlier, dressed in a flowing green chiffon gown. Men wore green uniforms adorned with multi-colored ribbons along with gold and silver medals.

"Those must be all the officials!" she pointed out to Hayden.

"This is pretty cool!" he said with the excitement of a little kid.

The band started to march. Jared climbed up on the float and joined the group. The cart began slowly moving down the street, following the band.

"This is it. Make sure to wave and smile your best! Make everyone wish they were *you!*" Jared said excitedly.

He switched on the TV, and The Wizard's face and upper body appeared. He smiled and waved.

The cart wobbled and creaked as the horses pulled it slowly down the road.

Grace recognized the tune. The crowd was jammed on both sides of the street, and everyone started singing.

*"Live good and life will be good to you!*
*Think good, feel good, look good!*
*Follow the Secrets!*
*And you will be good!"*

Grace sang along, waving at the cheering crowd, feeling like she was on top of the world.

She saw a little girl in the crowd being held up by her mom and waved at her. The girl waved back.

Grace was filled with pride and a sense of destiny.

She had always been a spectator in life. From now on, she would be a participant.

## CHAPTER 15

# THE BADLANDS

*"Being against evil doesn't make you good."*

— ERNEST HEMINGWAY

From the top of the float, Grace felt like a celebrity. The crowds around her cheered and sang off key. Some held up handmade signs saying things like:

*Good Luck on Your Journey!*

*Come Back with New Citizens for god!*

Grace's arm got tired from all the waving, but she didn't mind. They were nearing the city gates, which were open wide, revealing the long road ahead. The marching band stopped playing abruptly. This was the end of the parade. Grace turned toward the TV. She wanted to ask The Wizard a question, but the screen was already black.

"What a send-off!" remarked Tim.

They all got down from the float. A wagon being pulled by two large black horses came out of the gate.

"Here's our ride," Jared announced.

They climbed into the wagon. It was comfortable, with padded benches. Grace watched Leona shake her head.

"You don't have to do this," Grace whispered privately. "There is still time to turn back. We'll find you when we return."

"The more you try to talk me out of this, the more it makes me want to come." She smiled endearingly.

Jared stood up in the front of the wagon.

"All right, crew, remember what I told you. It's going to take a few hours to get there. I would suggest going over your material and memorizing the main points so it's easier for you when we arrive. Ready for an adventure!"

Grace shouted, "Yes!" The others didn't say anything but stared at her. She sat back in her seat.

The paved road soon ended, and the wagon bumped along the dirt path, heading away from the city. Grace looked back and felt a twinge of loneliness, even though she was in a wagon crammed with people. In the short time she had been in the EC, she had felt a real connection, like this was a place she could truly belong. She stared at the mountains beyond the EC and marveled at how far they had traveled.

She thought of The Wizard, how he was even more amazing than she had imagined. She felt guilty for the feelings she was harboring inside. Who was she to imagine herself with someone so... perfect? But he *had* noticed her out of the crowd. He *had* said she was special. He *had* chosen *her* for a special secret mission. She hoped she wouldn't fail him.

As they passed the carnival, everyone stared, but no one said a word. They could hear the faint sounds of carousel-style music and carnies shouting at patrons, wooing them to play the games. That same sickeningly sweet smell permeated the wagon. An image of the dancing temptress flashed in Grace's mind. *Come to me. Be powerful and free.* She blinked her eyes and shook her head to clear it.

171

She quickly turned back around, facing the front. As the carnival faded in the distance, the road split, going in another direction.

As time passed, the landscape began to change. The rolling green hills that surrounded the EC were replaced by a flat, barren, and dull landscape. Grace noticed a few scraggly trees with withered leaves. It looked even worse than Pleasant Grove, without the damage. Everything looked dead. She remembered the video they had watched in class. This was going to be a hard reality to face, she thought.

The cart creaked along for a long while, then stopped next to the old concrete foundation of a semi-collapsed building. All that remained standing was one wall.

Further down the road a crowd gathered in front of the town. People were yelling.

Angry graffiti phrases covered the old wall:

*The godvernment Lies!*

*The Wizard Is a Fraud!*

Jared stood up. "Welcome to the Badlands, team. Remember your training. Hand out your fliers, and engage with the residents. Tell them there is a better way of life. Show them what they are missing by not being in the EC. Beware of the protestors."

"Protestors?" asked Hayden. This was one thing Jared hadn't mentioned before.

"We're going to meet in the town square at noon. Don't get lost."

He looked at Leona. She gave him a sugary smile.

Grace and the others stepped out of the cart. The ground was cracked and dry.

"Watch where you step," murmured Tim. He did a little dance to avoid stepping on a dead rat.

Terrence sniffed at it.

"Gross, boy, no!" Grace called him away.

Tim leaned down and stared at the animal.

"That poor thing," he said, squeezing eye drops into his eyes.

Jared and the wagon driver began to pass out silver thermoses with straps.

"Good," said Tim. "I haven't noticed springs around here, so fresh water may come in handy."

"*This* may come in handy," replied Jared. "These are filled with something much better than water."

"Don't tell me," said Leona.

Jared continued, "That's right, team, you are all being equipped with a generous supply of highly concentrated Formula for your mission! When you feel weak, the Formula will give you strength to carry on."

Hayden unscrewed the cap and sniffed the contents, and Leona bit her tongue and glared at Jared.

Grace was too nervous to think about the Formula. This was a scary place, and unlike Pleasant Grove, this time they weren't just passing through. This time she was on a mission.

Jared approached Grace and motioned for her to follow him to a corner near the old wall, away from the wagon so no one could hear.

"So are you ready, Grace?"

She had some questions stirring in her mind, but she felt ashamed to ask them. She was supposed to represent the EC, but she really didn't know anything except what she had been told in class.

"I have a few questions I'd like to ask before we go in."

Jared nodded. "Go ahead."

"Well, um, I know this place is controlled by the godverment, but there is so much I don't understand. Like who is this Zay guy and why is this book so important?"

"You won't understand everything now. That's okay. You're just going to have to trust me. Trust The Wizard."

Jared looked her straight in the eyes and said in a serious tone, "He is counting on you, Grace. As soon as you complete this small task, he will answer all your questions. He'll give you everything you've ever dreamed of and more."

Grace considered this for a moment. Something else was nagging her, though.

"But what if I can't find Zay? What if I fail?"

"You won't. Remember, you were *chosen* for this task. Time to get going. I'll meet with you in the town square when we all gather there. I need to take care of some business. Good luck! Oh, and one more thing I meant to mention. If I were you, I'd keep a close eye on that creature of yours."

"What do you mean?" Grace asked, puzzled.

"These people are desperate. Many are refusing to work for the godvernment and that means no vouchers. There are starving people in there, and hunger makes people do…"

"You aren't saying…uhhh. Seriously? Terrence?"

"I am sure everything will be fine. Just keep an eye on him, that's all. Gotta run."

Grace went back to the wagon, confused and a little stunned.

Hayden, Leona, Tim, and Terrence were waiting for her. The others had already formed small groups and moved on.

"You ready to go, Grace?" asked Hayden.

"Yeah, sure. Let's do it."

Grace picked up Terrence and held him tight. He struggled in her arms unhappily until she finally put him down. "Stay close, boy, real close."

The four friends and the dog marched into the Badlands.

Leona unceremoniously ditched her thermos in a barrel of trash. "Feel lighter already," she announced.

They heard all kinds of commotion as they entered the town. There were tents lined up on the edge of the main road, some of them stamped with "property of godvernement". There was a table with a line of desperate-looking people. Around the line were pro-testers, marching with signs and chanting slogans.

As they approached, Grace read a few of their signs.

"Rolls NOT Rules!"

"The godvernment feeds us poison!"

"Will Work WHEN Fed."

It was all complete chaos. The godvernment officials were try-ing to herd people back into the lines, but nobody was listening. The four new EC ambassadors carefully walked around the crowd and line, trying to get through without being harassed.

"Come on, let's get away from here. Jared said to avoid these people," Grace said quickly.

Hayden was looking all around, his eyes wide.

"Whoaaa, man. This is so not peaceful!"

"Yeah, it's a good thing we have that propaganda to hand out," murmured Leona sarcastically.

They had made it through the crowd and were now on the oth-er side, looking around and taking everything in. Small children ran barefoot, some of them naked. Frail-looking men and women walked quickly through the streets, avoiding the protestors.

They passed a group of young adults who were sorting and stacking bricks. The youths paid little attention to the group of strangers, but Grace noticed that Terrence was getting a lot of stares.

"Stay close, boy," she told him again. Terrence obediently stayed at her heels.

Hayden walked up to the group.

"Hey!"

They stopped working and looked at him suspiciously. A few of the girls whispered to each other and laughed.

Grace approached one of the girls and asked softly so the oth-ers couldn't hear, "Do you know a man called Zay?"

The girl shook her head and turned away.

Hayden had his hand in his pocket and was pulling out a pamphlet. He handed it to another girl with pretty, dark eyes.

"Hey, I know you are, ummm, working really hard and that's cool, but if you come to the EC you won't have to work like this. It's a great place, really."

The girl looked at him and then burst out laughing, revealing a mouthful of decaying teeth. This shocked Hayden.

She turned to her friends. "He wants *me* to join the *EC*."

They all laughed.

"Yeah, I guess he doesn't get that you're not EC material! But hey, maybe you will clean up well! You and the mighty Wizard might just become best friends!" a rough-looking guy said, laughing.

Hayden wasn't sure what to do.

"I was just trying to help..."

The guy who spoke up interrupted him.

"Help us! With what, pamphlets? Look at us! No, really look at us, you idiot! Do you really think words will help us? Now, if you've got any food on you, we can talk."

"Sorry, man, no food, just info."

Hayden looked sad. He placed the pamphlet on the pile of bricks next to the girl.

"If you change your mind, we are meeting in the town square soon."

The girl snickered at him. "You don't really believe this, do you?" She pointed at the pamphlet. "I can tell you're not one of them. Hey, have you been to the carnival?"

"Yeah, I've been there. Why?"

"We are all planning to run away and join the carnival as soon as we can. We've heard that they're looking for people to work the concessions. We've heard there are games there that will make your dreams come alive."

"Yeah, and maybe your nightmares, too," Hayden responded quietly.

The girl just stared. Hayden had no more to say, and he turned back to the group, looking dejected.

Leona was trying to hide her laugh. "Well, that went over well. Cheer up, Hayden. Maybe the next girl will come with you."

They continued on, leaving the youth at the brick pile behind. Grace was a little disturbed by the scene. The training videos had portrayed the people as being desperate and thankful that the EC had come with an offer of a better way of life. Instead, they mocked Hayden without even looking at the pamphlets. Maybe this would be harder than Grace had imagined.

They walked past kids kicking a ball around in the street. One of the little boys wearing an oversized ripped T-shirt stopped the game and ran over to the group. Instinctively, Grace pulled out a colored pamphlet and handed it to him.

He took it, looking it over.

"Do you have anything to eat?" he asked eagerly.

Grace felt guilty. "No, I am sorry."

The boy threw the pamphlet down in the dirt and ran back to his game.

"This is tragic," said Tim, watching the kids. "They are barefoot, there is trash and probably broken glass all over the place. Too bad we don't have shoes to give them instead of this literature."

"Come on, Tim, use your head!" said Hayden. "They could give the flier to their parents and the whole family could move to the EC. Their quality of life would be ten times better than if we just gave them shoes."

"Who knows if they even *have* parents," Tim said morosely. He looked like he wanted to cry, but everyone knew he couldn't.

He approached the barefooted boy. "Son, I care and I want to help."

"Do you have any food?" the boy answered as if programmed to ask the same question to everyone.

"Sorry, I don't. All I have is…errr…um…a sort of drink. You are welcome to have some." Tim unscrewed the lid to his canteen and offered it to the boy.

The child sniffed the liquid. "Got any food?" the child repeated with a blank expression.

"Sorry, no food…only Formula." Tim looked dejected.

The boy ran back to his friends.

"Come on, guys, let's keep walking toward the town square." Grace forced herself to ignore the suffering and stay focused on the mission.

They passed a tent where an old man was sitting outside on a crate. He was wearing dark glasses and an old, dirty hat.

He looked up at them.

"Are you from the godvernment, here to arrest me?"

Tim approached him gently. "No, sir, we are not in the godvernment, don't worry. Can you direct us to the town square?"

The man replied, "The blind shall lead the blind. It is those who think they see that will remain blind. Yes, when those with sight look to the blind for answers, the storm is near."

"The town square," asked Leona. "Are we close?"

Tim elbowed her. "I think he's blind," he whispered.

"Town square…yes. There's a broken statue. It wasn't always broken, you know. Strange things happen here. A strange man walks there. Beware."

Grace looked at him quizzically. Could this strange man he spoke of be Zay?

The man kept babbling.

"The two great forces, always at war with each other. Both think they are good and the other is evil. Oh, the blindness of vanity. What they don't know is that there are more powerful forces at work, one dark and the other light. Light is not white, you know. Sometimes, somewhere, truth is like a rainbow."

The man leaned back, appearing as though he had expended his energy and needed a nap.

The group kept walking, not sure what to do.

"Hold on."

Grace ran back to the man, leaning in close to him.

"Do you know Zay?" she whispered.

The man just mumbled, keeping his eyes closed. "Trying to find a man? He could disappear, just like all you think you believe in. What you really seek is not a man, but a story with a happy ending. All you have is your story." Within seconds the man began to snore.

Grace frowned and joined her friends.

"What were you doing?" asked Tim.

"Never mind," Grace quickly replied.

"And *that guy* is one more reason why," began Leona matter-of-factly, "this place gives me the creeps."

"You think *every* place is creepy," Hayden pointed out. "Maybe you're the one that's creepy."

Leona rolled her eyes.

They continued walking, with Grace managing to discreetly approach several people to inquire about Zay. No one would answer, and she was getting frustrated. Her legs were tired, and her head ached from the events of the day so far.

Finally, they came upon the edge of what appeared to be the town square. It was littered with cardboard boxes, trash, and people.

"I think this is it," Grace said solemnly.

A large statue of a man stood in the middle of the crowd. The head had been knocked off, and the remainder of the monument was covered in graffiti, making the inscription at its base illegible.

The people were buzzing around, like they were waiting for something to begin. Grace noticed some wooden boxes that had been fashioned into a kind of platform. She gulped; panic gripped her. They were waiting for a show, and she was it.

Jared appeared out of the crowd and approached her.

"There you are! Right on time," he said, smiling at Grace, ignoring the others. "Are you ready?"

Leona gave Grace a strange look. She nodded a yes to Jared, even though her heart was about to beat out of her chest.

Hayden patted her on the back. "Good luck, Gracie. We believe in you."

Grace watched Leona turn to Tim and ask him something. She followed Jared over to the platform.

"Did you find him?" asked Jared.

"No...I tried. No one would help me." She felt like a failure, though she was irritated that her secret mission was so obscure. She was also terrified at the prospect of speaking.

"Keep searching," said Jared. "Ask around. The rebels know him. They are just afraid to admit it. Use your womanly persuasion. After they hear you speak, I think they will trust you."

The crowd was murmuring. There were protest signs but nobody held them up. No one was chanting or shouting. They didn't look angry, only tired and defeated.

"These people have nothing, Grace. *We* have everything. Remember that. All you have to do is explain how wonderful it is to be in the EC. Just be yourself and remember, The Wizard is counting on you."

Grace nodded, too nervous to respond. She clutched her EC pamphlet tightly. Terrence stood at her side, looking up with his big black eyes.

"You can do this." Jared smiled and gently shoved her toward the platform. She stepped up, her legs shaking. The crowd settled down and stared at her, some amusedly, some with contempt, and others blankly. She looked around but didn't see one smiling face, except for Hayden, who was grinning wildly. Tim gave her a thumbs-up. Leona looked unusually concerned.

"Hello," she began. Her voice sounded small and lost.

Speaking louder and more forcefully she continued. "I'm Grace. I am here to talk to you today about a special place." She opened up her pamphlet, her hands shaking. The crowd grew silent.

"Umm, the EC is the place to be, where you are free. You don't have to work for food…"

The crowd murmured. Grace wondered if anyone had ever told them about the EC. She kept going.

"Everyone is happy, smiling. Life is good. We don't suffer like you do here."

"You don't know anything about us!" shouted a man from the middle of the crowd. His words created some murmuring.

Grace continued, terrified, glancing down at her pamphlet, trying to remember what she learned so it didn't look like she was reading a script.

"The *Secrets* to happiness are in The Wizard's teaching. You will know how to live…"

"Come on! We've heard this before!" the same man interrupted her.

"Tell us something we don't know!" someone else shouted.

"Yeah!" shouted a woman. "We're hungry. Don't tell us, show us!"

Grace gulped. She felt light headed. The crowd was working themselves into a frenzy. Some were yelling out obscenities; others were dancing and waving their protest signs. Her chest felt constricted with panic. She searched her mind desperately for something to say.

Suddenly, a thought came into her mind:

*Tell them your story and only speak what you know.*

She closed the pamphlet and spoke in a loud voice that echoed through the crowd.

"Look, I am not from god. I am from...from...Texas!" Memories came flooding back to Grace, about the day she landed in god.

The crowd gasped. The man yelled out, "Texas isn't in god!"

"Don't say that!" Grace shot back. "It is so, I mean, it isn't... but..."

She paused, took a deep breath, and began to tell her story. In that moment she felt strangely calm, at ease.

"Please listen. I am lost in this strange place, simply trying to find my way home. On the way I met these people...my friends." She gestured toward the front row, where the others stood. "I don't know where I'd be without them. Anyway, I thought all I wanted was to figure out how to get home. But now I'm trying to figure out what *home* means...who I am...why I am here...where *is* here..."

The crowd fell completely silent as if spellbound. Grace, emboldened, continued.

"I am hungry just like you! We would have starved if it weren't for this strange man who keeps showing up, feeding us, for no reason. I just feel lost. My heart goes out to you people, I really want to help you, but...I don't have anything to give. I hope the EC will be all I...*hope* it will be. But at this point, that's all it is...hope."

Tears began forming in her eyes; she stopped talking and looked into the crowd, upon faces of suffering and desperation. Without saying another word, she stepped down from the platform. Spontaneous applause erupted through the crowd. Jared grabbed her arm.

"What are you doing?" he hissed in her ear. "You have the people in the palm of your hand. Close the deal!"

"I thought all you really cared about was getting this book?" Grace retorted, pulling her arm away, drying her eyes her sleeve.

"Yes, The Wizard wants this book, but we also need to attract new citizens to the EC. They need us, and we *need* them in order to sustain our way of life."

Grace was confused by Jared and wanted to question him, but a crowd had gathered around them and was pressing in.

"Please, tell us more!" one girl said pleadingly.

Jared whispered to Grace, "Don't forget, The Wizard is counting on you." He smiled and retreated back into the crowd.

Hayden, Tim, and Leona pushed their way through those gathering around Grace. People were asking about Texas, about the man who gave away food. More people came and pressed in to try to touch her.

"Oh gosh, this is insane," said Grace, beginning to panic.

"Let's get you out of here," said Tim.

Leona agreed and pushed her way through the throng, as Hayden and Tim, each holding one of Grace's arms, followed in her wake.

"Tell us more. We've never heard words like this! Grace!" A woman grabbed onto the hem of Grace's jacket.

"I don't have anything else…" She jerked away, trying not to cry again.

The four friends were fighting their way through the crowd when Grace remembered Terrence. She looked down, but he wasn't there.

"Oh my God! Terrence!" she shouted. "Hayden, Tim, Leona, have you seen him?"

"He was just here a minute ago," Tim replied, still holding Grace's arm, trying to break free of the unruly mob.

"*Terrence!*" Grace screamed as loud as she could and began to push people out of her way as she tried to run.

"Oh God, if anything happens to Terrence!" Her mind was racing, and raw panic gripped her.

They were almost through the crowd when a wild-looking man suddenly appeared directly in front of them, blocking their way. He had wispy brown hair that fell to his shoulders but stood up in the back. Bushy, nearly connected eyebrows were the most prominent feature on his face, making him quite ugly.

"Out of our way!" yelled Leona, about to shove him.

The man looked at Grace, then pointed to his feet, where the tiny dog sat, looking bewildered. "Lose something valuable?"

"*Terrence!*"

At the sound of her voice, he ran to Grace and jumped up into her arms as she bent down.

Grace hugged him tight until Terrence squealed.

"Hey, boy, don't ever leave my side. I thought you were going to be eat..."

Grace stopped herself from finishing the sentence.

"Thank you so much, sir," Grace gushed at the strange man. "How can I ever repay you?"

His dimpled chin quivered with excitement as he spoke. "I heard you are trying to find someone."

Grace froze. "You mean...Zay?"

"Who's Zay?" asked Leona.

"Shhhh," the man said. "Follow me. I'll take you there."

"What's going on?" asked Tim.

"We've got to follow him," Grace announced. "Trust me, I'll explain later."

They followed the man away from the crowd. He led them toward a building, one of the few left standing.

They stopped in front of the door, and the man opened it quickly. "Come on, in here."

"Who is this guy?" hissed Leona to Grace. "Why should we trust him?"

"No time to explain now," said Grace. "I have to do this. If you all want to stay outside, I understand."

"Are you crazy?" Hayden said. "We're totally with you."

Grace was relieved by their loyalty. They followed the man through the door into the building that looked like an old warehouse. There were no windows, although light came in through the cracks in the ceiling, which looked like it was about to cave in. Birds were nesting in the rafters. It was extremely dusty and Grace sneezed, followed by Tim, who was also blinking his eyes rapidly.

"God bless you," said Hayden. "Wait, is that what I say here?" he joked.

The man stopped in the center of the room. He smiled widely at them, making him look even scarier.

"I liked your speech," he said to Grace. "Honest, straightforward, humble, clear as a bell...except that part about Texas." He threw his head back and laughed, like the wild man they all thought he was.

Grace asked pointedly, "Where can I find Zay?"

"Hmmmm. You came for Zay? What would you like to say... nay, what do you *need* to say? There's no time for *likes* in times like these."

Grace sighed. "Where is he? You know him, right?"

The man laughed again, this time sounding more like he was cackling.

"Where he *is, is* not your real question. What you really meant to ask was 'How can I get him to give me what I came for?' did you not?"

Grace looked startled. "How do you know what I want?"

The man waved his arms about, as if conducting an invisible orchestra.

"What do we know? What we know is of no consequence compared with *who we are*. But that, I'm afraid, you can't see yet. Do you know why, oh inquisitor?"

Terrence was sniffing the man's feet and wagging his tail. Grace played along. "Why?"

The man gestured toward the door. His eyes widened even further till his thick eyebrows almost hit his hairline.

"Curtains," he whispered.

The group looked back and forth at each other. The unspoken consensus was that this man was a lunatic.

The man kept going, his voice starting out in a whisper and ending with a shout.

"You see, at first the curtains were for our own safety. Children don't know how to live, you know. They see the big bad world and want to stick their hands in every mud pie that's really cow dung, or every beehive, or every bear cave. The curtains kept the bad out, kept us from seeing it. But the problem is, we couldn't see the *good. No damn light could come in!!*"

Grace took a step back, startled by the volume of his voice. Clearly she would have to speak gently but firmly to him.

"Sir," she tried, "I really need to find Zay. I've come to ask him an important question."

The man twirled his hair around his finger until he couldn't wind it any tighter.

"Ask away. Zay is listening."

Grace looked around, confused.

"Uh, are you Zay?" Hayden asked.

The man started to laugh.

"Now you're catching on! You must be the brains of the group!"

He continued laughing, this time so hard that he began to sway as if he might fall down.

Grace felt stupid but didn't want to show it.

"Mr. Zay, I have been told you have a book, a very special book, and I was wondering if I could borrow it?"

Zay's expression changed instantly. He seemed to sober. He unwound his finger from his hair as a wide smile spread across his face.

"The book...yes..."

He reached out his arms and embraced Grace.

"I am Zay."

"Grace," she said, pulling away, feeling awkward.

He went in to hug the others. Leona backed away, but he caught her anyways.

"So…who are you?" asked Hayden.

Zay turned his back on them, dramatically.

"I am a nobody. I used to be a *somebody*, but then everything fell to pieces. But I'm glad. Sometimes you have to fall to pieces…. There is somebody to talk about who is so much more important than me. In comparison to his shadow, I am a nobody. But the strange thing is, because we have become acquainted, once again I am a somebody. A somebody, living as a nobody, nowhere… somewhere."

He spun around again, facing them. Grace couldn't tell if he was really insane or just toying with them. She stayed focused on the mission.

"The book?" she asked again.

"Yes, yes, the book. It's always about a *something*, isn't it? Or is it? People wage war, people sleep apathetically, people fight, people hate, people starve, and then say nice things to each other. Maybe it shouldn't be all about the book after all. The real power doesn't live in ink. The magic lies in the heart of the author. Why don't you inquire of me who wrote the book?"

Grace had a hard time following him.

"Ummm…who wrote the book?"

The man laughed again.

"Yes. Yes. Now that…*that* is a question worth asking!"

The man disappeared into a small room in the corner of the building.

"What the…" Leona said. "Who is this guy? What book?"

"Whoa, this dude is intense," Hayden said with a grin.

"Well, he seems safe enough," Tim whispered.

Grace hoped he was right.

He opened the door again, coming out like an actor to a stage. He held a small leather-bound book in his hand.

"Here you go," he said simply, handing it to Grace.

"You're just…giving it to me?" she said, shocked it had been so easy.

"A gift in appreciation of your speech. Has been a long time since someone spoke as you did."

Grace looked down at the book. "What's it about anyways?"

Zay grinned. "The Menu."

"The Menu?" she asked.

"Menu. Map. Names can be misleading. Choose your words carefully. Like your food, you are what you eat, and what you believe, you *will* speak, but you already know that."

"I do?" said Grace. It was a half question.

"Taste and see!" the man shouted, laughing hilariously. "Taste and see!"

With that, he turned and shut himself back into the small room.

The group looked at each other, hardly believing what just happened.

"So are you gonna tell us what's going on?" asked Leona.

Grace sighed. "Jared asked me to do this," she said, not wanting to explain any further.

Just then the door burst open and Zay returned, wearing dark glasses and an old hat. They immediately recognized the disguise.

"You…you were the *blind* man?" Tim asked incredulously.

"You assumed I was blind, but you didn't know. Everyone *here* thinks they see so clearly, I thought I would be blind, that I might see. Those who protest are blind to the problems, and therefore ignorant of answers. They build no shelter, only curse the storm. It is always about exchanging one dead thing for another, one tyrant for one who is cleverer."

He was now talking in a calm, thoughtful tone and didn't appear crazy anymore.

"Bad questions can only lead to bad answers. So choose your questions wisely, kids."

With that, he tipped his hat, winked, and walked back into the back room, closing the door behind him.

"Well, okay then!" proclaimed Hayden.

"What a nut job," said Leona.

Grace was silent. Nothing Zay said had made any sense, but had left her feeling dizzy, like she was barely holding on. She shook off the feeling, determined to focus on how pleased The Wizard would be to get the book.

"All right, we got what we came for," she said to the group. "Now let's get out of here."

# CHAPTER 16
# LOST

*"None are more hopelessly enslaved than those who believe they are free."*

— GOETHE

G race held the book tightly in her hand as they walked outside. The crowd was still gathered in the square, but no one had noticed the four strangers and pup walk out of the abandoned building. Grace looked anxiously into the crowd, hoping no one would come after her again. She had been so nervous before; it had all been a blur. But now, as she passed by, her attention was drawn to the weary and hungry men, women, and children who milled around the town square. Not merely hungry—Grace could tell by their gaunt faces that they were starving.

They skirted around the edge of the crowd, trying to leave the area without being recognized. At first it seemed to be working, but then a young girl with short red hair grabbed Grace by the arm.

"I know you. You are the one who spoke to us earlier."

The girl let go of her arm. "Can you tell me more?" she asked desperately. Grace looked down at the ground. The book was still in her hand, hidden behind her back.

"We, um..." The thought crossed her mind to give the girl a flier and invite her to come to the EC, but for some reason, she couldn't bring herself to do it.

"Do you have something for us?" the girl continued, excited. "I can tell you are not like the others. Can you show me how to get what you have?"

She was so desperate looking and Grace wanted to help, but something was stopping her from opening her mouth. Maybe it was something Zay had said. Maybe it was the book practically burning a hole in her hand. She felt guilty and torn.

"Here," she mumbled, taking the thermos from around her neck and holding it out to the girl.

The girl stared at it for a moment, confused. "What is this?"

"It's all I have."

The girl tilted her head to the side and looked at Grace with an expression of hopelessness. Without saying a word, she turned around and disappeared back into the crowd.

Grace felt a gnawing inside her but pushed it aside. She set the thermos on a nearby box. Maybe the girl would come back and get it.

"Let's go," Grace said sharply to Hayden, Tim, and Leona, who were standing by her. They had remained silent during the entire exchange.

"Let's go this way, we'll avoid the people," Grace suggested, pointing.

"Uh, okay, as long as you know where you are going," Hayden said.

"Yeah, I think this is a shortcut."

They walked an unfamiliar street, but a pile of rubble taller than their heads made it a dead end.

"Uh, let's go over here," she tried, leading the others into an alley.

"Man, I am really *starving*," sighed Hayden, pausing for a moment. He unscrewed the lid to his thermos of Formula and took a sip.

"Blehhhh!" He spit it out on the ground. "Man, it wouldn't be so bad if it was hot, or ice cold, but lukewarm this stuff is disgusting!"

"There are some things worse than hunger," Leona responded, amused.

Grace ignored the growl in her own stomach. She was beginning to feel light-headed, but pressed on. They wandered around for a while until Grace realized she had no idea where they were.

"It's probably going to be dark in a few hours," Tim said, sounding worried.

"Yeah, I think if we keep walking down this way, we'll connect with the main road," Grace said, not wanting to admit they were lost.

They passed rows of burnt-out buildings and piles of bricks and rocks. Nothing looked familiar. The streets were pretty empty except for a few people here and there cleaning up. They ignored the strange group, but Grace kept a close eye on her dog. Nobody bothered handing out fliers.

"What's all that noise?" asked Leona, stiffening.

The group stopped walking for a moment and listened. Someone was talking over a loudspeaker, but it sounded muffled. Cheers and shouts echoed the garbled voice.

"More protesting?" asked Hayden.

Rounding the next corner, they came upon a crowd gathered around a platform, where a woman stood speaking into a megaphone. On both sides of the platform were tents with "property of godvernment" stamped in white across their fronts.

As they got closer, Grace gasped. "Linda!" It was the woman from the first day, the one who had warned her not to eat from the table. She was wearing a black business suit and speaking authoritatively.

Leona watched as Grace stared at the woman, mouth open. "Do you know her?"

Grace nodded slightly. "I met her when I first arrived. I guess she must be a leader in the godverment. She is not friendly at all."

They stayed in the back, trying to look inconspicuous, and listened to Linda's speech.

"...and the godvernment program is fair and just. It is the way we have been doing things for many generations. People work for a fair wage. They get vouchers. The more they work, the more they eat. Simple, fair, and just! It works!

"The EC promises freedom, but don't be deceived! Freedom is a lie, a myth, a pipe dream. People are lazy, selfish, weak, and bad to the bone. We need a system of laws, penalties, and a godvernment that judges righteously! Those who don't work must starve! That is the only way they will learn to obey!"

The crowd cheered. The woman continued.

"The EC *has forsaken god*! They ignore the old ways and think they can live on Formula. Don't be deceived by their watered-down Formula. You must have solid food to survive! Traditions that have been passed down through generations cannot be abandoned! Things written in stone cannot be erased!"

Applause, whistles, and shouts erupted.

Grace noticed a man standing nearby was staring at her and the others. He finally approached them and handed everyone a piece of paper. "Please read this!" he said zealously. "Do I know you?" he asked Grace. He smiled, seeming harmless enough.

"No...I don't think so," she said.

"We are here to help, you know. We are good people, just trying to do the right thing. We are trying to maintain order and a stable society. Look at this town! This is what rebellion with no rules looks like. Is this what you want? Is this the kind of place you want to live in, where you want to raise your kids?

"My daughter ran off to the EC with her boyfriend when she was only sixteen. We didn't hear from her for months. She finally stumbled back home one night half starved, mumbling about *Secrets*. She talked about her boyfriend being taken away to be rehabilitated and never seeing him again. She begged for something solid to eat. Of course, we made her work first, but then she ate and seemed to be happy to be back.

"Just like Linda said, freedom is dangerous and will lead to the collapse of families, as well as society." The man began to tear up. "My little Georgiana."

"Is your daughter doing okay now?" Tim asked.

"Sadly, she took off again after being home a few weeks. She left a note saying she was joining the carnival."

"That's very tragic," Grace murmured, looking around. She felt nervous. If this man found out they had come from the EC, it might cause problems. It was time to get out of there.

"We better go. We have, uh, work to do," Grace said, hoping the man would leave them alone.

"Go where? What work? Now is the time to make your decision to stand with the godverment. Putting it off today will lead to destruction tomorrow!"

Just as Grace started to panic, Tim walked over to the man and gave him a hug. "I understand what it feels like to lose someone that you love so dearly. Maybe someday she will return." Tim shook the man's hand firmly and turned away.

Stunned by Tim's loving gesture, the man was rendered temporarily speechless.

"Let's get out of here," Leona said in a low voice.

Still holding godverment pamphlets, and wearing serious expressions so as not to arouse suspicion, they took the opportunity to slip away. Grace noticed a man on the outskirts of the crowd wheeling a small pushcart. He stopped to chat with a couple of people who were standing off to the side listening to the speech. As they got closer, Grace realized it was the Orchard Owner!

"No way!" she gasped, adrenaline rushing through her body.

He looked up and smiled as they were walking by, but Grace averted her eyes. She tried to conceal her panic, as the situation was growing more bizarre by the minute.

Tim noticed him. "Hey, that's…"

"Shhhhh, just keep walking!" Grace said, pushing Tim in the back.

Once they were clear of the crowd, they stopped to regroup.

"That was him! The baker. He's here!" Tim said excitedly.

"What!?" asked Leona, puzzled.

Hayden looked back but couldn't pick him out in the crowd. "Are you sure? What's he doing here?"

"I don't know!" said Grace. "Following us maybe?"

"So, he's part of the godvernment then?" said Hayden. "That must have been why he was hiding in the EC."

Tim looked perplexed. "No, no. That doesn't make sense. Remember at the barbecue when the woman from the godvernment blasted him for feeding people?"

"Well, I wasn't at this barbecue, but right now he is here, hanging around a godvernment rally," Leona remarked.

"It can't just be a coincidence that he keeps showing up everywhere we are," Grace said, perplexed.

"Hey, I wonder if he brought along some of that awesome pizza!" Hayden chimed in, licking his lips.

"Let's just forget about it. Either way, it's not safe here," Grace said. "We need to figure out how to get back to the wagon before it gets dark."

Grace longed to be walking the safe and friendly streets of the EC. Her throat hurt from the dusty streets, and her eyes burned. Feelings of stress, fatigue, and hunger overwhelmed her.

"We're going the wrong way," Leona said in a tired, deadpan voice.

"Hmmmm, I don't think so," Hayden said, pointing. "We want to keeping heading the way we came from."

"Uh, no, you're getting turned around because we came out the other side trying to avoid the crowd," Leona retorted. "It's *this* way." She began walking down another street.

Hayden looked at Grace for help. She hated to admit it, but Leona was right.

"I think she's right," Grace said.

Leona stopped in her tracks.

"Excuse me? What did you say? Would you mind repeating that for my own pleasure, Grace? A little louder this time."

Grace sighed. "I think you're right."

Leona smiled and started back down the road. Tim shook his head in amusement.

They walked down the street, up an alley, and around several corners until they came upon another group. Once again, they heard a voice booming over a loudspeaker. Immediately, Grace recognized a couple who had come with them on the wagon from the EC. One of the men, a wiry, pale man with slicked-back hair, was standing on a portable stage. He had a wireless microphone in his hand, and small speakers were set up in front of him. A crowd was gathered around.

Grace breathed a sigh of relief to be among "her people." Drawing closer, they stopped to listen to the man speaking.

"We are here to bring peace! The old godvernment has oppressed you for too long. We want to empower you! We are about people living Happy, Healthy, and Wholesome lives. And we accept you for who you are!"

The crowd cheered.

"We want to help unlock the potential that lies dormant within you. There are *Secrets*, friends, mysteries to life and god, hidden for ages, that The Wizard has discovered and wants to share with you. The godvernment wants you to remain ignorant, to always be on the outside looking in. We invite you to come into the inner circle of wisdom, beauty, and awesomeness!"

"The godvernment says you are nothing. We say you are everything! They say you are beyond help. We say, *help yourself to freedom!*"

Thunderous applause and cheers rippled through the audience.

Some movement on the other side of the crowd distracted Grace. It was the Orchard Owner with his cart, chatting with a group of people.

"He's stalking us. I knew it!" Leona had noticed him too.

Grace watched him take out a small object wrapped in white paper from his cart and offer it to one of the men he was speaking with. The man took it, peered under the paper, and then shoved it back at the Orchard Owner.

"What's he doing?" said Grace, having lost the ability to be surprised.

Part of her wanted to talk to him, as he had been nothing but kind and generous. But she knew there was danger in going against the established order, and trouble was the last thing she wanted. Still, maybe she should go over and talk with him? Before she could suggest it, the speech ended. The speaker got off the box and immediately made eye contact with Grace, smiling and waving. He approached the group.

"Hey! Good to see you guys here. My name is Eddie! Having any luck handing out fliers?"

The group shifted uncomfortably. Hayden's pockets were filled. Tim had given most of his out. Leona had left hers in the wagon.

"Yeah, great luck, great," said Grace, scanning the dispersing crowd, trying to keep an eye on the Orchard Owner. She couldn't find him.

"Great! I'll see you back at the wagon in a few minutes. We're gonna follow up with some of the people who made their decision today to come to the EC. Nothing more satisfying than knowing we're making a difference. See you in a bit".

As soon as Eddie had left, Grace began nervously scanning the crowd.

"Where did he go?"

"Where did who go?" Tim asked.

"Who else? Our friendly stalker!" she replied.

"How'd he get here so fast?" asked Hayden.

"Easy, he knows where he's going, and we *were* lost," said Leona.

Tim looked around. "So maybe he isn't with the godvernment? Is he with the EC?"

"I think he is with the EC. He seems enlightened. Maybe he's one of us," Hayden suggested.

Leona snorted. "*Us? Really?* Speak for yourself!"

Grace thought it was odd, though, how he seemed to fit in everywhere, but nowhere. He never asked for anything, and he was always with the strangest people.

"Should we wait for the other New Members?" she suggested, hoping the Orchard Owner would appear again.

"Let's just go," said Leona. "I know the way from here."

Grace didn't argue. As the group walked in silence, she thought of Linda and the nice man who represented the godvernment. What they were saying rang true. Then again, what her EC team member had said also made sense. She didn't want to admit it, but now she could see both perspectives.

She wondered if somehow both could be right. But that couldn't be possible. They hated each other and had completely opposite beliefs. Walking past another gang of desperate-looking kids, she shuttered. She remembered what the godvernment man said about the need for rules. She wouldn't want to live in a lawless society like this.

Besides, she was loyal to The Wizard. The EC wasn't like this place, anyway. The godvernment man just didn't understand. She would give The Wizard the book, and he would take care of her. He would help her friends and give them all they needed. As she walked through the mean streets, her stomach growled. She cursed it silently, wishing she didn't have to ever eat again.

Grace recognized some of the landmarks now. They were approaching the entrance, where the wagon was parked just on the other side of the protesters. The godvernment tables were torn down. All that remained were angry-looking, dirty people. One man was standing on a mound of trash, precariously balanced, shouting.·He was handsome, but rough looking.

"We need a resistance!" he shouted. "We need to rise up and become our own town again! Some people think the answer lies in joining the EC, but let me tell you, the oppression there is just as bad. We need true freedom! We need food without becoming the godvernment's slaves! So many of our youth are running off to join the carnival. Friends, that is not the answer. Their games are like a virus that attacks your mind and turns you into a zombie. The godvernment, the EC, and the carnival are all the same trap. The only thing that separates them is the bait. They are all puppeteers stealthily tying strings around their ignorant, sleeping prey!"

One man, who looked like a godvernment worker, shouted, "You have no food, no freedom to offer, only words. You are against everything but stand for nothing."

Grace felt uncomfortable. They walked around the edge, trying to blend in, experts by now.

Then she saw him, The Orchard Owner! He had his cart, and he was pushing it around. This time, Grace noticed more people crowded around him. As he began to hand out the packages, more people came. They unwrapped them greedily.

Sandwiches! He was handing out sandwiches.

Grace pushed her way through the crowd, abandoning all concern about being recognized.

"Grace! What are you doing?" Leona followed her. Then she saw him as well. She joined Grace, and they slowly made their way to the man.

He continued to hand out sandwiches. The people who were listening to the man shouting from the heap of trash began to swarm around the food cart. Suddenly, another man appeared and started helping distribute the sandwiches. Zay.

Grace approached him first. "What are *you* doing here?"

He grinned. "Everyone around here is looking for answers," Zay said. "I say the answer is sandwiches. Have one!" He handed one to Grace.

She looked down at the package in her hand, unsure what to do with it. The boys had arrived, and Hayden was already digging into his unashamedly. Tim was carefully unwrapping his. Leona wasn't convinced. She confronted the Orchard Owner again.

"Why are you following us, man?"

"So good to see you again, Leona," replied the Baker. "You look hungry, have a sandwich."

Darkness was descending quickly. People were shoving and pushing and trying to get to the sandwich cart. Grace felt someone shove her in the back. She wanted to stay and ask questions, but she was afraid of being left behind. She stuffed her sandwich in her jacket pocket and summoned the others.

"We need to go, it's getting dark! Hurry!" The group broke away finally. Leona and Tim ate their sandwiches quickly as they hustled along, occasionally tearing off pieces for Terrence. Hayden had already downed his.

"Hurry up with those," Grace said fearfully. "Remember, we were told not to accept food from strangers."

Leona rolled her eyes like she didn't care, but she ate quickly anyway. They walked faster, nearly running. Grace breathed a sigh of relief when she saw the wagon in the distance. But as they got closer, she saw that it was surrounded by protesters.

And it was moving!

"Don't leave us!" Grace shouted at the top of her lungs. The group ran as fast as they could. The protesters shouted obscenities, and a few were throwing things in the direction of the wagon.

"God help us," Grace panted

Just then an opening formed in the group of protesters, and a clear path appeared that led directly to the departing wagon. The group seized their opportunity, ran through the gauntlet of angry humanity, and jumped into the back of the wagon.

The wagon quickly picked up speed and began to draw clear of the angry mob.

Jared shouted from the front to the group in the back.

"You made it! We were about to leave without you. I hope your mission was successful."

"*About* to leave?" Leona shouted back

"Mission accomplished," Grace said, out of breath.

No one spoke after that as the horses trotted down the road. Grace sat in the very back of the wagon. The tiredness that had been gnawing at her all day threatened to envelop her as she watched The Badlands fade away.

# CHAPTER 17
# THE HOSPITAL

*"The logical end of defensive warfare is surrender."*

— NAPOLEON

Grace leaned back in the wagon seat, exhausted from the day's events. Her body wanted to shut down and fall into a deep sleep, but her mind was too active to allow that to happen. She kept replaying the happenings of the day, almost too much to take in and understand.

She fell into a daydream and imagined how it would be to finally meet The Wizard. She imagined walking into his office with the book in hand. He would smile and tell her what a good job she did. Tell her how special she was, how set apart. She would blush and say something modest...

"Grace?"

Jared interrupted her fantasy as he squeezed into the small space between her and Leona, who glared at him but then moved over.

He leaned in toward Grace, his face looking intense and serious. Grace sighed, still thinking about The Wizard.

"Did you get *it?*" He smiled through clenched teeth. Grace could tell he was on edge.

She reached into her pocket but then stopped and pulled her hand back.

"Wait a minute, I thought *I* was going to give it to The Wizard, personally."

"It's okay, I'll just give it to him, take it off your hands. It will be safer this way."

Grace frowned slightly. "I don't mind holding on to it. I'd really like to give it to him myself."

Jared leaned in closer. His eyes narrowed ever so slightly, but he kept his constant smile.

"He told me to get it to him as soon as possible. I'll be able to see him sooner. He is going to be so thrilled! I know as soon as he has it in his hands, he will want to have a special meeting with you and your friends."

Grace considered his request for a moment. She should have been glad to give the book to Jared and rid herself of the responsibility, but she wasn't. It was *her mission*; she wanted to be there and place the book in The Wizard's hand herself. She decided to take a stand.

"No, Jared, I will give it to him. Please." She tried to smile.

Jared sighed, exasperated. "You have no idea how important..." Jared stopped himself mid-sentence. His face was red, and he was gritting his teeth while still maintaining a half smile. Grace could tell he was carefully considering his next move.

"All right, have it your way. There is a meeting tomorrow evening. The Wizard will be there. You can give it to him then."

Surprised it had been that easy, Grace sat back and relaxed. "All right. Thank you."

Jared offered her a smile that was more of a half grimace, then switched to his loud announcer voice so everyone could hear, "You did a superb job out there, Grace! Because of you, many lives are changed." He got up abruptly and went back to the front of the wagon without looking back at her.

Leona, who had been sitting on the other side of Grace listening to the conversation, had a look of triumph on her face. She leaned in. "You did the right thing. Don't trust this faker." She put her hand on Grace's shoulder. "I'm glad you are thinking for yourself again."

"What do you mean? I always think for myself!" responded Grace defensively.

Leona gave her a little smirk. "Okay, girl."

Grace fell silent, thinking about what Leona was saying. She didn't see Jared as a faker. He was just doing his job. The Wizard was certainly too busy to be bothered by just anybody. But she wasn't just an "anybody" anymore. Despite her fears, she had finally done something important, something courageous. Her life had a purpose again.

She heard Terrence chewing on something and looked down. He was shredding one of the fliers that had fallen out of her pocket. She managed a smile, even though she wasn't feeling well.

Grace noticed Eddie, the man who had been speaking at the rally, speaking loudly. "...and an entire family has committed to come to the EC. Isn't that great?" He looked around at everyone, expecting a reaction, but no one said a word.

Grace watched Leona grab the fliers she had left in the back of the wagon and let them fly out the back. A gust of wind took them up, and they danced for a moment before landing like confetti on the trail behind them. The night soon swallowed them as the wagon rolled on.

She locked eyes with Grace.

"Oops," she said casually.

No one else seemed to notice. Tim, who sat next to Hayden on a bench in front of Grace and Leona, turned around. "I overheard you talking to Jared. That means we're meeting The Wizard soon!" He smiled.

Grace nodded, not wanting to discuss it. Hayden rubbed his eyes and yawned loudly.

"I'll believe it when I see it," said Leona, her eyes flashing.

"Shhhh. Keep it down!" Grace said, annoyed.

She wished the time would pass more quickly. The EC seemed so far away. Now that she was silent, she began to realize how terrible she was feeling, like her mind was slowly disconnecting from her body. She tried to shake it off, but she couldn't escape the feeling like she was spinning. She hated the bumpiness of the wagon and the obnoxious noise of everyone's chatter, and she wished she could make it all stop. She felt annoyed with everyone and everything and was now feeling worse by the minute.

Feelings of uneasiness began to take shape; unwanted past memories flashed across her mind. She had no idea how to deal with them. Panic began to set in. The more she tried to resist, the more it seemed to grow, her will like sand trying to stop a rising tide. She no longer felt in control of her mental processes.

She leaned over, putting her head between her knees. Terrence, who was at her feet, sniffed her hair concernedly.

"Are you okay?" Tim asked, slightly worried. But to Grace, his voice sounded a thousand miles away.

Tim whispered in her ear, "Grace, you should eat something. Do you still have that sandwich?"

Grace could feel the lumpy object in her pocket but ignored it. In her dizzy state, the thought of food was repulsive.

She closed her eyes and managed to whisper, "I am fine, Tim. I am fine. We are all *fine*."

But she was anything but fine. Her gut was lurching. Everything inside of her wanted out. She stood up quickly, knowing she was going to vomit, but there was nothing to come out. She leaned over the edge of the wagon just as it hit a large bump, launching her forward with nothing to grab onto. Someone screamed. She felt herself falling. Her head struck the hard ground.

*THUD!*

Pain.

Blackness.

*Dust covers the old wood floor of the church. Nobody notices Grace. She hides under a pew in the back of the sanctuary. She likes the old mothball smell of the burgundy cloth covering the wooden bench. She is lying down, staring up at a cobweb hidden in the corner of the bench. Grace listens to the boring chatter of grownups engaging in small talk after a long Sunday service. She has only been living with her aunt and uncle for a few weeks, but she's getting used to it.*

*Grace sees four legs approaching, both sets with nylons and brown pumps, and hears the creaky voices of two old ladies in the church.*

*"And that poor girl! How anyone could be selfish enough to abandon a wife and child is beyond me. And then the mother dies, so young."*

*Grace freezes.*

*The other voice speaks.*

*"No one knows where the father is, so they can't contact him. Not that he would want the poor little girl anyway. That's why Emily and Pastor Harry were forced to take her. Poor child."*

*"Poor Emily and Harry! They already bear so much responsibility, and now to be forced to take on this..."*

*Grace can't move a muscle.*

*She wants to roll out from under the pew and tell these gossips they are wrong, that her daddy is out there looking for her, and that her aunt and uncle want her.*

*But she can't move. So she lies there, breathing heavily, trying not to make a noise.*

Grace's head ached. Her eyes blinked open. She was in a white room, lying on a white bed.

All the memories of her time in the strange land of god rushed back to her all at once.

"Are you awake now?"

A rasping voice from the other side of the room startled her. She craned her neck to see who was speaking and then saw someone lying in a bed a few feet away. It was a girl, so thin her skin was almost transparent. She had big blue eyes that were sunk into her gaunt face, a face that would be beautiful if it weren't so skeletal.

"Yes. Where am I?" Grace asked.

"You're in the EC Rehabilitation Center."

Grace breathed a sigh of relief. She was safe. How did she get here? She remembered the wagon. She must have fallen. She tried to sit up, but her head still hurt.

"Ahhhhhh," she groaned softly. "How long have I been here, and do you know where my friends are?"

"They brought you in yesterday, and sorry, but I haven't seen your friends," the girl responded. She sounded tired and weak.

"What's your name?" Grace asked, her voice also sounding hoarse and weak.

"Anna. Yours?"

"Grace. Why are you here?"

Anna was silent. "They don't know," she answered after a moment. "I did everything they told me to do. I followed all the *Secrets.* I wore the smile. I did all the extra assignments. But I still ended up here. I am so pathetic; I have to drink so much Formula these days, because I'm so weak in my mind. I always try as hard as I can, but it's never enough. I guess there's just something wrong with me."

Grace didn't know how to respond. Just then the door opened, and a professionally dressed man and a woman walked in. The man wore a white lab coat and steel-rimmed spectacles. The woman wore a nondescript kind of tunic with an EC insignia above the left breast.

"You're awake," the woman said to Grace, as if surprised. The man stood in a corner, staring at Grace, but said nothing. There was something about him that made her uneasy.

The woman leaned over her bed and put her hand on Grace's forehead. "My name is Dr. Gladworth. I am here to help you, Grace."

She was pretty, with straight brown hair and well-shaped eyebrows.

"Where are my friends and my dog?" Grace asked.

Dr. Gladworth glanced at the man who stood by the door and then back at Grace. "They are fine. You'll see them once you feel better."

"I would really like to see them now," Grace pleaded, feeling a twinge of panic.

The doctor ignored her. She pulled up a chair that was on the other side of the bed and sat down. The man stood behind her, glaring with an expressionless face.

"Grace, I need to ask you a few questions."

Grace nodded, trying to calm down. She reassured herself that everything was fine, that her friends were probably waiting in the lobby.

"All right," Gladworth began, "have you made sure all your thoughts are positive?"

"Huh?"

"Have you been thinking happy, positive thoughts? You know, sunshine instead of rainclouds?"

"Uhhhh, I guess. What does this have to do with what's wrong with me?"

The woman smiled condescendingly and checked something off on her clipboard.

"Have you been following the *Thirteen Secrets?*"

"Yes, of course. I mean, I have tried to...but...I think I fell out of a wagon and bumped my head! I don't see how following the *Secrets* has anything to do with me being here. This is a hospital, right?"

Gladworth rapidly scribbled on her clipboard. She then handed Grace a packet of papers stapled together.

"This is a rehabilitation center, for the mind. If you were thinking correctly you wouldn't have fallen out of that wagon, now would you?" The woman flashed the same condescending smile.

"I need you to read through these papers and commit all the *Secrets* and helpful hints to memory. They will help you feel better in no time."

Grace frowned at the papers on her bed. She leafed through them briefly. They were more *Secrets*, X number of steps to success, etc.

She suddenly felt claustrophobic and anxious, and she wanted to jump out of bed and run out to find her friends. But instead she took a deep breath and collected her thoughts.

"Okay," she managed through her teeth. "Could you at least get me something for my head? It hurts."

Dr. Gladworth smiled and got out of her chair. She whispered to the man, who nodded and left the room. Grace felt relieved to see him gone.

"A nurse will be in shortly to take care of you. You'll be just fine, Grace."

Grace mumbled thanks.

"By the way, Jared sends you his best wishes for a speedy recovery. He will be coming to visit you very soon. You must be a very special girl to have such important people looking after you."

Gladworth walked over to Anna. "And how are you doing, Anna? Any improvement?"

Grace kept her eyes on the papers but wasn't reading them. She was listening to the conversation next to her.

"No, ma'am." Anna sounded ashamed.

"Well, just keep it up. You'll begin to see progress real soon. Our program never fails."

"Good-bye for now, girls."

She walked out of the room. As soon as the door shut, Grace shoved the papers off her lap. They fluttered onto the white floor.

Grace looked at Anna lying in her bed, silent and still.

"Anna, you're going to be okay. Don't worry."

"I wish I could believe that." She sniffled and wiped her eyes.

"I'll help you get out of here," Grace said, her voice full of emotion. "We'll find my friends, figure out what's going on…. I know who can help you! I have an appointment with The Wizard to give him a…wait a minute!" She looked around frantically.

"My jacket…the book! Someone must have taken them."

Just then the door opened. A tiny woman in a white nurse's outfit wheeled in an IV drip machine.

"Hello, Grace. Counselor Gladworth sent me to give you something to help your head."

"Uhhh, okay." Grace looked up at the device. A plastic bag filled with a cloudy brownish liquid hung from a hook. The nurse wheeled the machine over next to Grace's bed.

"What is this for? I have a headache. Can't I just have a couple of aspirin?" Grace asked.

"Don't worry, Grace, you are new here. Don't feel bad for needing a little Formula." She held out a huge needle attached to a tube coming from the IV bag. She took hold of Grace's arm. Grace quickly pulled her arm free.

"I don't need this. What I *need* is to get out of here! I have an important meeting with The Wizard. I need to find my friends!" She started to get out of the bed, but the nurse pressed her back down with one arm across her chest. She was much stronger than Grace. The nurse jabbed the needle into Grace's arm. She cried out it pain and pulled away, her arm bleeding.

The nurse stumbled back in surprise. She came back at Grace with the IV again, sounding annoyed. "Just lie down. You'll gain your strength in no time. Please don't try to resist!"

"Get your hands off her!"

A familiar voice filled the room. The nurse jerked her head around to see who it was. There stood Leona, hands on her hips and a snarl on her face. Terrence ran in, barking.

Leona approached the nurse aggressively but then stopped abruptly upon seeing the blood on Grace's arm.

"Leona! Please help! Get me out of here!"

Leona stared for a moment, completely frozen. Before Grace knew what was happening, Terrence lunged at the nurse, nipping her on the calf with his sharp little teeth.

"Ow ow ow!" the nurse cried out, dropping her needle on the floor.

Clutching her leg, she yelled, "Get that creature out of here! This is a sanitary environment!"

"Oh, I'll get them both out of here!" shouted Leona, who was back to her normal self. She rushed toward Grace, helping her to stand up.

Terrence barked and growled at the nurse, who hobbled out of the room. "I am coming back with help! Security!" she yelled down the hall.

"We were getting a little worried about you," Leona said, trying to conceal a smile.

"Thanks for coming for me. I'm okay now. Where are the guys?"

"They created a diversion so I could sneak past security and find you. We need to go, now…" Leona stopped mid-sentence and stared at Anna, just noticing her.

"This place is crazy and sick," she mumbled. She pulled a wrapped sandwich from her pocket and handed it to Grace. "You need to eat, and we need to *run.*"

"Where did you find that? My jacket! Do you have the book?"

Leona laughed. "It's with Tim. Don't worry, Grace. We wouldn't let anything happen to our ticket to see The Wizard."

Grace held the sandwich, still feeling light-headed and confused.

"What happened anyway?"

"I'll explain once we are out of here. Come on." Leona grabbed Grace by the arm and led her toward the door.

"Wait!" Grace looked back at Anna, who was lying there, silent as a corpse.

She broke her sandwich in half and handed a piece to Anna.

The girl looked at it for a moment like she was contemplating the offer, but then she turned her head away.

"No, thanks. I don't need it. The doctor is right, I just need to get this stuff down." Her bony finger pointed to the stack of books and papers on her bedside table. "I believe in the power of the *Thirteen Secrets.*"

Leona looked at her, incredulous. "I'll tell you a secret, if you don't eat soon you're going to starve to death! Come with us now."

The girl just stared at them with her sunken blue eyes.

Grace set the sandwich half on her table. "I am leaving it here. Please eat it, Anna. We can come back for you later."

Anna smiled and shook her head. "No, thanks. It was nice to meet you."

Grace didn't want to leave her, but she knew they needed to get out before the security arrived. She turned to Leona.

"We have to move now," Leona said authoritatively. They walked briskly out of the room, Terrence following.

They walked quickly down the empty corridor.

"How did you find me?" Grace whispered to Leona.

"Terrence," she said. "Take a bite of that sandwich while we are walking. It will give you energy."

Hands shaking, Grace unwrapped it, held it up to her mouth, and bit down.

It was delicious. Meaty and cheesy, soft bread, savory, and still amazingly fresh.

They heard voices approaching.

"Quick, this way!" Leona pulled her through a door. They stumbled into a large rectangular room. Grace and Leona stopped in their tracks, stunned. The room was lined with beds on either side, too many to count.

A person, or what remained of one, lay in each bed. Many were mostly skin and bones. A faint groan could be heard from one bed. Other than that, it was silent. It smelled like antiseptic and death.

Grace put her hand over her mouth in shock. These people were worse off than Anna. "This place gives me the creeps. Let's get out of here as soon as possible."

Leona cracked open the door they had come through and peered out into the hall. "It's clear. They're gone," she whispered. "We need to make it to the end of the hall, where there is a maintenance elevator."

Grace nodded. She stared at a man in the bed closest to the door. His sunken eyes gazed straight at her. He blinked, and then his lips formed words:

"Hhhhelp..."

Grace turned away, overwhelmed with emotion. Tears started streaming down her cheeks, but she knew there was nothing she could do for the man. She picked up Terrence so his nails wouldn't clack on the floor and quietly followed Leona out into the hall.

They crept down to the elevator. Leona pressed the button. "Come on, come on."

The elevator opened just as Gladworth appeared at the other end of the hall with two security guards.

"Stop! Come back! We are only trying to help you!" she yelled

Grace and Leona got in and pressed the "close" button. Grace saw the doctor's frowning face disappear as the doors shut.

"Close one!" said Leona. She quickly pressed the "B" button. They both breathed out sighs of relief.

*Ding!*

The elevator stopped on the bottom floor. It opened up into a dark, cold basement.

"This is the maintenance floor. It's how I snuck in," Leona said calmly.

Grace put Terrence down. She started following Leona, though it was taking every ounce of her mental and physical energy just to put one foot in front of the other. She took another bite of the half of the sandwich she still gripped tightly in her hand. It helped.

"This way," Leona said, noticing Grace was still struggling. "Grab my hand."

With her free hand, Grace gripped Leona's hand, and they walked down a dark hall. It was musty and hard to breathe. Leona pointed toward a red exit sign. She pushed a door open, and they stumbled out into sunlight. They were in the alley of the hospital. It was empty except for a large covered wagon that was backed up to large double doors.

Printed across the side of the wagon was written:

"EC Formula Processing Plant."

As they walked away quickly in the opposite direction, Grace looked back and saw two men coming out of the doors. They were wearing masks and rubber gloves and each pushed a gurney covered by a white cloth. Stopping at the back of the wagon, they loaded up the white cloths and placed them into the.... *Oh, no!* she thought. These weren't just cloths. She remembered the room, the man who cried out for help.

She turned away in shock, refusing to believe what she had just witnessed. It couldn't be. She figured she must be hallucinating from her head injury.

Grace followed Leona out onto the main road, where Hayden and Tim were waiting, pacing nervously. The two girls looked at each other and awkwardly let go of each other's hands.

"Thanks, Leona," said Grace quietly.

"Don't worry about it. You would have done the same for me," Leona said, looking at Grace at first but then at the ground.

"You made it!" Tim grinned. Both Tim and Hayden embraced Grace.

"Welcome back, Captain," Hayden joked.

Tim helped Grace slip into her jacket. She put her hand in the pocket and felt the book. She didn't know whether to laugh or cry.

Maybe later she would do both. For the moment, she was just glad to be out of the hospital and with her friends again.

The group continued up the street away from the Rehabilitation Center, Leona looking back suspiciously to make sure no one was following them.

"You okay, Grace?" asked Hayden, looking concerned.

"Yeah...I think so." But she wasn't. The thought of Anna lying there, and now the scene in the alley, haunted her. She wondered if Leona had seen what the men were loading into the wagon. She thought about asking but couldn't bring herself to talk about it.

"I still don't know what happened," she said, quivering.

"You fell off the wagon!" Hayden said, his eyes widening.

"We thought you were dead at first. Terrence jumped out right after you. You must have passed out. We brought you back and they took you here, to this hospital or whatever it is, but they wouldn't let us upstairs. Something about that place didn't feel right..." His voice trailed off. "We all decided that we needed to get you out of there, one way or the other."

Grace nodded. She bit into her sandwich, already feeling a little better. The food gave her energy and new clarity.

"That's why I fell out," she said.

"What?" Hayden turned to her.

"I fell out because I was so weak. I hadn't eaten all day. I thought I could live without it."

"Live without food!" said Leona angrily. "I've seen my share of weirdness, but this place takes it to another level. Did you see those people in there? They were starving." Her voice was filled with sadness.

Grace knew Leona was right. Anna and the others were starving. But The Wizard was good and kind! There must be an explanation for this. He must not know what was going on in there. Surely, he would take care of those people right away when he found out.

*But does Jared know about all this?* she wondered. *The doctor lady said he was coming to visit me in the hospital.* So many questions remained unanswered, but Grace knew one thing for sure: People needed real food; no one could survive for long on a diet of Formula or Secrets.

CHAPTER 18

# THE WIZARD

*"Vice, in its true light, is so deformed, that it shocks us at first sight; and would hardly ever seduce us, if it did not at first wear the mask of some virtue."*

— LORD CHESTERFIELD

The wind was beginning to pick up. The weather had been consistently sunny and mild in the EC, but now, dark clouds were looming over the spotless city. It was afternoon, and the group was headed back toward the main hall.

Grace was silent and feeling weary. Tim noticed and approached her.

"Are you okay?"

She nodded slowly.

"I'm worried about you," he said with a fatherly look of compassion on his face. "Did anyone take a look at your head?"

Grace put her fingers on the back of her head where a small bump had formed.

"I'm okay...really. It's a miracle I didn't have a more serious injury. Falling out of a moving wagon is not something I want to ever do again."

"Well," Tim said, "I think you need more to eat. We all do. We've got a little bit of time before the meeting tonight."

Hayden spoke up. "Man, it seems like all we are ever doing is trying to find food. The people here seem to be doing just fine drinking the Formula stuff. I wonder what's in it?"

Grace grimaced. She didn't want to think about *that.*

"Hayden, come on, you don't believe that bull Jared is trying to feed you?" Leona blurted out. "It's all a big lie! People need solid food. You didn't see what we saw in that hospital."

"What did you see?" asked Hayden

"Forget it. We've got to get to a meeting. In the meantime, someone around here must know where we can get something to eat!"

She approached two women who were walking by.

"Uh oh, here she goes," said Hayden.

Leona walked out into the road and stood right in the women's path. They stopped, frozen like animals about to be pounced on.

"Could you please tell me," Leona said, her voice dripping with forced politeness, "where to find some *food* in this city?!"

The women looked at each other, taken aback.

"And don't direct me to some fake restaurant with nasty Formula! My friend is hurt, we are all hungry. Just tell me where to get *solid food*!"

The women didn't respond but smiled and walked briskly away from the demanding girl with the wild hair.

Leona came back to the group, a smirk on her face.

"I guess I scared them. Looks like we may have to wait 'til this Baker dude shows up again."

They continued on to the Great Hall without incident. They were a little early, so they sat on a bench near the front door and rested.

Grace inhaled and caught that earthy electric scent of a storm coming. She hoped it wouldn't start raining until after they were inside.

She had a flash of memory...the small country house, the old church, and her aunt and uncle. Home. It felt so far away, like another lifetime.

Another image entered into her mind of a gurney being wheeled into the alley of the hospital. She shuddered. She really needed to talk to The Wizard. Surely, he would make everything right.

Tim interrupted her thoughts.

"This smell, it's so familiar." He closed his eyes and breathed deeply.

"A storm is coming," said Leona, looking up beyond the buildings into the darkening sky.

"I guess this must be the calm before the storm," Grace said softly

The group was still for a moment. Tim broke the silence.

"Well, our mission is almost complete. We are really going to meet The Wizard tonight."

He smiled at Grace, who managed a half smile back.

Leona played with her hair; twirling it around her finger until she wound it so tight she couldn't release it. She tugged for a moment then laughed, lightening the mood. Grace felt it was the first time she had actually seen Leona laugh.

Soon it was time to go, so they walked over to where the line was forming outside The Great Hall. "Dude, I guess this is it," Hayden said.

"Time to face the music," said Leona with a smirk.

"We've been promoted to the front row!"

Hayden was like a teen at a rock concert. Grace felt a small thrill when the same usher who had denied them access in the last meeting led them to seats in the second row, right near the stage.

*The closer, the better,* Grace thought. The small book still sat comfortably in her pocket. She felt for it, running her fingers over the smooth leather cover just to make sure it was still there.

Tim looked at her.

"You think they are going to call you on stage?"

"Maybe? All I know is Jared told me that I could give the book to The Wizard tonight. That's all I care about."

Tim patted her on the knee.

"You've got this. You have confidence, Grace. You open your mouth and people listen. It's a gift. We've all followed you here. We believe in you."

"Thanks," mumbled Grace, not feeling worthy to receive Tim's compliments. But he was correct, the others *were* there because of her. More than anything, she didn't want to let them down.

She looked around and saw the room was filling up. There were easily several thousand people already seated. It seemed like the whole city showed up for these meetings.

The lights began to dim until the room was nearly pitch black. The chattering ceased, and Grace found herself holding her breath.

Several spotlights came on, and the dancers took their places, men in green suits and women in green dresses.

Another spotlight illuminated the orchestra positioned on the other side of the stage. The music started, and the dancers danced and sang in unison.

*"Try harder! Follow the steps!*
*Dig deeper, you'll find your purpose yet."*

The lights flashed off and on, and a giant screen lit up and played a video that was in sync with the song: people of the EC with big grins, all looking perfect, beautiful, and content.

The dancing and singing continued.

Grace felt sick. She thought of the young people they had met in the Badlands, covered in filth, sorting bricks all day long just to earn a piece of disgusting, dry meat. The carnival, with its zombie-like patrons, lost in the futility of escape, hypnotized by worthless games. She thought of Anna, lying in the hospital, a skeleton, literally starving to death trying to be a stronger person.

Grace felt like she was having an out-of-body experience. She didn't know how much more she could endure. The lights, dancing, and video images were too much. The music was very loud, as they were right near the speakers. It all grated on her soul.

"I've been here…many times before…"

Then as if on cue, the music stopped, and Grace opened her eyes. The dancers hurried off the stage.

Jared appeared out of nowhere, like a magician. He was dressed to the nines in a fine tailored black suit and light-green shirt with a dark-green tie. He flashed his perfect white teeth at the audience.

"Greetings, wonderful citizens of the EC! I'm Jared, as most of you know. I am going to be your emcee for tonight's very special meeting. Who is ready to see some amazing things?"

The audience clapped and cheered on cue. There was a palpable sense of excitement and expectation in the room.

"I am very happy to introduce to you tonight a group of individuals who have dared to be more than they thought they could be, a group who have learned *The Secrets* and are not afraid to share what they have with those in need. Please rise, everyone, and give a huge EC welcome to the New Members!"

Everyone clapped. Grace wasn't sure what to do. The others who were seated around them, all stood up. Grace and her friends eventually stood up as well, awkwardly. Grace had often imagined how wonderful it would feel to receive such praise and recognition, but now that the moment had arrived, she felt nothing.

Jared smiled, and then his gaze fell directly on Grace. His smile disappeared, his eyes looked like saucers, and he froze for a second. He gave her a quizzical look and then regained his composure. Grace wondered if he'd thought she was still in the hospital.

Jared talked a little about their journey into The Badlands, showed some video clips of the destitute residents, and finished with an obligatory, irrelevant, and what was supposed to be an amusing anecdote. Then it was testimony time.

First, Eddie went up on stage. He spoke about his experience in The Badlands, about the family he had convinced to come to the EC, pointing them out in the audience. Eddie went on and on for what seemed like forever, but no one seemed to mind because everything he said always ended with superlatives praising the awesome EC and the wonderful Wizard of god.

"And now I want to thank you, Jared." Eddie was mercifully finishing his monologue and his brief moment in the limelight.

"Without you, I wouldn't have ever thought I was good enough to become a citizen. I now feel I'm worthy."

Jared looked pleased. He approached Eddie and put a slender gold bracelet on his wrist. Everyone clapped enthusiastically.

Eddie took his seat, waving his hand with the bracelet and receiving high-fives from others.

Several other people went up to receive their bracelets.

Grace fidgeted in her seat. Where was The Wizard?

Jared looked directly at her from the stage and smiled. It was a devious smile. He was up to something. Her stomach fluttered.

"And now," Jared said, "we'd like to introduce a very special young lady. I didn't think she'd be able to make it tonight, but here she is. She is brand new to the EC but has already made quite an impression on The Wizard. Friends, join me in giving a big EC welcome to Grace!" Jared motioned for her to come on the stage.

Grace stood up without thought or intention, as if playing her part in one of the choreographed dance numbers.

She walked up the side steps onto the stage, trying not to look at the sea of people clapping for her. Terrence tried to follow her, but Tim held him back.

The camera zoomed in on her face. She was terrified but managed a smile. As soon as she did, the audience cheered louder.

"Introducing Grace, the new face of the EC!" Jared spoke with passion into the microphone, trying to incite the crowd into an even louder ovation.

Grace felt flushed and dizzy, and her cheeks reddened.

"And now, friends, someone special has come tonight to personally congratulate Grace on a job well done. Ladies and gentlemen, the one, the only...*The Wizard*!!!"

The crowd roared. Grace's heart quickened as she looked around the stage, waiting for him to make an appearance.

But he didn't. Instead, he appeared on the screen yet again. Her heart sank. She turned to the screen, where The Wizard was smiling down on her and nodding his approval.

"You did a great job, Grace! Jared has told me all about it, and about your bravery and dedication! I am so proud of you."

Before she could say anything, Jared spoke into the microphone again.

"That is so true, my Wizard. As you know, Grace has demonstrated a great ability to understand and implement the Secrets. She has shown great courage in the face of adversity. When I asked if she would be willing to accept a special assignment for the EC, she took it on wholeheartedly! And so, Grace, before I give you your New Member's bracelet, please present me with what you captured from The Badlands, and your mission will be complete!" Everyone leaned in and looked at her expectantly.

Grace stood still, unable to move. This felt like a nightmare. She clenched her fist tight and pulled it out of her pocket, leaving the book behind. She turned and faced Jared, filled with a new-found boldness and resolve.

"No, I will not," she said firmly.

The audience gasped, murmuring to themselves. Jared had an incredulous look on his face. He had obviously calculated that manipulation and peer pressure would force Grace to comply. He had underestimated her and now had to think quickly.

"Gracie", he said, smiling condescendingly. He said it smoothly, trying to regain control as always. "It's time give up the book, which is meaningless to you anyway, and receive your EC citizen bracelet. You are one of us now!"

"I am not one of you." Dead silence filled the huge auditorium.

From the front row, Leona gave her a double thumbs-up. Bolstered with confidence, Grace continued.

"I am not brave or dedicated. I am lost. My friends and I didn't come for here for meetings, citizenship classes, or Formula. We didn't come here to learn *Secrets* about the benefits of smiling, attend pep rallies, or to battle the godvernment for new recruits. We came here for help!"

She turned to the screen, where The Wizard was looking down, watching the whole scene play out in silence. Jared was horrified, frozen, and, for once, speechless.

"Please, Wizard, wherever you are, please help us! My friends and I have traveled so far to see you. We've done everything you've asked. Why do you still hide yourself from us? I believe you can help my friends and me. I believe that you have the power to change our lives, today. I believe in you…I…I *love* you. Please…"

She looked up at the man on the screen. The Wizard said nothing, his face not moving, as if the screen had frozen.

There was an eerie silence in the room.

Grace snapped. All the frustration that had been building poured out of her.

"Where are you?!" she demanded in front of the now shocked audience, pointing at the screen. "I need to see you *in person*! Tell me where you are and I will come to you. I'll give you the book! I believe you have the answers. I need to talk to you!"

Jared's face was now reddening with fury, but he kept his voice calm. He approached Grace and took her elbow, trying to lead her away from the screen and off the stage. "Excuse us a minute", he said to the murmuring audience, trying to smile but not succeeding very well.

"Grace, The Wizard *is* with us," he tried to whisper in her ear. "This is the way we do things. Now, just give me the damn book."

Grace jerked her elbow away and ran back to the front of the screen.

The Wizard's face was still frozen.

"Where are you!? I'm not going to be sent away again! I'll come to you! I can't do this anymore. I need to see you, *now*!"

As if someone had pressed a play button, The Wizard on the screen began to move again. He spoke to Grace gently.

"Grace, please give Jared the book."

"No! Tell me where you are! I'll give it to you myself!"

Jared was still trying to usher her off stage. This time he grabbed her aggressively, his perfectly manicured fingernails digging into her arm.

He whispered gruffly into her ear, "You don't question The Wizard this way. You are nothing. You have no right to…"

"Hey, let go of her!" Tim stood up, trying to hold onto Terrence, who was flailing in his arms and growling fiercely at the stage.

Jared released his grip on her arm. He grabbed the microphone off the stand.

"I apologize for this, everyone. Grace had an accident earlier, got a nasty little bump on the head and isn't thinking straight right now. She just needs a little Formula and she'll be back to normal in no time…"

"Lies! All lies!" Leona stood up, shouting and interrupting Jared.

Before anyone could react, Leona ran up onto the stage and grabbed the microphone out of Jared's hand. She turned to face the audience.

"This is all a sham!" She shouted to the stunned audience. "We've been told over and over again how great, good, and powerful The Wizard is, but all I've seen is special effects on a screen! You don't have to live like this, drinking that nasty Formula crap and starving to death. It will kill you! I've seen it! Run while you still can!"

In a split second, Jared lunged at Leona, ripping the microphone from her hand. She immediately reached to grab it back, and they both held onto it. Seeing she could not outwrestle him, Leona released her grip on the microphone, the momentum causing it to strike him on the nose. Jared recoiled in pain but quickly recovered and angrily grabbed one of Leona's arms and twisted it behind her back. She cried out in pain.

"All right, that's enough!" Tim shouted, leaping up from his seat.

Tim and Hayden ran up on the stage, preceded by Terrence, who had broken loose of Tim's grip.

"Leave her alone!" Grace shouted at Jared.

Leona struggled out of Jared's grasp, as the others had distracted him.

Several security guards were running up the aisles toward the stage but were slowed by some of the crowd who were heading for the exits. The Wizard on the screen was encouraging everyone to calm down. No one listened. It was pandemonium.

Grace noticed a door at the back of the stage. The guards were coming fast, and it looked to be their only way out.

"Come on!"

She grabbed Leona's hand, and they sprinted past Jared to the back of the stage. Hayden and Tim followed, with Terrence at their heels.

Pausing, Grace turned over two tables that held gold membership bracelets and certificates, causing the items to spill and scatter across the stage, distracting Jared, who was in pursuit.

They ran through the door and slammed it shut.

"There's no lock!" said Tim.

"Here!" Hayden wedged a large box under the doorknob just as it started to turn.

"Let's go!" Grace yelled frantically. "I'm sure there's another way backstage, and they'll catch up to us soon."

They ran down a long hallway with doors on both sides.

Grace tried one. It was locked.

"Where are we going?" asked Leona, looking panicked.

"We're gonna find The Wizard," Grace said, panting.

The group made their way through a maze of corridors until they couldn't have retraced their steps if they tried.

The hall split and offered two directions to go. Terrence ran ahead of them down the hall to the left. They raced after him until they came to a dead end. There was one door at the end, and Grace thought she heard a noise coming from inside.

Terrence sniffed at the door and barked.

Grace stepped forward and turned the knob.

The door opened.

It was a small room with desks and tables lining the walls, all with computer screens and assorted electronic devices on them. One table held a bowl with a single goldfish swimming around, right next to a microwave and toaster. Crumbs covered the table, and it smelled like old food. An overflowing trashcan sat under the table, revealing a mess of papers and wrappers. A short, wiry man with a thin comb-over sat in the chair, facing one of the screens.

He had headphones on that looked enormous compared to the rest of his head. Several of the screens showed different shots of the auditorium. The audience was still buzzing, and Jared was attempting to calm them down.

The man's back was turned to the group standing in the doorway, and he was rapidly typing on a keyboard. He leaned down and spoke into a microphone hanging down from a wire attached to the ceiling.

"It's okay, everyone, please take you seats. The program will continue in a minute. I have everything under control. Pay no attention to what just happened."

Grace watched, too stunned to say anything. As the man typed and spoke, the figure on his screen moved and repeated the exact same words.

The Wizard!

All at once, Grace realized what was happening.

"You!" she yelled.

The man spun around in his chair, terrified, nearly knocking over his keyboard.

As if instinctively, he grabbed the microphone and repeated, "Pay no attention to what you have seen. The Wizard has everything under control."

"Well, now!" said Leona. "What do we have here?"

The man got tangled up in his headphone wires but quickly unwrapped himself and stood up to face his guests.

He smiled sheepishly and nervously took off his glasses, attempting to polish them on his tucked-in shirt. His pants were too short, and he wore a bowtie.

"Uhhh...H-H--Hi..."

His voice trailed off, sounding small. Grace walked into the room and pointed at the screen where the image of The Wizard was now silent and frozen.

"What is this?" she said angrily, thudding her finger on the screen.

"Please, don't, you'll smudge the screen…"

Leona walked forward and got in the man's face. He was barely taller than her. "So *you* are the great and powerful Wizard?" She choked on a laugh.

Hayden and Tim were right behind Leona.

"No way, man! Not you!" said Hayden, staring at the screen, bewildered.

"You mean, The Wizard is a computer program you control from this little room?"

The man just nodded, unable to look any of them in the eye.

"Who are you? What's your name?" asked Tim.

"B-B-B…Bill," the man stammered. He sniffled and then wiped his nose with the back of his hand.

Grace collapsed into his spinning office chair.

"This can't be happening. *This can't be real,*" she muttered, shaking her head.

Leona was boiling. "You fraud! You faker! You…you…I *knew* we were being conned!"

Tim slumped onto the floor beside the desk and rested his head in his hands.

"I was so hopeful. I had so much faith," he sighed.

"Dude, this is not cool at all!" Hayden said, raising his voice at Bill. "Pretending like you are some guru guy who can help people! What gives? You're nothing but a phony."

Bill was still staring at the ground. "Yes, I am," he admitted.

Grace felt a twinge of compassion, but it was quickly replaced with anger.

"So The Wizard, you just, what…made him up?"

Bill shook his head slowly but didn't say a word.

Leona grabbed his arm.

"We are going to expose you! Show these people that the perfect, strong, charismatic leader they have been worshipping is nothing but a nerdy computer programmer."

Grace, operating on pure adrenaline, stood from her chair.

"You! You need to go out there and tell all those people you have been fooling that The Wizard is a fake!" she said angrily, pointing at the audience on the screen.

Bill looked up at them pathetically, wiping his nose again.

"All right, but it won't be easy. You don't understand." He seemed strangely calm, almost relieved. He walked over and absentmindedly fed the goldfish.

The others stared at him.

"The truth must be told," Tim said, putting drops in his eyes. "No matter how much it hurts."

"I agree with you." Bill had resignation in his voice. "I've been tired of this charade for a very long time. But this won't go over very well, not well at all."

The group all proceeded toward the door and waited for Bill.

The small, weary-looking man walked out of the room, the four friends and the dog following close behind.

"You better tell them the whole truth!" Grace demanded. "No more magic tricks!"

As they walked back down the maze of hallways, waves of thoughts and emotions filled Grace's mind. It was all a big, fat lie; she had been in love with an illusion. If it weren't for her rage and desire for justice, she would have collapsed from the pain of it.

As she walked through the halls, her mind raced. She thought of Anna! An imaginary man was running the system that was starving her to death. Her anger intensified, and she knew that she had to expose the lies to help save people like Anna and the man on the gurney who had cried out for help. They didn't have to live on Formula any longer. Once the people heard the good news, they would be set free!

This time she really did have a mission.

# CHAPTER 19

# THE UNMASKING

*"Where ignorance is bliss, 'tis folly to be wise."*

— THOMAS GRAY

The group followed Bill until they reached the door that led to the stage. They didn't see any security, so Grace assumed they must have still been searching for them somewhere in the maze of passageways. Hayden pushed away the box he had wedged under the doorknob.

Leona pointed dramatically to the door. "There it is, *Bill*. You just have to walk in and tell everyone that The Wizard is a fraud. It's time to end this."

Bill sighed and turned the doorknob.

Grace and her friends followed Bill onto the stage. Jared was in the middle of a pep talk. There were some empty seats, but most of the audience had remained.

"...and we are always going to be the greatest in god! Just keep try...."

He stopped dead in the middle of a sentence when he saw the group coming onstage. As he looked at Bill, Jared turned the pale color of Formula.

Grace was pleased to see him finally caught off guard.

Leona took advantage of Jared's momentary shock, grabbed the microphone from him, and handed it to Bill. Grace looked around for the security guards, but there were none to be seen.

Bill held the microphone like it was a bomb about to detonate.

"What are you doing out of your office?" Jared hissed. He walked forward to grab the microphone back from Bill, but Hayden and Tim blocked him and he backed off. Leona gave Bill a little shove to the center of the stage.

"Come on, Bill," she encouraged the nervous man. "You've already been exposed. Game over. Time to bring the curtain down on this farce."

Bill gulped, and his Adam's apple bobbed down his thin neck. He began to speak.

"I...I-I-I...was pretending to b-b-be...The Wizard. He is gone. It is all f-f-fake. Hope you enjoyed the show. You can all go home now."

Bill shoved the microphone into Grace's hand and began to walk toward the exit door, but Tim's strong hand on his shoulder changed his mind.

A murmur arose from the audience.

"I knew it!" someone yelled. A few people got up and began to make their way to the exits.

A man from the front yelled, "Why should we believe you?"

Another yelled, "The man's lying! We know The Wizard is real. You can't fool us!"

A woman from the back shouted, "Who are you? Why should we listen to you?"

"He is telling the truth!" Grace spoke into the microphone. "None of this is real. You don't have to pretend anymore. You don't have to try to live on the *Secrets*. You can go home now and get something to eat!"

Grace was expecting uproar, but with the exception of those few initial comments, the crowd was relatively calm. They talked amongst themselves, the stadium buzzing with discussion. Nobody seemed sure about what to do next.

Just then the door to backstage flew open and several guards ran out. Tim and Hayden moved out of Jared's way, seeing the guards were too much for them to handle.

Grace shouted into the microphone while she still could. Leona stood next to her holding Terrence.

"Why are you still here? You don't have to live like this! Throw away the fake smiles and just be real for once!"

The audience started booing. The guards were just about to grab Grace when Jared held his hand up. He was smiling his fake smile now. Something was up.

Grace leaned in to whisper to Leona.

"What's Jared up to and why aren't these people listening?! Instead of booing Bill and Jared they are booing us!"

Bill was cowering in the corner of the stage, not sure what to do. Tim and Hayden were standing nearby. It was like they were all frozen in the spotlight, taking part in some strange play where no one had rehearsed their lines.

Leona took the microphone from Grace.

"Didn't you hear them? Don't you understand? You've been scammed!"

"Turn the music back on!" a man yelled from the crowd.

"Yeah, bring the dancers back on! This is boring! I'd rather watch a video than listen to you blah, blah, blah," a teenager shouted toward the stage.

"We want The Wizard!" a woman screamed from somewhere in the upper balcony.

"Yeah! Bring back The Wizard!" The audience was cheering and screaming.

"The Wizard doesn't exist!" Leona yelled into the microphone, but the voices of the crowd drowned her out.

Soon a chant started:

"We want The Wizard! We want The Wizard!"

Grace looked back helplessly and saw Jared standing next to the security guards, his arms crossed, smiling and looking pleased.

It began to dawn on her that the people lacked the capacity to comprehend what they were saying. The truth didn't resonate, so all they heard was blah, blah, blah. They just wanted to get on with the show.

Grace felt invisible and naked all at the same time.

The chanting kept getting louder and louder, and many in the crowd were now getting out of their seats. Some people in the New Members section rushed forward toward the stage. The guards looked at Jared, at Grace and the others, then at the crowd, unsure what to do.

"They are liars and traitors!" Jared yelled, pointing at the group. Rage swept through the crowd, and there was a rush of people toward the stage.

Leona threw down the microphone. "We need to get out of here. I thought we were doing them a favor, but they are turning on us!"

Bill snapped out of it. "Let's go backstage. This is about to get ugly."

With Jared and the security guards focused on the rowdy crowd, they seized the opportunity and ran back through the door, racing down the maze of hallways, Bill leading the way. Grace scooped up Terrence, and they ran as fast as they could until they reached the computer room again.

They followed Bill back to his office, and he shut the door, closing his eyes and breathing deeply. "I have to breathe deeply or my stammer will come back," said Bill, opening his eyes. "We are safe in here for now. Jared will have his hands full dealing with the crowd."

Grace collapsed on the floor, momentarily relieved and trying not to focus on the reality that her whole world was crashing down all around her.

Tim looked distraught but addressed Bill calmly. "Bill, could you please tell us what this is all about and how The Wizard came to be? I am so confused."

Bill sighed, sitting in his chair. He fiddled with a few buttons on his computer. The Wizard on the screen began moving again.

"What are you doing?" asked Leona.

"I am putting it on auto-Wizard to keep them occupied. Jared is focused on the audience. He's not concerned about us right now. He knows he's won the battle, so now all that remains to do is some minor damage control.

"I'll be glad to tell you the whole story, if you want to hear it," Bill offered

"Yeah, let's hear it, and don't leave anything out," said Leona.

Bill began.

"The Wizard was a *real* man. He was good, wise, and charismatic. He was a great leader, and we learned how to gather and grow our own food. He knew that if the godvernment lost control of the food supply, they would soon lose control of the people. The godvernment fought hard to put us in fear, but we resisted and slowly learned how to feed ourselves. Oh, how good that food was in those days!

"Instead of abusing followers like the godvernment, The Wizard wanted to empower people to become world changers, independent and free. This is where the *Secrets* came in. The *Secrets* were something he condensed from a special book he discovered.

Initially, The Wizard tried to get others to read the book for themselves, but they couldn't comprehend it, so he figured it would be best to feed the citizens truth in bite-sized morsels. This is how the *Thirteen Secrets* came to be.

"It was wonderful for a time, everyone working together and sharing food with one another; but as our numbers grew, many citizens began to demand more and more, while at the same time becoming increasingly lazy. Instead of building a better world, the 'empowered ones' became self-absorbed and narcissistic.

"They looked to The Wizard to feed them. He used to say he had created a monster that he had no idea how to continue feeding. What had begun as pure had now become polluted and self-absorbed. He knew how to use the *Secrets* to temporarily modify behavior, but he had no clue how to change selfish human nature.

"The Wizard started to doubt the *Secrets*. He isolated himself from everyone except for Jared, his personal assistant, and me. I was the techie of the group."

Bill stopped speaking for a moment to wipe his glasses. There was a certain look of pride on his face, and maybe a little regret.

"Hey, what's up with you not stuttering anymore?" Hayden asked.

"I only stutter when I'm nervous. I'm grateful to be able to tell my story to people who will listen."

He put his glasses back on and continued.

"Jared was the one who kept it all going when The Wizard would shut himself up in his room. The Wizard would open up to me and say how he wanted to help the people but didn't know what he was doing anymore. He believed the dream of the EC had become a dead end.

"By this time the Special Meetings had replaced shared meals as the center of community life. The Wizard put Jared in charge of the show, and he thrived in the spotlight. In the beginning, The Wizard spoke at every meeting, but eventually he became too depressed to speak at all. This is when Jared and I developed the digital Wizard. At first the people were skeptical and demanded The Wizard show up in person. To appease them, Jared introduced video productions, special music, dancers, and special-recognition ceremonies. Heartwarming personal anecdotes replaced The Wizard's old brand of teaching. The people ate it up! Soon they forgot all about the old days, and the meetings exploded in popularity.

"Amazingly, the people quickly adjusted to never seeing a real person and fell in love with the digital Wizard."

As he said that, Grace felt a cold chill come over her.

"So, where is The Wizard now?" Hayden asked.

"The bigger and more successful the EC became, the easier it was for him to hide behind the virtual version of himself. He started disappearing for long periods of time. He spoke of meeting with this mysterious man, and he would come back and try to explain to Jared and the others on the Leadership Team about his experience. He was so excited and we listened, but we really didn't understand what he was talking about."

"You haven't told us where he is now!" Leona demanded.

"One day he just vanished. He left a note saying, *Gone out for dinner.* He hasn't returned, and I doubt he ever will.

"The Leadership Team was concerned but had bigger problems to solve. Nobody wanted to gather food anymore. The food supply was scarce. The people were growing increasingly thin, weak, and sickly. They held a series of closed-door meetings. Within a few weeks they introduced The Formula. I don't really like to talk about that stuff."

Bill's voice was beginning to crack. He stopped talking and stared off into space for a moment.

The group sat still, captivated by his story. In a few moments, Bill regained his composure and continued.

"So, Jared convinced me that we had to keep the show going or the EC would fall apart and the godvernment would take control. He said that even though what we had wasn't perfect, it was better than the alternative. At the time, I believed him, but for a long time now I have just been going through the motions, doing my job. It isn't that hard. Between the two of us we know what the people want and how to put on a good show. We don't even have to write new scripts anymore, we just recycle the old ones. It always amazes me that the audience never catches on. We just keep promising how wonderful everything is going to be tomorrow."

Bill lowered his voice to just above a whisper. "I hope The Wizard is alive and well. I miss him every day. He was my friend, and now I'm alone except for my little goldfish, Bob, but he isn't much company."

Bill pointed to the bowl on his table, where the orange goldfish was moving his fins listlessly in the brown water, staring ahead into nothing, as fish do.

No one knew what to do next. The room fell silent. The only sound came from a hidden air conditioner malfunctioning somewhere in the ceiling and the noise of Bill's heavy breathing. A surreal atmosphere permeated the room.

"Bill." Leona spoke up so unexpectedly that everyone flinched. "When you said The Wizard was meeting with a man, did he ever tell you who this man was? Do you know anything about him?" Her tone was warmer, higher pitched, and her anger had vanished.

Bill shrugged.

"It was a long time ago. He'd come back after being gone for weeks, bright eyed and excited. He'd talk about parties with great food and other stuff. I remember a day or so before he left for good he snuck into my office and sat down. He said, 'Bill, I've found it. I've seen! I've tasted!'

"He kept repeating that over and over. That was the last time I saw him."

Leona was pacing back and forth in the room, occasionally shaking her head up and down as if trying to figure something out. She had a wide-eyed yet determined look on her face.

"I have to go," she said. "Don't follow me. I'll find you later. I just...have to go." She ran out of the room, slamming the door behind her.

Tim got up immediately to go after her. Hayden put his hand up.

"Tim, man, stop. She said not to follow."

Tim looked concerned. "Where is she going?"

"Just let her go," Grace said with resignation in her voice.

"Was it something I said?" asked Bill.

"She just does whatever she wants to do," replied Hayden. "There is no point in arguing."

"Now what?" Tim asked.

Grace wrapped her arms around her knees, and the tears she had been fighting back welled up in her eyes and overflowed before she could stop them.

Hayden sat down next to her and put his hand on her back.

"Why?" she asked through her tears. "Why would people rather believe lies? Doesn't anyone care about the *truth anymore?*"

The room was silent except for Grace's soft sobs. Bill finally spoke.

"Truth isn't something people here are looking for, miss," he said. "You can't find something you're not seeking."

# CHAPTER 20

# THE BAR

*"And the day came when the risk to remain tight in a bud*
*was more painful than the risk it took to blossom."*

— ANAIS NIN

B ill's words echoed in Grace's heart. Maybe that was her problem; maybe she didn't know what she was really looking for. She had started out searching for a way back home but ended up pursuing a man, who turned out to be an illusion. Nothing made sense anymore. Nothing was good or true. If it weren't for the numbness she felt, she would be screaming in pain.

Bill sat as his computer staring at the screen, occasionally typing on his keyboard.

Tim was leaning against a desk, staring blankly into space with his arms crossed.

Hayden sat on the dusty crumb-covered floor near Grace. He shook his head slowly back and forth.

"I don't know, man. I just don't."

Grace still had her head in her hands. She looked up for a moment, feeling restless and antsy. The room felt small and stuffy.

Tim glanced at her. "What do we do now? Where do we go from here?"

"I don't know anymore, Tim," Grace said softly. "The whole purpose of our journey was to find The Wizard. Well...we found him, and he can't help anyone, because he isn't real. There's nothing keeping us together anymore. Maybe we should all go our own way, like Leona."

Tim looked slightly crushed.

Hayden frowned. "Don't talk like that. We need each other now more than ever."

Grace ignored him, stuck in her own dark thoughts. Her sadness turned to guilt.

"This is all my fault. I convinced you to come. Hayden, you would have been happier in that field where I found you. The same goes for you, Tim. You shouldn't have followed me. I gave you both false hope. I was lost and had no business telling others where they should go."

"I don't regret following you," Hayden tried again. "This is not your fault. We'll figure this out. We're friends. We'll stick together."

Grace stood up. "I am not a good friend. You guys are better off without me."

She avoided eye contact with them as she picked up Terrence and walked out the door and into the corridor.

She held Terrence tightly, tears streaming down her face. "It's just you and me now, buddy. Just like it's always been."

He yipped and looked back at the door, Grace turned and saw Hayden standing in the doorway, looking dejected.

"Where are you going! Grace?"

"Please don't follow me!" she said, holding back tears unsuccessfully as she walked briskly down the hall.

She wandered for a long time, going in and out of hallways. Nothing looked familiar. She could hear the music coming from the Great Hall, but it sounded far away. In despair, she tried a door, hoping it would lead to an exit. Instead, she found herself staring into a large storage closet. There were shelves stacked with cardboard boxes, a pile of dusty stage lights, a few fold-up chairs, and an old couch that was pushed up against the wall. She flipped the switch, and a bare light bulb lit up the room.

Grace was exhausted, and the couch looked inviting. She entered the closet, still carrying Terrence, closed the door, flipped off the light switch, and collapsed on the couch. It was dusty and lumpy but fairly comfortable. She felt safe there; no one would find her. She closed her eyes and immediately had a flashback of hiding in her closet at her aunt and uncle's home.

Home...

*Grace stands in a field, alone. The field is filled with broken glass. She looks down, and her hands are bleeding. She tries to run but can't make her legs move. She's afraid that if she falls, she will be cut into pieces by the sharp glass. She is trapped.*

*Grace looks down and sees a framed sheet of glass with a jagged hole in the center. In the glass, she sees her mother's face, but it isn't a photograph. She's there, alive, moving, and clear despite the broken glass. She calls to Grace, but instead of reaching out, Grace begins to shout at the image.*

*"What did you do to make him leave? Why did you have to get sick? Why did you have to leave me all alone?"*

*Slowly, her mother's face begins to fade. Grace panics.*

*"Wait! Where are you? Come back!"*

*It makes no difference.*

*She disappears into a bright swirling haze of fragmented pieces of colorful glass, and Grace realizes it's nothing but a broken mirror. She's yelling at herself, at her own reflection in the broken pieces.*

Grace awoke, startled from her dream, not knowing how long she had been sleeping. She sat up quickly, and her head throbbed while her eyes adjusted to the darkness; the only light came from under the door that led into the hallway. Suddenly, the tight space didn't seem comforting anymore. She fumbled out of the closet into the hallway, momentarily blinded by the bright lights. She shivered violently. She felt cold and dazed.

"Let's go, Terrence. We need to get outside."

They wandered up and down hallways for a while. It was silent; she didn't hear music or crowd noise. Finally, at the end of a hallway, she found a fire exit and walked outside. It was very early morning, just after dawn. She had slept through the night in the closet.

She put Terrence down and looked around, not knowing what to expect. It was the sort of weather where the sky can't decide if it wants to drizzle or rain, so it just stays a depressing, dull grey. There seemed to be a melancholy atmosphere lingering over the city, although Grace realized it was probably just her mood. She could see people milling around and chatting, while posters of The Wizard still hung everywhere despite the previous evening's events. She couldn't bring herself to look at them.

Grace didn't know where to go or what to do, so she walked around to the front of the big building, found a bench, and sat down.

She wondered about the others. Where had Leona gone? Was she coming back? What about Hayden and Tim? Had they been looking for her? Grace tried not to think about her friends, but she couldn't help it. The fact that she was sitting on a bench within sight of the entrance to The Great Hall indicated maybe she wanted to be found.

She shivered and stuck her hands in her pockets. The book. She had forgotten all about it. Just a few short hours ago she had seen it as her greatest achievement and ticket to see The Wizard, but now it was basically worthless. She took it out of her pocket, a bit curious but mostly out of boredom.

Why had Jared wanted it so bad anyway? Looking at the cover, she remembered the man with the round glasses. He had a book that looked just like this one. She seemed to remember him saying his was some sort of map book. Zay called this one a Menu, but of course he was completely insane. Grace sighed from deep within and dropped her chin to her chest. She had dreamed that The Wizard would explain everything, including the meaning of this book.

She opened to the first page. It was printed in a foreign language. The letters were beautiful and scrawling, but their meaning was as incomprehensible as a child's scribbles. She flipped through and found that the rest of the book was the same.

"Some special, sacred book! What good is it if nobody can understand it?" she mumbled to herself and threw it on the ground in disgust.

It landed in the street on the edge of a puddle. Terrence began barking and wagging his tail. Grace looked up and saw Leona walking briskly toward her, It appeared she was actually *smiling.*

Without saying a word, Leona walked over and picked up the book, brushing off specks of dirt. She sat down on the bench next to Grace with the book on her lap and began petting Terrence.

"You're back," said Grace with no hint of emotion in her voice, though deep down, she was relieved.

"Yeah, of course I am," said Leona, smiling almost shyly. "I've been looking all over the city for you since late last night."

"I didn't expect to ever see you again. Where did you go, anyway?"

"I had to check something out on my own. I was always planning on coming back. You guys are the closest thing to a family I've ever had."

"*Family?*" Grace looked at her suspiciously.

"I know I haven't always been the nicest person..." Leona began.

Grace didn't say a word, but she couldn't deny that there was a real change in Leona's demeanor.

"So...what were you checking out?" Grace's curiosity was growing

"I'll tell you if you'll listen. Like, *really* listen. I'll warn you, it's going to sound kind of crazy."

"Okay, sure," said Grace.

"So...when Bill was talking about what had happened to the old Wizard, I had a thought. Remember when he mentioned The Wizard leaving for long stretches to spend time with some mysterious man? Well, somehow I *knew* the man Bill was talking about *had* to be that cook guy, the guy who kept giving us food. I figured even if he wasn't the one, he would be someone we could trust for some straight answers. I wanted to find the real Wizard. I wanted to do this for the group, for you, for all of us."

Grace nodded. "How'd you know where to find him?" she asked.

"Well, I didn't really...I just had an idea. I ran back to where the wall was painted like a mural. This time I couldn't find the door, no matter how hard I tried. Strange, right? I thought of climbing over the wall, but it was too steep and there was no way around it. Finally, I just said screw it, and gave up."

Her eyes got really big, her hands gesturing wildly.

"My mind was racing. Was he in the Badlands? There was no way I could make that trip on my own. I didn't know what to do, and I didn't want to come back to you with nothing. By the way, where are Hayden and Tim?"

Grace shrugged. "I don't know. I left them shortly after you did..." Her voice trailed off, and she looked away. Leona sensed Grace didn't want to discuss it further and continued her story.

"Oh, that's fine, we'll find them later.... So, I was sitting outside on the curb by those ugly apartments past the wall. I was feeling pretty hopeless and confused. Kind of how you look sitting on this bench right now." Leona smiled, but Grace was still staring off at nothing.

"I had been sitting there for some time when Charlie came walking down the street and sat down beside me. I demanded he open the door and take me to find the Baker guy, but Charlie said that door didn't work anymore. He said it was hard to explain but I looked like I could use a drink, and he invited me to come with him to a bar down the street owned by a friend of his. Ha! I had no idea they had bars in *this* place. So, I followed him, because what else was I going to do? I decided to take him up on his offer. I was a little afraid, but it turned out to be legit. There really was a bar hidden in the apartment building! It looked like a nice place. There were a few people hanging out there that I recognized from the pizza dinner.

"Charlie offered me a drink on the house, but no man buys you a drink unless they want something from you. I remembered I had a voucher left in my pocket. I pulled it out and set it on the counter, but Charlie wouldn't take it. I was so pissed. I stood up and got in his face, trying to get him to take my money, yelling, 'Do you know what I *did* to earn that?'"

Leona shrugged her shoulders. "Grace, you may have guessed by now, but I'm not really ashamed anymore. When I first got dumped into this crazy place I was confused and desperate. I let Dirty Frank take advantage of me. I felt dirty and used, but instead of crying, I got angry and decided to take care of myself, no matter what it took."

Grace had a pained look on her face. She said nothing and kept listening.

"So anyway, I ranted at Charlie for a while about how all men are jerks. It was like all the hurt I had stuffed inside of me came out. I was a volcano erupting. He just sat there and listened.

"When I had finally finished venting on him, Charlie just smiled and said, 'So, ready for that drink now?' He really was just a nice guy who saw I was having a bad day and wanted to buy me a drink.

"Then I saw *him*. The owner. He was sitting in the far corner of the bar, all sneaky like, watching the whole thing. He came over and sat down on the stool next to me. I didn't know if he was going to tell me to quiet down or...what. But he just said, 'Hello, Leona, good to see you again. I'm so glad you decided to stop by.'"

Grace could see Leona's eyes beginning to tear up.

"The baker?" she asked.

"Yeah, there he was again. I didn't know what to say. I was a mess. I couldn't look at him at first. I felt guilty, like somehow I had hurt him. I broke down and starting crying. He put his hand on my shoulder. Normally, I would have jerked it away and pulled back to throw a punch, but strangely this time I didn't even flinch. Then he looked me in the eyes, and Grace, I will never forget what he said.

"'Leona, you have been scratching and clawing for life as far back as you can remember, but life is a gift, the most precious gift, and true gifts are *always* unearned and undeserved.'

"'You're thirsty, but afraid to let anyone buy you a drink. You have been afraid for so long. The problem is, your vouchers aren't any good here. All the drinks at my place are on the house, or not at all. You'll just have to trust me. If you ask, I'll give you a drink that will truly quench your thirst!'

"'Yes, please,' I answered without realizing the words were coming out of my mouth. But instead of pouring a drink, he began to talk to me about things in my life. Things nobody else knew, painful things I had buried deep in my memory."

Leona was getting excited; her eyes, though brimming with tears, sparkled like a child's.

"He spoke about my father. I knew from the time I was a little girl that my dad had wanted a boy. He was going to name him Leo. He was very disappointed and angry when I came out a girl. When I was growing up, he was always working and didn't have any idea how to relate to me. I acted tough and did everything I could to act like a boy so he would like me, so he would love me. It didn't work, and I just became more screwed up. If you pretend to be someone else long enough, you forget who you are.

"It hurt like hell to hear what the Baker was saying, but I listened and I *got* it. I saw it. I saw the man who raised me for the broken man he was, and I knew I had to forgive him. I saw myself, how I had always run away, trying to find love but instead just getting hurt and running again.

"Like, before I ended up here, I was with this terrible guy. I thought he loved me, but I caught him cheating. I freaked out, stole his scooter, and drove as far away as I could until I was in the middle of nowhere and ran out of gas. I hated myself and had nothing left. Then that crazy storm blew up, and I'm not sure what happened next. It's still kind of a blur. All I remember is blacking out and waking up in Pleasant Grove with nothing."

Leona's voice was cracking and she was wiping away tears.

"The Baker somehow knew everything about me, but instead of judging, he really seemed to understand, and care. He told me my deepest desire was also my greatest fear. Love.

"He told me real love must be freely given and received. I told him that I was ready for that drink. This is where it gets hard to explain and a little crazy. As we continued talking, I had a growing sensation of being hugged. It started out small, but soon it felt like a bear hug! At the same time warmth came over my body, and I knew I was safe, and so loved.

" I felt so alive and free. I didn't know what to say or do! Without thinking I blurted out, 'Man, this is one hell of a damn drink!' Then, embarrassed by my foul mouth, I panicked and said, 'Oh shit, sorry for cussing.'

"I looked at the Baker, he looked at Charlie, and Charlie looked at me and then the Baker, and...we all busted out laughing. I'm talking the intense, falling on the floor with your side hurting, kind. I've never laughed so hard or for so long. It was amazing!

"Once I was able to pull myself together, I told him I needed to leave to come and find you guys. I asked him what we should do next. He told me to just go find my friends and to not to worry about anything.

"All I can know is that I'm not afraid anymore. I can't remember a day, a minute in my life, when I wasn't afraid. I have no idea what is going to happen next, but I'm not afraid. That's it, Grace. Crazy, isn't it?"

As Leona told her story, Grace could feel something inside her chest open a little. She wanted to believe what Leona was saying, to be happy for her, but part of her resented what Leona had experienced.

Grace knew Leona was waiting for a response.

"That's...great. Good for you," Grace said matter-of-factly.

After a few moments waiting for more response, Leona looked sort of hurt but seemed to brush it off quickly and stood up. She gave her face a quick rub.

"We need to find the guys."

Grace got up slowly, still in a daze

"Okay."

She began following Leona back down the same road they had traveled before.

# CHAPTER 21
# THE FERRIS WHEEL

*"Your pain is the breaking of the shell that encloses your understanding."*

— KAHLIL GIBRAN

Grace followed Leona through the streets of the EC, her head hanging down. She didn't want anyone to recognize her from last night's show. Leona hadn't said where they were going, but she didn't bother asking. She hardly cared anymore, but just plodded along. Occasionally, Leona would stop and wait for her to catch up. She never complained, which surprised Grace.

When they got to the entrance of the city, Grace stopped and looked up at the big walls.

"We are going out *there?*" she asked.

"Yeah, you didn't think we would stay in here forever, did you?"

Grace looked back at the city. Though it didn't hold as much appeal to her as before, it was still safe. Out there it was wild and unknown.

"I'm so tired."

"Grace, what do you have left here?" Leona asked gently.

"Nothing," Grace said after a long pause. Terrence whimpered quietly on the ground beside her.

"It's time to move on then," Leona said, continuing toward the gate.

Grace looked back at the city one last time and then followed Leona.

The guard at the booth didn't pay much attention to them, even though Terrence barked at him a few times on the way out.

"Funny," Grace muttered. "The last time we left here they gave us a parade."

"Yeah," said Leona, smiling. "We're definitely not rock stars anymore."

They walked along the road in silence, Grace picking up her pace once they were outside the walls of the EC. Before long they could hear the eerie music of the carnival. Grace realized where Leona was leading her.

"What makes you think Hayden and Tim will be in there?"

"Well, I don't know for sure, but I bet they felt abandoned by us. The carnival has games. They're guys."

Grace sighed. "Okay."

Taking a short cut, they soon arrived at the carnival and entered the familiar scene. Lines of people with vacant faces and zoned-out eyes, blankly staring straight ahead, hardly talking or moving except to shuffle forward when the line moved. Leona scanned the crowd. She held her hand over her nose.

"What *is* that disgusting smell? It's like rotting food mixed with something sweet. Weird, I don't remember smelling that before, do you?"

Grace hardly noticed. She stared at the tents they passed blankly.

"Girls, girls, do we have a game for you!"

A sleazy-looking worker was trying to coax them into a tent filled with bright lights and the sounds of upbeat music. They ignored him and pressed on. Grace stopped for a moment, suddenly feeling dizzy. She leaned over, putting her hands on her knees. Terrence rubbed against her leg.

"Are you okay?" Leona asked.

"Yeah, I think so..." Her voice drifted off.

"Here, why don't you sit down on one of those crates? I'll go look around for the guys and be back here in twenty minutes or so." Grace didn't argue. She sat down and watched Leona wander off.

A man dressed up like a clown walked by carrying several cotton candy cones. He stopped in front of Grace and looked down at her. His painted smile looked creepy, and Grace wished he would leave. Clowns had always frightened her. Terrence growled.

"You look like you could use a little pick-me-up," the clown said, handing her a cotton candy. "Here, take this! It'll do you good. Once you have a little, you'll keep coming back for more."

Grace took it from him. "Thanks," she mumbled, hoping he would go away. The clown smiled deviously and then moved on to a group waiting in line at a nearby gaming tent.

Grace stared at the fluffy pink cotton candy in her hand. Suddenly, she was hungry. She took a bite. Sugar evaporated in her mouth. The sudden rush of sweetness was wonderful, although the aftertaste was unpleasant, and strangely familiar. She took another bite, and then another.

"Come in and see into the future!"

She heard a deep female voice and turned around, dropping her cotton candy on the ground. She picked it up. Brown dirt freckled the otherwise perfect pink cloud. She attempted to wipe it off and casually took another bite.

Grace's attention was drawn to a small tent she hadn't noticed before. An overweight old woman was sitting in a folding chair, her fat legs jutting out of her dress and resting on another chair in front of her. She looked directly at Grace while her wrinkled face twisted into a sly grin.

"Come on, sweetie, don't you want to know who you'll marry? How rich you'll be? When you will die?"

Grace got up and walked to the tent without thinking, as if some unseen force was drawing her, attracting her. She didn't notice when the cotton candy fell from her hand and onto the ground.

The woman grinned, moving her feet from the chair where they were resting, and pointed for Grace to sit down. She did so and called for Terence to lie at her feet.

"You want to know your future, pretty girl?" the woman asked.

"No. Not really. It's not looking too promising right now," Grace started. "Can you tell me about my past?"

The woman stared at her with eyes that were dark and expressionless. "Usually, if one can't remember their past, it's for a good reason."

"I don't care," said Grace stubbornly. "I have nothing to lose."

The woman offered a toothless smile, showing a little of her pink gums.

"All right, dearie, let's see then. Give me your hands."

Grace complied with the woman's request.

Terrence was now sniffing at the woman's feet, trying to decide if he liked her or not. He growled a little.

"Hush, Terrence!" Grace said.

The woman's hands were cold and rough. Grace closed her eyes. She thought about how her aunt always told her that fortune-tellers were evil, but Grace never took it seriously. Too much of the world was evil to her aunt, as far as Grace was concerned.

The woman spoke very slowly. "I see a pretty little girl in a blue dress. She is playing a game of hide-and-seek. She is in a very big building."

Grace froze.

"I see a cross in the front of a large room. The girl is giggling, running even though she knows she may get in trouble. She runs down a hall, away from the cross, and finds a large closet. It's dark and a little scary. She is waiting for her friend to find her. Then the door opens. It is not her friend, but a man with a purple-striped tie. He puts his finger on his lips and comes into the closet to sit next to her..."

Grace opened her eyes.

"Stop," she said. She ripped her hands away from the old woman. "That's enough!" Her voice was shaking.

"I told you, the forgotten past is better left forgotten. But if you want to know your future..."

"No!"

Grace stood up abruptly and stormed away from the tent, leaving the woman looking surprised. Terrence followed her, barking, as she moved quickly and clumsily back into the carnival, ignoring the calls of the workers, pushing and shoving her way through the mob. Her heart was pounding, and her mind was racing.

She just wanted to escape, to get as far away from the ghosts of her past as possible. So many people, so much noise, too many lights, no way out. She was in a full-blown panic when she looked up and saw the Ferris wheel just ahead. Up! The line was short, but she cut it anyway, picking up Terrence and pushing her way to the front.

"Hey, what are you doing?" someone asked.

"Stop!" another person yelled.

Grace ignored them. She walked past the attendant just as he was going to let on a couple next in line.

Grace jumped into the swinging basket. The attendant looked at her like he was debating whether or not to kick her out.

"Hey, it's our turn!" the people in line shouted at her angrily.

The attendant shrugged his shoulders, shut the door, and pushed the lever on the control panel so Grace's basket moved up. Slowly, the basket ascended until it stopped with her at the very top. Grace gazed at the carnival below, and then beyond, over the land of god. The sun had broken through the clouds, and the late-morning breeze caressed her face. *Free at last,* she thought. She looked around and marveled at the view.

She could see the towers of the EC sparkling in the distance. She wished for a moment that she were back there, back to the well-dressed rows of people, back to the loud, happy music, to the people singing, to the safety and comfort of sitting next to her mother...

No.

She felt dizzy and closed her eyes. The ghosts had found her!

*The man in the purple-striped tie puts his finger over his lips to motion he wants her to be quiet. He is sitting very close to her. He asks a question:*

*"Can I hide in here with you, Grace?"*

*What is he doing in here? He is supposed to be out there, helping the old ladies out of the sanctuary like he always does after service. That is his job, helping people sit down and get up. He is too important to play kids games, and she giggles at the thought. He takes her giggle as an invitation to stay, pressing closer to her in that small storage closet.*

*She looks up into the man's face, with his slight moustache and skin stretching tightly over his face as he gives a thin-lipped smile. His breath smells kind of stale as he whispers in her ear. She can feel warm breath on her cheek.*

*"That's a very pretty dress."*

*She feels special. She never knew her own father. He thinks her dress is pretty. She likes the feeling. Nobody has ever made her feel like that before.*

*What is he doing now?*

*Blackness. Numbness. Confusion.*

*Later, in the car ride home, she is chattering away to her mom.*

*She says something about how funny it was that the man liked to play games with her.*

*Her mother looks over at her, her eyes wide and fearful.*

*"What do you mean, Gracie? Tell me more."*

*She tells her mother what happened.*

*She has never seen her mom so upset. Grace is scared. Her mom speeds home, wiping tears from her eyes and cursing out loud. Her mom never speaks like that. When they gets home, she tells Grace to play in her room, but instead she listens, her ear pressed against the wall as her mother yells and cries on the phone.*

*They never go back to that nice big building with the giant cross in the front. After that her mom often cries at night when she thinks Grace is asleep.*

*Grace lies awake in the darkness, thinking,* It's my fault. I made my mommy sad. I made her sick. I shouldn't have said anything.

Grace opened her eyes, tears blurring her vision now. The motion of the Ferris wheel was making her nauseous. She held Terrence close, and he licked her hand.

"If only I had kept my mouth shut that day," she whispered to Terrence.

They reached the very top of the Ferris wheel for the second time round. It creaked to a stop again. Grace put Terrence down on the seat next to her and spontaneously stood up.

The basket creaked back and forth slightly in the wind. Grace held onto the lap bar and leaned over. The people below looked like toys, wind-up dolls just going through the motions.

*"Can I hide in here with you, Grace?"*

She leaned further over the bar. *Why? Why do good people die and bad people thrive? Why did my dad leave me? Why isn't The Wizard real? Why doesn't anyone love me? Why am I here anyway?*

Grace leaned over the bar a little further as the wind blew her hair straight back. She began to wonder what would happen if she leaned over just a little farther and…. Would she wake up back in Texas? Would she die? Was she already dead? Was this hell?

Terrence yipped loudly, and Grace opened her eyes. Looking down at her dog's sweet face and wagging tail, she sat back down. She stroked his furry head and had an overwhelming sense of being insignificant and *small*.

*So small, but so loved.*

Those words startled her. Tears came rushing down her cheeks like a blanket of water, and a deep guttural sob rose up from her soul. The Ferris wheel was moving again. Grace couldn't hold back and cried out everything she had left inside. *Home…where are you?*

*God!*

*God?*

CHAPTER 22

# THE WAGON

*"And now here is my secret, a very simple secret; it is only
with the heart that one can see rightly, what is essential is
invisible to the eye."*

— ANTOINE DE SAINT-EXUPERY

B ack on the ground, Grace's legs felt rubbery. Her face felt like
it was on fire, her eyes swollen and red, but she didn't care.

She wandered back to the area where Leona had left her,
avoiding the fortune-teller's tent. She spotted Leona sitting on the
same crate she had been sitting on. She looked upset. As Grace
approached, Leona looked up and sighed, relief washing over her
face.

"There you are. I was scared I lost you."

Grace didn't respond and shifted her eyes to the ground, not
wanting to talk about where she had been.

"Well, I haven't found Hayden. Let's go over and look in the
area near the freaky funhouse."

"All right."

The girls walked through the carnival. Grace felt lost in the chaos of people. She followed Leona, grateful for a friend who was strong. She never imagined seeing Leona in this way.

"Look!"

They spotted Hayden across from the game he had been playing the last time they were at the carnival. He was sitting on the ground, looking dejected. His face was covered in pink splotches. He was holding an empty cotton candy cardboard stick. The ground around him was scattered with leftover sticks. Terrence ran up and started sniffing at them.

Leona burst out laughing. "Hayden! What happened! Did you get attacked by a fluffy pink cloud?"

Hayden didn't laugh. He was staring straight ahead, hardly blinking.

"Hayden?" Grace tried. Her voice sounded hoarse from crying.

Hayden looked up, hardly moving. His eyes looked vacant, like he had lost his spark.

"Huh?" He looked shell-shocked.

Leona leaned in closer to him. "Hayden, how many of those things did you eat?"

Hayden glanced at the ground where dozens of the empty cardboard holders lay. "I, ummm…I don't know."

"Are you okay?" Leona said. Hayden blinked slowly, like he was coming back to reality.

"I was walking down a dusty road…trying to get far enough away to feel free. Then the storm came…" He said it faintly, with hardly any emotion at all.

Grace and Leona looked at each other.

"Where's Tim?" Leona asked.

Hayden kept going. "I've been trying so hard, trying to wrap my mind around the meaning of life. Why? Why struggle and strive when it's all futile and meaningless?"

Leona sat down beside Hayden, took his hand, and held it warmly. "Breathe, Hayden, and don't try to talk for a few minutes." Leona spoke softly to him.

Finally, Hayden inhaled deeply and let it out slowly. "Wow, that was heavy." He squeezed Leona's hand and smiled. "Grace, Leona! It's good to see you! I was so sad after you both left. I didn't know if I would ever see you again. Tim was there, but I missed you both so much. I felt so lost. I..."

He broke off.

Leona let go of Hayden's hand and moved over to sit across from him, next to Grace. She asked again, "Hayden, do you know where Tim is?"

"Before I came here and started to eat the cotton candy, Tim told me to sit down and wait for him, that he was going somewhere and would come back for me soon. He said if he wasn't back in a few hours to wait for him outside the carnival gate."

"Okay," Leona said. "We will wait here for a little and see if he returns." Grace nodded in agreement, and Hayden continued to speak. His eyes were clear again and opened wide.

"When Tim left, I was all alone with my thoughts once again. So I sat down and watched the gamer-zombies wander back and forth between booths. I listened as the carnies shouted at them, hoping to set their hooks into new prey. Empty promises served up to gullible seekers. Then it hit me, and I saw in them the story of my life.

"All the gurus I've followed, they were all just carnies trolling for new victims. I realized my whole life had been spent wandering from booth to booth, game to game.

"We're all like thirsty pilgrims desperately seeking where to *dig our well.* Someone comes along and says, 'Dig here, this is the spot where you will tap into an unending water supply.' But it never works, and it never lasts. Empty words rattling around like stones tossed into dry wells. The source of life has to be beyond nature, because nature is all doomed to decay. Life is *alive!*

"For a moment, my thoughts were crystal clear, but soon my epiphany had vanished and all I felt was lonely and hungry. So I wandered over here and began to eat cotton candy. I thought if I zoned out and ate enough of it I would feel better, but all it did was make me feel more confused and really sick to my stomach."

Grace kicked a cardboard stick into the dust.

Leona stood up. "Wow, Hayden, sounds like you have really figured some things out. We're all learning here, and changing. Maybe The Wizard gave us what we were looking for after all." She smiled at Grace.

Grace did not smile. She had never felt more lost in her life.

Leona spoke up again. "Hey, I think we should blow this popsicle stand and go look for Tim outside. Are you ready?"

Grace and Hayden nodded in agreement.

Trying to avoid the crowd, they ducked behind the booths and skirted along the backside of the carnival. After a few minutes they came up to the side of a very large tent they hadn't noticed on their last visit. That sickening, sweet smell was more intense than ever. Making their way around to the front they saw an entrance with a long line of people waiting to go inside. Above the entrance was a sign that read "Food Program."

Even though they were hungry, they bypassed the line and walked around to the other side of the tent. There they saw a wagon backed up to a large opening. Terrence began to bark loudly. Grace gasped. "Oh my God." On the side of the wagon was written "EC Formula Processing." Grace grabbed onto Hayden's arm to steady herself. It took all her strength to prevent herself from being sick right there and then.

"Well, that's weird," said Hayden. "What's an EC wagon doing here?"

"Let's just get out of here as fast as we can," Grace said, her voice quivering.

"Sounds good to me." Leona was focused on finding the way out and wasn't paying much attention to the wagon.

Within seconds, they found themselves outside the carnival compound. Grace began to feel a bit better. She was glad to put the carnival, with its distractions and temptations, behind her forever.

They sat down on some rocks on the side of the road and waited. "Now what?" Grace asked.

"Well, let's hope Tim shows up here," Hayden replied. The three sat in silence for a while.

"What's that sound?" Leona looked up and listened.

They could hear the creak of wagon wheels turning and the clip-clop sound of horse hooves. They stood still for a moment, waiting to see who was approaching.

Grace held her breath as a wagon pulled by two horses appeared over the crest of a hill.

They recognized the three people seated on the driver's bench.

"Tim! Cal! Madeline!" Leona called out, waving.

Cal pulled on the reins, and the wagon came to a stop.

"You need a lift?" said Cal, his eyes shining. "You look like you could use one!"

The three climbed onto the wagon, with Grace carrying Terrence, and settled into seats near the front. Tim reached out to hug Leona, Grace, and Hayden.

"We were just coming to rescue you guys!" Tim said, smiling. "What happened? Where did you two go?"

Leona launched into her story of meeting with the Baker, with everyone but Grace listening intently. Madeline and Cal were both grinning from ear to ear.

Once Leona had given the short version of her story, Cal looked back at Grace. "So, Grace, Tim tells me you were successful in finding The Wizard. I'm sorry it wasn't all you hoped it would be."

His wife elbowed him and gave him a funny look, but Cal ignored her.

The others turned to Grace, expecting her to tell the story.

Grace swallowed. "Yeah, it sure wasn't what I expected. The Wizard was an illusion, a computerized special effect created and controlled by some guy named Bill. The real Wizard took off long ago and nobody knows where he is."

Cal looked thoughtful for a moment.

"Ah, yes...Bill. How is Bill?"

Leona looked at him. "You know Bill?"

Cal smiled slightly. "It's been a long time...but yes. I know him very well. Good man."

An awkward silence filled the cart. Grace stared at Cal, in an almost dreamlike state. His gruff beard covered most of his face, but his eyes shone a brilliant green. Something about him seemed incredibly familiar. Suddenly, her eyes opened wide, and her mouth dropped open. A flood of emotions hit her all at once.

"No, it can't be! Are you..."

She stopped, unable to form the words.

Cal kept staring forward, looking wistful.

Madeline frowned. "You need to tell them, dear. It's time."

"I am...at least I was, a long time ago...The Wizard."

"*What?*" shouted Leona.

"*No way!*" Hayden said.

Tim just stood staring at Cal, mouth gaping.

Grace's face reddened deeply, and she gripped her seat to steady herself. She looked at Madeline, embarrassed at the thought of the feelings she once had for The Wizard. Although the digitally enhanced Wizard was younger and perfect, the more Grace stared at Cal, the more she could see it. If he lost about twenty pounds and shaved his beard...

"How could you do this?" Grace said bitterly. She felt betrayed and made a fool by this man.

Cal cleared his throat. "I hope you can forgive me for any pain I may have caused you. At one time I was privileged to serve as leader of the EC. But The Wizard...that was never me. He was a creation of technology, marketing, and hero worship."

"But why?!" shouted Grace, overwhelmed and upset. "You knew the truth! Why didn't you tell us when we stayed with you that The Wizard was a fake, or rather that you were, or used to be...you know what I mean!' Why did you let us go off to see The Wizard without telling us the truth?"

"You weren't seeking truth. You were seeking The Wizard, and you needed to find him for yourself. Some things can't be explained. They have to be experienced."

"But...but you knew I was lost and looking to The Wizard for help! You could have told me what you knew!"

"I wanted to tell you many things, but you couldn't bear them at the time. Only the lost listen to directions. You weren't lost, you knew exactly where you were going—to see The Wizard. Tim told me how you brought Bill onstage. You were trying to do a good thing, but the people had no context, no ability to understand what you were saying. The effect is that now they are even more hardened in their beliefs.

"Think about it, Grace. If I would have told you that night that I was The Wizard, would you have believed me?" Cal waited for a reply.

"I don't know," Grace admitted

Madeline spoke up. "Sometimes you have to fall to pieces before you can fall into peace."

The friends sat in stunned silence for a few minutes, not knowing what to ask or say.

Finally, Hayden spoke up. "Just when I think god can't possibly get any more surreal, my mind is blown again. So...what now?"

"Now, we are going to meet some friends for dinner," Cal said calmly. "Once we are all dining together, everything will be fine.

Rest your minds, some problems are too much for the brain and can only be solved through the stomach."

The sound of the horses clopping down the dusty road made a soothing soundtrack for the otherwise silence-filled cart.

Grace wanted to shake Cal and ask "Why?" again, but she didn't move from her seat. Her body felt stiff, like it had decided to stop struggling and let the wagon take it wherever it was going. Grace had lost all illusions of being in control and had no desire to move anywhere on her own; she only wanted to be drawn along and allow someone else to be in control for a change.

# CHAPTER 23
# OLD FRIENDS AND ENEMIES

*"When I discover who I am, I'll be free."*

— RALPH ELLISON

G race woke up, startled. Her head had been resting on Hayden's shoulder. She rubbed her eyes and saw they were approaching The Badlands.

"Oh no, not this place," Grace said, yawning.

"Here we are!" said Cal enthusiastically. They could see smoke rising from the city of rubble.

"Smells awful," commented Hayden, scrunching up his nose. "So, what are we doing here, Cal? Hopefully not handing out fliers again?"

Cal laughed. "No paperwork to hand out, my friend. This time *we* are the fliers!"

They passed the graffiti-covered building they had parked beside just a few days earlier. Cal didn't stop the wagon.

"Are we taking the wagon in?" Leona asked.

"Yep. Gotta pick a few people up," responded Cal. "We have plenty of room for more passengers."

The wagon slowly approached the entrance to the city, where there was a gathering of people. As they entered, Grace could tell by their uniforms that they were from the godvernment. A few officials approached the wagon on foot, blocking their entrance.

"Stop! You are entering godvernment territory," one man said.

Cal didn't seem bothered. "It's all right, we just need to pass by. We'll be out of your way soon."

"I am afraid I can't let that happen." A woman emerged from the crowd.

"Linda," said Madeline.

Grace's stomach began to roll, and her chest tightened.

Linda ignored Madeline. "Where are your papers?" she demanded.

Cal looked at his wife then back at Linda.

"Well, now, let's see, I think they are somewhere."

The guards were whispering to one another. One of them pointed at Cal. "You look familiar. I think you are with the EC."

Linda looked at him more closely, cocking her head as she stared at his face.

"*You!* I recognize that face, despite that scraggly beard you hide behind."

Linda turned her gaze to Grace.

"And you? I remember you. What is your name?"

"Grace."

"Ah yes, you're the girl who tried to eat from the sacred table. And that creature!" She pointed at Terrence.

Grace held onto Terrence tightly.

"I am going to have to ask you to step out of the wagon and confirm your identity."

The toughest-looking guard stepped up on the wagon and grabbed Tim by the arm.

"Come out of the wagon now!" Tim looked at Cal, who nodded his head. They all followed Tim out, frightened. They stood together beside the wagon and were scrutinized by the godvernment officials along with a growing mob of onlookers.

"Hey, that guy was handing out EC literature here a few days ago," yelled a man from the crowd, pointing toward Hayden.

Linda looked pleased.

"Well, it looks like we are going to have to detain you for a while until we get this sorted out. We can't have people roaming around god with unconfirmed identities. You are going to have to prove that you belong here before you are allowed to pass."

Terrence was struggling in Grace's arms, barking and growling at Linda.

A man in the crowd leaned over and whispered in Linda's ear. She smirked. She walked up to Leona and looked at her, her eyes full of judgment.

"I know who you are." She pointed her long, bony finger in Leona's face. "You're one of Frank's girls, aren't you?"

Leona's face turned red, but she didn't respond.

"I know who—or rather, what—you are, young lady. We've worked hard to rid god of immoral filth like you."

"That's enough!" said Cal authoritatively, stepping away from the wagon toward Linda. "You have no right to speak as a representative of god. We've all done things we're not proud of. Her name is Leona, and she is not filth. She is a precious young woman of god."

Undaunted, Linda pointed her finger at Cal. "Who are you to talk, you washed-up old wizard!"

A voice in the crowd shouted out, "Linda, don't you have some paperwork to alphabetize?"

Zay stepped out from the crowd, looking as wild and crazy as ever. This time he had fire in his eyes.

Linda turned to him, smirking. "Ah, Isaiah, you have come out of hiding. This is none of your business. You have no authority here anymore. Move along now."

"*You* are the one who needs to move along, you big bully," said Zay, pointing his finger at Linda.

"The fact is," Zay shouted, addressing the whole crowd, "Linda here has no real authority. Her power lies only in deception, accusation, and fear! But look around! The old kingdom is collapsing, but a new one is at hand! It's in the air! Can you smell it? Can you taste it?" He laughed out loud, like a madman.

Zay moved and stood directly in front of Linda and stared into her dark eyes.

"The first thing you do with hungry people is feed them! You think you control the food through your little 'program'"—he dramatically made his fingers into quotation marks—"but in reality, you control nothing! The land of god is abundant, and its fruits are free for the taking! The air we breathe, sunlight, water, the gravity that keeps us from flying out into space are all gifts granted to all, with no strings attached. Only a masterful, diabolical deception could cause anyone to imagine earning favors from god. What an insane and prideful thought! There is no shortage of food. The only famine lies within the hearts and minds of those starved of truth and blinded by fear and lies.

"*You* are one of the deceived ones, dearest Linda! Oh yes, I knew you when you were young and zealous for justice and fairness. You imagined yourself the arbiter of god, but instead you became a dictator. But you are also starving, snared by your own trap. If only you could see.

"Ah, yes! Taste and see! That is the only way! The feast is at hand and the preparations completed! No more time for chitchat! The food will get cold, and the ice will melt in the drinks!"

Zay jumped up and down with his arms raised over his head, as if he was trying to touch some invisible ceiling.

Linda took the opportunity to regain control. "You are a madman! Where do you get these foolish notions! Security! Restrain the lunatic Zay and take rest of these rebels into custody."

The guards didn't move. The crowd was murmuring.

"What are you waiting for? Do as I have commanded!" Linda's expression was a mixture of anger and horror.

One by one, the guards turned and walked away. The spectators began to disperse as well.

Linda was incensed and grabbed onto the arm of one of the deserting guards. "Where do you think you are going? I make the rules around here! I command you to arrest these criminals!"

He turned and faced his leader. "What's their crime, speaking the truth? They aren't hurting anyone, and I'm too hungry to fight them." His sunken eyes looked weary and vacant. Linda loosened her grip and let him go on his way.

"You think this is a victory, don't you?" Linda turned her attention back to Zay. "Well, just wait and see what happens when they discover that all of your words are cheap and the freedom you preach is a lie! Fear will drive them back. It always does."

Zay didn't respond. Linda then cast an evil look toward Grace, "And you...*Grace*! You have been nothing but trouble! Go back to where you came from. There is no place for Grace in the land of god!"

Linda turned and walked away.

Grace felt a cold chill run down her back.

Cal ran over and embraced Zay.

"My old friend. It's so good to see you again!"

The others looked at each other in amazement.

"Well, I think we can get back in the wagon and be on our way now that our identity has been established," Madeline said with a wink.

Zay shouted, "Yeeeeeessssss, maaaaaaaaaaaa'am!" He hugged Madeline and swung her around like a small child.

She laughed. "You crazy man, put me down at once!"

They all climbed back in the wagon, Cal grabbed the reins, and the horses began moving slowly forward.

"I don't understand, why did they let us go? I thought we were about to be thrown into some *godforsaken* jail," Hayden said, nervously laughing.

Zay stood up at the back of the wagon as it started to move. He held onto the frame, leaned out, and shouted to the remnants, "Anyone, whoever wants, we invite you to come with us! Leave the godvernment and be free! This invitation is open to all the weary and hungry! Come, celebrate with us!"

The reaction of the crowd appeared to be a mixture of curiosity, amusement, and anger. No one responded.

Zay continued shouting his invitation until the wagon had cleared the crowd; then he took a seat next to Hayden.

"My young, deep-thinking friend, they retreated because once a lie is revealed it loses its power to deceive. Linda knows that her time is running out. Fear is a finite motivator. Freedom is not merely an ideological pipe dream, it is imbedded in our nature, and the essence of what makes us humans. To be enslaved *is* to die, and to live *is* to be free.

"But more essentially, Linda's kingdom hinges upon binding her subjects in selfishness through propagating the lie that god's providence is feeble and its benevolence limited. This is the lie that gives birth to all manner of selfishness, greed, and lust. Linda knows that once people see, really see, that god's goodness is infinite, selfishness will die of starvation."

Zay paused then slapped Hayden on the back and laughed his wild laugh and kept speaking.

"Once upon a time, Linda and I were very close comrades. Back when old Cal and I were sworn enemies, I was her second-in-command. More like she was the pretty face and I was the power behind it."

The group all looked at him, surprised.

"You were a godvernment leader?" said Leona, half laughing.

"The best of the best!" announced Zay. "I had charisma—people always like that. I was moral, honest, an upstanding example of piety—at least, that's how others saw me. I knew better, and one day I simply lost the ability to fake it anymore. I think that's when I finally snapped!"

He winked at Leona. "But falling apart was the best thing that could have ever happened to me!"

Zay's expression turned somber as they passed by broken-down buildings charred from fire and covered in graffiti.

"This was once the capital of god. It was a magnificent city but now is in ruins because of the harsh laws of the godvernment. They condemned every building that did not meet their rigid code. They are masters of condemnation, yet they never rebuild." He smiled to himself, leaned back, and gave Hayden a big hug. "But some things you have to tear down completely before you can rebuild."

The wagon maneuvered around the rubble of half-demolished buildings and piles of trash. Once in a while, Zay, Madeline, or Cal would call out to someone they saw hauling garbage or sitting on the side of the road.

"Come with us! Leave your dead-end work and come join the celebration!" Several people looked at them longingly, but no one would risk abandoning their work for fear of judgment.

"What celebration?" Grace asked curiously.

"You'll see for yourself, very soon.

"The godvernment has such a stronghold of fear in this area," said Cal. "Such sadness and gloom. Once we get further into the city, hopefully there will be some people who will want to join us."

Grace had many questions, but she kept quiet and stuck with her plan to sit back and just go along for the ride.

"We are about to enter into EC territory," remarked Zay. "More fun ahead, boys and girls." He had a wild look in his eyes.

Cal stopped the wagon in front of a large crowd of people. They were mulling around aimlessly. Grace noticed some people handing out fliers, trying to engage with the people of the city. Another man was setting up a stage and a sound system.

"Here we go again," said Hayden.

Grace looked into the crowd. Her heart nearly stopped. She noticed Jared and several people she recognized from the EC.

"Oh no," she whispered. "Jared's here."

Grace slunk down into the wagon, hoping to become invisible. But Jared had already noticed them and was approaching the wagon, a fake smile on his face.

"Well! Hello! I wasn't expecting to see you all…together…so soon!"

Jared looked at Cal. "Calvin. What a surprise. Facial hair doesn't really suit you. You look like a lumberjack. We have been wondering what you've been up to."

"Good to see you, Jared. It's been a while," Cal replied, unfazed by Jared's remarks.

A small man cowered behind Jared.

Cal noticed him. "Bill! Hey, Bill!"

The timid man stepped out from behind Jared. "H-h-h-hello," he squeaked, adjusting his glasses and staring at his shoes.

"We are here to film a new and dazzling EC promotional video," said Jared, his white teeth flashing in the sun. "We want to show people the brutality of the godvernment in glorious 3D! Brutality is something old Isaiah there knows all about."

Zay responded, "Yes, I know all too well about brutality. That's why I'm no longer with the godvernment."

"Ah yes. Neutral just like our former great leader." He pointed to Cal. "I am afraid neutrality never got anyone anywhere."

"Standing for truth is not neutral, Jared," Cal said gently. "We are on the side of the people. People starving for bread and for truth."

"Truth?" Jared laughed. "Whose truth are you speaking about? What is truth, O wise one? Isn't it whatever makes the people happy, healthy, and wholesome?" His sarcastic tone made Cal cringe slightly.

"Speaking of truth, this young lady has something of mine." Jared pointed to Grace.

"You want the book, Jared?" Zay asked. "You could have just asked me yourself. But I'm afraid that you won't find any new and improved recipes in there."

Jared looked stunned for a moment, and then he regained his composure. "I don't know what you're talking about."

Cal spoke up. "I did get the *Secrets* from the book. I just repackaged the old set of rules into self-help principles in order to make them more digestible. I thought we were building a better, freer society, but in the end I realized we were serving up the same dish: death. We starved people in a vain attempt to make them good. The problem is that you can't 'eat' *Secrets* any more than you can eat rules or laws.

"The Formula is failing. It is slowly but surely poisoning the people of the EC. It was always a deadly mixture, though we began with good intentions. You and I both know why it's poisonous. I know that you aren't able to recruit enough members to make up for the ones that are dying off. The people are consuming one another, all the while believing they are making a difference for god. Jared, listen to me, the problem isn't badness, but deadness."

Jared was getting angry. "I don't know what you are talking about. Where's the book, Grace? Hand it over!"

Grace shrugged her shoulders, unwilling to get involved in the debate.

"I have it," said Leona. She reached into her pocket and handed it to Zay. "Here. This is yours. It belongs to you."

Zay took the book, grinning wildly. He hopped out of the wagon and approached Jared.

"There is nothing magical about this book, Jared. What matters is whether you can read it or not."

"What are you talking about, you lunatic! Of course I can read!" Zay smiled. "All right then, here you go!"

He handed the book to Jared. Jared had a look of conquering satisfaction as he snatched the book out of Zay's hands.

He flipped it open, staring at the contents. A puzzled look crossed his face.

"What is this?" He looked at Zay angrily. He flipped through the pages, becoming more confused and frustrated.

"Take it! This means nothing to me! Where is the real book, the one with the formulas?" He shoved it back in Zay's hand.

During this exchange, Bill had snuck around Jared and was now climbing into the wagon. The others welcomed him warmly.

Jared noticed his assistant in the wagon and approached him in a huff.

"Bill? Bill! What are you doing?! Get down here! We have work to do!"

Bill didn't budge from the seat tucked between Hayden and Leona.

"I am going with them,"Bill said softly but confidently.

Jared tried to hide his desperation. "What are you talking about? The EC is your home, and people are depending on you!"

Cal reached back and patted Bill's knee, not paying any attention to Jared. "It's good to see you again, Bill."

Bill's resolve thickened. "I won't be your puppet anymore, Jared. I am done with show business!" He began to raise his voice. The other people from the EC and some from the Badlands gathered around the wagon to listen in.

"The EC is a fraud! It is no better than the godvernment! They both produce the same thing: death!"

The crowd was stirring, talking, and many were becoming visibility upset.

Jared's face was bright red. "You will be sorry, all of you!" he said, his voice suddenly sounding high pitched and shrill.

For the first time since she had seen him, Grace felt sorry for Jared.

Cal looked down compassionately at Jared from the wagon seat.

"Jared, I knew you when you were a young man, so hopeful and full of vision. I know you are hungry and tired. Give up the lie. Come join us. Please!"

Jared shook his head, angry, but Grace could see a look of sadness and betrayal sweep over his face.

"I have work to do." He turned his back to the wagon and walked back to where the stage was being set up. A crowd of people gathered around him, demanding answers. He still looked upset as he tried to calm them down and supervise the stage construction.

A mother and two small dirty and barefooted children approached the wagon.

"Please," the woman said, looking hopefully up at them. "I believe you are speaking the truth. Can we come with you?"

"Of course!" said Zay, wildly happy. He tossed the book up to Leona and helped the woman and her kids into the wagon. Madeline got up and sat next to the woman and began talking with her.

Zay stood up in the wagon again.

"If anyone else wants to come with us, we welcome you with open arms! Come as you are!"

When they realized no one else was going to join them, Cal grabbed the reins, and soon the wagon began to move forward.

Grace noticed Madeline had her arm around the woman they had just picked up. They were both crying.

Grace started to get choked up but quickly looked away.

Leona held the book out, staring at it.

"I don't get it, Zay," she started. "If this book is so important, why is it written in a language that no one can understand?"

Zay held out his hand to Leona, and she placed the book in it. He then lifted the book to his nose and inhaled deeply, closing his eyes.

"Mmmmmm. Smell the fresh-baked bread!"

The others looked at him strangely.

"The reason people can't read it is because they see it as a manual."

"So, what's so wrong with a manual?" asked Hayden. "I could sure use one sometimes!"

Zay swept his hand across the landscape of the ruined city.

"This is what is wrong. Both the EC and the godvernment devised their systems from this same book. How ironic that two diametrically opposed systems would draw inspiration from the same source. Or are they really opposite?

"Leona, this book is unlike any other book. It appears to teach whatever the individual reader desires. If Jared had looked harder, he would have discovered words that justified his own prejudices."

He paused, smiling at the little girl with big eyes and a dirty face snuggled next to her mom.

"This book cannot be understood by the mind because it is not written for the minds of men. It is written to, and is in fact food for, the spirit of man. Unless you have new eyes, you will be an illiterate who imagines himself a sage. "

"I think I see!" said Leona excitedly. "This is what the Baker began to tell me."

"Man, that is some heavy, heavy stuff," Hayden said, letting out a deep sigh.

Zay placed his hand on Hayden's knee. "Rest your mind, my friend, and open up your heart."

Grace's own mind was reeling. What did this all mean? Nothing and no one made sense anymore. She buried her head in her hands as Terrence slept peacefully on her lap.

# CHAPTER 24
# THE FACTORY

*"A dead thing can go with the stream, but only a living thing can go against it."*

— G.K. Chesterson

The wagon stopped suddenly next to a big pile of rubble. Up ahead, they could see the front of an enormous building, almost the size of the Great Hall in the EC. Grace couldn't believe they hadn't seen it on their last trip. It was built of huge blocks of stone. There were no windows, just smokestacks billowing out black soot. A massive, imposing, heavy metal door stood in front.

As they got closer, Grace noticed inscriptions on a row of ten stones twenty feet or so above the entrance. It looked like numbers and letters, but she didn't understand the language.

"What is this place?" asked Hayden, wrinkling his nose.

Tim coughed. They all tried to cover their noses with their hands and shirts, but they couldn't escape the stench.

"This is death"," said Zay, gazing at the door. Madeline shuddered and buried her face in her hands.

Zay continued, "Believe it or not, a long time ago this building was a sort of school.

"That was a long time ago. For many years now it has served another purpose, a diabolical one. Handling dead things is a tricky business." Zay's tone grew somber, and his volume diminished to a whisper. "That which is dead must be kept away from the living. Death can only breed death."

"What are we doing here?" Grace asked, unable to keep quiet any longer. It was hard to breathe, and she was growing more anxious by the second.

Cal said slowly, "Sometimes, the truth is bitterly painful. But it must be embraced and exposed before freedom can flow."

He began to guide the wagon around the side of the great windowless monolith. As they proceeded, Grace saw a tall stone wall shielding the back of the building from view. The wagon slowly made its way around the wall and stopped at the corner.

Everyone in the wagon remained still and silent, waiting to see what would happen next. It wasn't long before another wagon was seen approaching from the distance. It finally stopped near the center of the wall. Just then two enormous iron gates began to open slowly toward the wagon.

Grace read what was printed on the side of the wagon:

"EC Formula Processing Plant."

Fear and dread shot through her body, as her stomach knotted and her face turned ashen.

"*No!*" she screamed.

Leona clutched Grace, trying to calm her down.

As the other wagon entered, Cal snapped the reins, and the horses quickly pulled their wagon through the gates just as they were closing.

The other wagon came to a stop near two large metal doors at the back of the building. Two men got out and opened the doors slowly.

Safely within the stone wall, Cal pulled the reins, and the wagon came to an abrupt stop. The gate closed behind them.

Grace suddenly pulled away from Leona, jumped out, and ran toward the men.

"Grace? What are you doing?" Leona called out. Cal and Terrence jumped down and began chasing after her.

"Stop, you need to stop!" Grace ran toward the men, who were climbing back into their wagon, preparing to enter the building.

"I know what you are doing! I know what you have in there! You EC people are just a bunch of well-dressed zombies!"

"Hey, who are you!" the driver said gruffly. "You're not authorized to be here!" Grace glared at him and ran around to the back of the wagon. Terrence was barking wildly.

Cal stepped in front of the wagon. The horses whinnied and stomped their hooves.

"Game's up," he said fiercely.

The others had gotten out of the wagon and were running to join Grace.

"What's going on?" Tim asked as the others joined Cal and Grace.

Grace took a deep breath and lifted the canvas on the back of the EC wagon.

Everyone gasped.

Lying in the wagon were stacks of emaciated human corpses.

Leona turned away. Madeline wrapped her arm around her. Hayden covered his mouth as if trying to stop himself from being sick. Tim just stood with his mouth open. Bill shook his head sadly.

Zay stood next to Grace and said, "I didn't realize you knew."

He spoke to the others.

"When someone grows too weak to function in the system, they are considered disposable. They are isolated until they die and then processed out in order to feed the new arrivals. The leadership justifies the turnover by proclaiming *god is just separating the chaff from the grain.*"

Grace shuddered, and then slowly her eyes fell on a small girl towards the back of the wagon. The girl's eyes were shut, but her face was unmistakable.

"*Anna!*" she cried.

Before anyone could stop her, she rushed to the back of the wagon and climbed inside. Ignoring the rotting corpses and the stench, she lifted the girl's emaciated frame and carried it reverently back toward her friends.

The others stared at her in disbelief. Zay didn't seem fazed. He walked over, held out his arms, and Grace reluctantly handed him Anna's body. He carried her back to their wagon and laid her down in the back.

The driver and his partner hadn't noticed what Grace was doing, as they had been occupied arguing with Cal. "I don't care who you say you are. If you don't get out of our way, we will run you over!"

Their horses began to move forward. Cal jumped out of the way, tripping over a rock and falling down right under their feet.

"*No!*" Leona screamed in a panic.

"Cal!" Madeline shrieked, rushing over to him.

He rolled out of the way just in time. The wagon pulled through the doors, which then quickly closed.

"Are you okay?" Madeline asked, helping her husband to his feet.

"Yes, dear, I'm fine." He brushed himself off.

Zay came over to check on Cal. "Glad to see you're okay, old buddy. We rescued one! She's safe now."

"But Zay…it's too late…she's dead," Grace sobbed. She put her face down on the dead girl's wasted frame and cried bitterly. Leona put her arms around Grace and hugged her tightly.

Everyone was shell-shocked.

Zay shook his head. "Don't be afraid, Grace. In the end, life always triumphs over death."

Leona spoke up. "He's right, you know. Death doesn't have to be the end. Nothing in this land is as it appears on the surface. You just have to believe there is something better waiting for all of us. We just don't see it clearly yet."

But something inside Grace made her more determined than ever to change the present situation. She dried her eyes and listened to the others talking.

"The EC is evil!" proclaimed Tim.

"I can't believe we were helping to recruit victims for them!" Hayden said in shock.

"Don't rush to conclusions," said Zay. "Evil has many faces. There is another side to this you must see."

"Come on!" Cal yelled, jumping back up into the wagon. They all piled in. He drove it around the other side of the large building.

Nothing could have prepared them for what they saw next. Turning the corner they saw another entrance identical to the one they had entered. A couple of wagons were lined up, preparing to enter through large doors leading into the side of the building.

On the sides of these wagons was written, "godvernment Work for Food program."

"Zay! I don't understand! What does this mean?" Grace cried out loudly. "I though the EC and the godvernment were enemies?"

"They are in competition with one another, but long ago they agreed it was mutually beneficial to join forces in order to meet the growing demands of their respective 'food programs.' It was strictly a relationship of convenience based upon economies of scale.

"The godvernment is serving up the same deadly concoction as the Formula, just in a different form. Their people prefer their death served straight up, dry and tough. Their palate is a reflection of their society. They prefer structure, rules instead of *Secrets*. They fancy discipline over philosophy and admonishment over encouragement. They like something they can sink their teeth into!

"The EC crowd enjoys their deadness watered down, smooth, and easier to swallow. They enjoy the esoteric, the mysterious, and the relevant. They demand freedom that goes down easy, a freedom without sacrifice or pain. The smoothie crowd."

He continued, "The food processing joint venture allows both parties to maximize food production by minimizing waste, and in the end they are using the same deadly mixture. Oh yes, it's the mixture that makes all this so insidiously dangerous. If they were serving up pure poison, nobody would consume it, so they deceive their people by adding good food to the mix. But tragically, it only takes a small amount of dead human flesh to poison the whole food supply, and they are adding it by the wagonloads. "

Everyone gasped.

"Why is everything in god so corrupt and evil?" Leona asked.

"Yeah, it's like one big power struggle," Hayden chimed in.

"Where is love in all of this?" Tim was reaching for his eye drops.

Cal spoke up. "The truth is, some have given themselves over to evil, but for the most part evil flourishes because of ignorance. People *trying to do the right thing*.

"My friends, don't fall into the trap of cynicism, as that path always leads directly to the carnival. There is no escape. There is only the choice to make the world better or worse."

Grace, who had been sitting quietly, stood up quickly and spoke. "Something has to be done!"

"Yes, we have to do something!" said Leona forcefully.

Cal grabbed the reins and began to lead the horses back around to the rear of the building. "I have an idea. Tim, Bill, come with me. Zay, you and the others wait here. There will be a shift change in a few minutes. Zay, you know what to do! We'll be back!"

"You got it, my friend!" Cal stopped the wagon, and Zay and the others climbed out and watched as Cal quickly guided the wagon out of the gate just as it opened to let in another delivery.

"I have a feeling things are about to get real interesting around here!" Zay said, wild eyed, belting out his best madman laugh.

"You see, this factory is located in a very important place! This is the location of the main spring that flows out from an enormous underground artesian well. This spring provides the necessary energy and water to power the factory," Zay explained.

"They've installed an elaborate *flow restriction mechanism* over top of the wellhead. They restrict the water flow to accommodate their processing needs."

"So that's why the land around here is like a desert!" said Leona

Just then the large metal doors opened up, and a steady stream of factory workers began to file out. At the same time, the outer gates opened and another group began to make their way toward the factory door.

"Shift change!" Zay proclaimed.

He turned to Grace and said, "You and the others wait here. But when the time comes, I want you to speak the truth as loud as you can."

Grace looked at Zay incredulously. "Why do you want me to speak? These are your people, and you seem to have all the answers. I'm just as confused as they are!"

Zay smiled, took Grace's hands, and spoke softly. "It is strange, but true, that most often people will listen to a stranger, someone from outside their family and tribe, before they will listen to one of their own. The heart grows calloused towards truth that has been ignored or rejected, and the familiar becomes despised."

Zay squeezed her hands slightly and then released them gently. "There is something else. We all have been granted gifts, and yours is needed right now. I know you understand what I am saying."

Grace looked into Zay's eyes and nodded, taking in a deep breath.

The little group and the dog stood there, wondering what would come next. Leona sat down on the ground, and Terrence jumped onto her lap.

Zay grabbed an old crate that was lying in a pile of trash, ran toward the middle of the courtyard, leapt up on the crate, and began jumping up and down, waving his arms and screaming, "Taste and see!"

The spectacle caught the attention of the crowd, and people stopped in their tracks to stare.

"People of god!" he began. "Today is the day of truth! You've been deceived! You've been working so hard, just trying to survive! You have been brainwashed into believing you live in a desert, but god is a land of great orchards, rivers, and meadows teeming with life and an abundance of food!"

"You're insane!" someone yelled out.

Zay laughed his crazy laugh, as if to agree with his heckler.

"Open your eyes and see what *is*! An enemy has blinded you from beholding this beautiful, abundant land of god. Your land has been made to appear desolate. It's a lie!"

"What does that mean?" a woman shouted.

Zay pointed to the factory. "The product of this factory is *death* itself! This place is recycling dead flesh and calling it food! You have forgotten, or may never have known, the taste of real food. But I have good news! Everything you need, all that you have dreamed of, is right here. It's all around you."

The crowd grumbled and began to argue among themselves.

"Why should we believe you, crazy man?" someone shouted at Zay.

Another man yelled, "Yeah, you are just the latest know-it-all to come along and lead us to *the truth*! Leave us alone and let us work." He started laughing, along with several others. The crowd was becoming unruly.

Grace knew this was her time. She knew what she had to do and made her way through the crowd and finally to Zay. She felt something powerful inside of her churning, waiting to be revealed. Her gift was coming out one way or another.

"I'll take a shot at it," Grace said, smiling at Zay. He smiled back and stepped off the crate. Grace stood up straight and addressed the crowd in her loudest voice.

"It's true, people are dying. My friend, Anna, is already dead. She was taught the lie that if you try hard enough you can make it on your own strength, along with a little Formula, of course," Grace ended with a sarcastic tone.

"Well, we can't. You can't. It is time to stop pretending!"

The crowd grew silent. Something about Grace captured their attention.

She continued, "Traveling through this land I've seen evil and destruction, but I've also experienced goodness. I wish you could meet the Orchard Owner. I don't understand him completely, but I can tell from experience that every time we were lost and starving, he showed up and fed us the most awesome food! Just about everyone else in god who offers food is after something, but he never asks anything in return! You've just gotta meet this man. You've just gotta meet him." Tears began to stream down Grace's face.

"We have been promised things before. Why should we believe you?" someone shouted from the crowd.

"I will take you to him! You can…taste and see."

Zay yipped and jumped up with his hand out like he was high-fiving the air.

The mood of the crowd was shifting from anger and distrust to bewilderment and confusion.

"We have never heard anyone speak like this before," a woman shouted. "How can this be?" The crowd began to argue amongst themselves. Grace thought she noticed some pushing and shoving, but as the people were so tightly packed together, she couldn't be sure.

"They just don't get it!" Grace said, looking down at Zay.

"They will have an opportunity soon. Don't worry," he said, smiling.

Just then Grace saw the wagon, with Cal at the reins, coming through the gates. He slowed the horses down to a slow walk as the wagon made its way to the center of the yard. The crowd parted to allow a path for the wagon, and soon Cal called out "Whoa" and the horses came to a stop just a few feet away from where Grace and Zay stood.

Bill and Tim jumped out of the back and began to set up folding tables. Cal and Zay joined in to help. As soon as the tables were set up, they began to unload boxes of food and place them on the tables. Cal called for Madeline, Hayden, and Leona to come and help. The crowd seemed transfixed by the scene that was playing out in their midst.

While the others continued putting out the spread of roast beef sandwiches and fresh fruit and vegetables, Cal jumped up on one of the tables and began to shout.

"People of god, I know a little about putting on a good show! I know about smooth words, promises, and *Secrets*, which in the end leave you hungry and lost. But today we ask you to, as my friend is so fond of saying, *taste and see!*

"The godvernment seeks to make you their slave, while the EC would recruit you as a mercenary. It's only a matter of whether you prefer the stick or the carrot. Whichever way you choose, you lose your freedom and slowly starve to death.

"We are inviting you to dine! Come as you are, with no strings attached!"

"We have been warned not to accept food from strangers," a man shouted from the crowd. "It may be poisoned!" The crowd noise grew louder, and Cal realized he was losing them.

Cal spoke out, loud and strong. "A long time ago I was...*The Wizard* of god! People came to me for answers, but I was lost myself! I was hungry. One day I met someone and tasted real food! From that moment on, my life has never been the same! Listen to me! There are *no Secrets*! Come, eat and see for yourselves!"

Gasps could be heard among the crowd. Some people rushed to the tables, others approached cautiously, but most of the growing crowd just stood around and debated with each other. A steady stream of workers filed out of the factory, while others continued to come in through the open gates.

"This is becoming quite a scene!" Hayden said to Grace as they continued to serve.

Grace looked at the people gathered around the tables. She saw expressions that could only be described as stunned ecstasy. She remembered how hungry she had been when she first met the Baker in Pleasant Grove. She remembered the amazing food and the effect it had on those who dined.

She marveled at the chaotic scene being played out in the courtyard of the massive factory. The range of human emotions all manifested in response to identical conditions: Anger. Confusion. Fear. Anxiety. Amazement. Inexpressible joy.

Suddenly an angry man dressed in a suit and holding a bullhorn ran out the factory door.

"Return to your work stations at once!" he screamed.

Even with the bullhorn he was barely heard over the crowd.

"I repeat, return to your stations! You are breaking the rules and will be punished severely unless you return immediately!"

A few workers ran back in, but the majority ignored him and continued to mull around, looking at the food and eating the sandwiches.

The man in the suit ran into the crowd, screaming into the bullhorn. "Anyone caught not working will be punished and banished from god!" A small group of workers who had been talking amongst themselves approached the man and snatched the bullhorn away, knocking him to the ground in the process.

A tall, thin man from the group spoke into the bullhorn. "*No!* We're tired of being worked and starved to death! What are they going to do to us that they haven't already done! What are we afraid of? What's the worst they can do, kill us? We're already dead! We're just waiting our turn to be processed!"

"*Yeah!*" a large number from the crowd shouted in unison.

A large group of men, along with a few women, rushed toward the factory door. The man in the suit stood and screamed at the top of his lungs, trying to restore order, but his voice was drowned out by the frenzied mob. He was still pleading with the workers to stop as he followed the last ones storming through the door.

Grace and Hayden, who had stopped serving to watch this scene unfold, stared at each other wide eyed.

"What's going to happen now?" Hayden asked Grace.

Grace shrugged. "I've stopped trying to figure things out."

The scene outside continued on as before. Small groups of workers huddled together having heated discussions, while others dined on the gracious feast that was spread out before them. Others simply stood in silence, waiting to see what would happen next.

*BANG!*

*POP!*

*WHOOSH!*

The ground shook as loud, strange sounds echoed from inside the factory.

Within seconds, the tall man emerged from the factory door, followed by a rush of other workers, some wearing suits. He shouted into the bullhorn, "The cap is off the well! We're *free!*"

Grace noticed water beginning to trickle through the doors then quickly intensifying into a stream that began to flood the platform and spill onto the ground.

"Clear out!" someone shouted.

"Quick, everyone into the wagon," Zay called out. "Now! Hop in!"

The group all returned to the wagon and climbed in. Several people from the crowd also jumped in, until the wagon could hold no more. Some hung off the side.

The scene was now total pandemonium. Some were celebrating, dancing with joy and shouting, "*Freedom*," while others were running back inside the factory, hoping they could somehow repair the damage that had been done. A good number simply stood around in a daze, watching to see what would happen next.

"Leave now and come us! You're *not* free yet! " Zay shouted from the back of the wagon as Cal guided the horses through the gate. "You've torn down the lie, but now you must discover the truth, before new deception creeps in to fill the void! Come with us! We won't leave you stranded!"

A few more joined in and followed the wagon as it exited through the gates and headed back down the path. After a few minutes, Grace looked back and noticed streams of water gushing out through cracks in the wall that surrounded the factory.

The waters that had been held back for so long were flowing once again.

# CHAPTER 25
# AWAKENING

*"Blessed are those with cracks in their broken heart because that is how the light gets in."*

— SHANNON L. ALDER

"A re we going to bury her somewhere?" Grace was holding onto Anna's gaunt body to keep it from jostling too much in the back of the wagon.

Zay cocked his head to the side. "The life-giving waters have been released. The crops will grow once again."

"What?" Grace looked up at Zay, confused.

"Death is simply the absence of life. Life always triumphs over death! Don't be afraid, just believe."

The wagon stopped abruptly in front of a most odd-looking structure. The walls of the building appeared to be made up of bits and pieces from junkyards and demolished buildings. Concrete blocks that looked like they were about to crumble were awkwardly fused with pieces of wood, cloth, plastic, and an assortment of household items such as broken tables and chairs.

It was a giant piece of abstract art. As Grace stared at the structure, she was overcome with a powerful sense of déjà vu. The top of the building sloped up and was constructed with steel bars, wooden planks, and scrap metal, making a sort of steeple.

"We're here," said Cal, stopping the wagon.

The passengers began to climb out of the wagon.

Grace looked down at Anna, not sure what to do. Cal approached her. "I'll carry her inside," he said gently, scooping up the body. Grace nodded and followed Cal out of the wagon.

A large group of people had gathered in front of the strange building, talking and chattering. Unlike the usual residents of the Badlands, these people all looked happy. Some of the factory workers who had followed the wagon were now mingling with the others who had gathered.

Just then Grace saw a little girl she recognized.

"Rhoda!" she shouted, a smile breaking through.

Rhoda ran up and hugged her tight.

"You're so far away from home," Grace said.

Rhoda smiled and nodded, tugging Grace's hand and pointing toward the front of the building. Grace noticed Hayden talking to one of the girls they had encountered stacking bricks on their previous trip to the Badlands. Leona had found Charlie and was chatting with him, and Zay was introducing Tim to others. Cal had disappeared inside with Anna's body.

Grace knelt down on the ground, looking at the little, barefoot girl.

"How did you get here all the way from Pleasant Grove?"

The girl looked past her, her eyes as big as saucers.

"Mama!" Rhoda shouted. She ran toward the woman who had been traveling with the group through the Badlands.

The woman put her hand over her mouth, her eyes wide. She knelt to the ground and embraced the little girl, sobbing.

She picked Rhoda up, rocking her back and forth. The woman's other children, who had been playing nearby, ran over, embracing them both.

"My baby!" she cried.

She turned to Madeline and Grace, her eyes shining.

"I thought I lost her in the storm. I thought I had lost her..."

Grace stared at the miraculous reunion with tears streaming down her cheeks. Leona approached her. She linked arms with Grace.

"Let's go in," she said confidently. Tim saw the girls from the other side of the courtyard. He smiled, said something to Cal, and walked over to join them. He took Leona's arm.

When Hayden saw his friends linked together, he walked over and took Grace's arm, smiling.

"I don't know where we are, but there is something so familiar about this place!" he exclaimed.

"Are you ready?" Tim asked, looking at Grace.

"Yes."

Without another word being spoken, linked together as one, they stepped toward the door and into the building. Zay ran in front of them, flinging the front door open.

"After you," he said with a sweep of his arm. Standing in the doorway, they saw the entrance led into a small foyer. Directly ahead were large, wide-open double doors.

In the frame of the doorway stood the Orchard Owner, positioned as one who was charged with greeting guests of honor.

"Welcome," he said, smiling warmly. Beyond him, a huge room could be seen. Stained glass panels in the ceiling allowed light to pour in, illuminating an extraordinarily long banquet table lined with chairs.

Grace looked at the man standing in the doorway, his hands stretched up against the frame, as if he were holding it up, as if he were a part of the frame. A ray of light shone through the broken glass, illuminating his face.

Grace remembered the image from her mosaic.

"Come in and have a seat. Everything is ready now." He smiled.

The friends unlinked arms and walked through the doorway. Grace stopped in front of the Orchard Owner.

Terrence was at his feet, wagging his tail and looking up at him. He laughed, leaned over, and patted the dog, his eyes still on Grace.

"It's you. I have so many questions," Grace started. She looked beyond him and saw Anna's body lying on a bench in the corner of the room. Her face was uncovered, and she looked so peaceful, almost radiant in death.

"What about her!" Grace said, pointing. "Why didn't you show up and feed her, like you did us? We didn't do anything to earn it! Why did she have to die?"

The Orchard Owner looked at her kindly. "Tell me, did you offer food to Anna in the hospital?" Grace remembered Anna turning down the sandwich. "Why trouble yourself with questions beyond your understanding?

"I have many things to tell you, but first, we must dine."

"I know, I know, that's what you always say." Grace sighed, swallowed her sadness, and looked around the room. It was so beautifully decorated. The table was immaculate. She immediately felt dirty and underdressed. She was also very hungry.

She turned to the Orchard Owner.

"We've had a long journey. Is there any way I would have time to go and clean up..."

Even as she was saying it, she realized how ridiculous it sounded. She was no dirtier than anyone else and had no clean clothes to change into anyway.

The Orchard Owner smiled and gestured toward the table.

Grace felt like she was walking through a recurring dream. She followed her friends over to the table, and they sat down on intricately carved chairs. The back of each chair had a unique design: scenes of birds, waterfalls, picnic scenes. They were each extraordinary, exquisite pieces of art.

"He made all of those," said Cal.

"He's an artist too!" exclaimed Hayden, impressed.

The table was covered in deep-blue-and-green china set on a pure-white linen tablecloth. Pure-silver chalices sparkled in the sunlight. Though matched perfectly, each dish and cup was uniquely designed, like the chairs. Grace was thinking about how each item on the table told a story. There were also beautiful serving dishes on the table, but the food had not yet been served.

Grace was sitting between Leona and Rhoda, across from Hayden and Tim. Looking around the table, she couldn't help but notice how out of place the dinner guests appeared, seated at such a fancy table. Having felt like an outsider her whole life, normally she would have felt terribly self-conscious about being unbathed and underdressed in such a fancy setting. However, this time she fit right in.

Feeling more comfortable, she continued looking around the room, surveying the guests. Just then, she noticed a man seated across the table, several chairs down.

He looked familiar, like someone she once knew, yet strangely different.

Then she noticed his purple-striped tie.

"No," Grace whispered, dread and fear gripping her.

The Orchard Owner approached and knelt down beside her.

She turned in her chair, looking to escape. "What is *he* doing here?" she hissed angrily.

The Orchard Owner put his hand on her shoulder.

"He was hungry and accepted the invitation, just like you."

"But it's not fair!" cried Grace, lowering her voice to a whisper so she didn't make a scene.

"He *hurt* me. He ruined my life! But I...I shouldn't have..." Grace was aghast.

She looked at the Orchard Owner, tears running down her dirty cheeks.

The Orchard Owner looked her in the eyes.

"Grace," he said quietly. "It was *not* your fault."

"But why? Why me? Why my mom? She was so wonderful and so full of love. Why couldn't my father have died instead? Or better yet, why not *him?*"

She pointed to the man in the purple tie.

"Grace," the Orchard Owner began softly, "this land is full of broken people, some terribly so. To create something perfect takes great skill, but to redeem the hideous, the condemned, and unforgivable requires the hand of the master artist, the creator.

"Look around and feast your eyes on the miraculous beauty of redemption."

Grace looked up.

The stained glass, the walls, the furniture were all broken pieces made into works of art.

Grace looked next to her.

Leona looked at Grace. The angry, frightened little girl from the pawnshop was now so alive, so free and radiant—an exquisite work of art fashioned from broken pieces.

Grace couldn't deny what she saw but still didn't understand. "Why is the world so broken?"

The Orchard Owner was silent for a moment, and then he spoke. "The land of god freely grants every good thing to all who seek. The only famine is one of love, compassion, and vision. An evil deception has caused many to become lost in self-centeredness. The ignorant claw and fight each other for that which god has given freely. What they seek stands before them with open arms, but their eyes are turned inward.

"But be careful not to judge prematurely and superficially. Some have an appearance of good but are deeply flawed, or pure evil at the core. Likewise, some who appear diabolically wicked are simply horribly broken and starving. In the end, the hungry will accept the invitation and evil will disappear into the shadows.

"But your journey here wasn't about searching for answers, but about finding your way back home, remember? Well, what if I told you that you were home at this very moment, that all your dreams had come true, and all that remained was for you to wake up and open your eyes?"

Grace stared silently at the empty dishes. She felt empty herself, except for grief and sadness. She glanced over at the man in the purple-striped tie. He was looking the other way. She hated the rage that filled her. She didn't want to feel it, but she didn't know how to let go.

"Help," she whispered.

The Orchard Owner left her side and went over to the bench where Anna lay. He knelt over her and whispered something in her ear. Before Grace could comprehend what was happening, the girl opened her eyes and sat up.

Grace gasped.

"Anna! You're alive!"

The Orchard Owner picked the frail girl up and carried her to the table, setting her gently in a chair across from Grace.

"How? I thought you were…"

"It is good to see you again," Anna said. "It's good to wake up. I was having a bad dream… I was so weak. I was trying so hard to breathe. Then I let go and…now I'm here and so hungry! Are we having dinner?"

Grace searched for words but couldn't find any. Her mind was blank.

The Orchard Owner spoke to Grace. "Don't seek truth. Seek life. Life is everything. It sustains all things and is *always* true."

He approached Leona and whispered something in her ear. She grinned and handed him the book. He then took his seat at the head of the table.

"Friends," he began. The table hushed as he spoke in a voice that was rich, warm, and full of love.

"Welcome. I'm so glad you've all accepted my invitation. I have longed for this day to arrive. You've been promised better days to come, blessings to arrive tomorrow, but that day never comes, so you suffer *today*. Some of you have tried to flee death through isolation, starvation, or diversions, only to discover escape is impossible. You're hungry.

"Friends, I have good news! The better day is now. The bonds of deception are broken, and the time to dine and be refreshed has come! *Today is the day!* Everything I have been given, I freely give to you."

He opened the book and began to read.

His voice, as he read, was like a song. It was rich and melodious, and as it resonated through the room Grace found she wasn't processing the words so much as she was breathing them in. At the same time, she began to experience an odd sensation in her chest. She felt as if invisible arms were embracing her and liquid love was purging her heart.

As he continued, Grace's senses heightened, and she caught the scent of something incredible, a heavenly aroma that words couldn't describe. She became aware that her eyes were closed, and opening them slowly, she beheld what her nostrils had already perceived. The serving dishes were filled to overflowing with the most exquisite food!

She gasped, struggling to catch her breath.

Roasted turkeys that must have weighed more than Terrence sat alongside massive sides of ham and beef dripping with juice. Other dishes were filled with every imaginable roasted vegetable, mashed potatoes with flecks of butter, and steaming hot rolls. There were exotic dishes, including fragrant Chinese noodles, towers of sushi, and rows of whole lobsters.

Piles of bright-colored fruits, plates with twenty types of yellow and white cheeses, skewers and kebobs filled with grilled seafood, chicken, white onions, and red peppers. Desserts galore: giant cakes intricately decorated with frills of white and colored frosting, crisscrossed pies, and piles of cookies, even tiramisu. The carafes were filled with deep-red wine and white bubbly champagne. Others contained fruit juices in colors she had never seen. There were crystal pitchers filled with chilled water that sparkled so brilliantly it appeared illuminated.

There were many more dishes Grace had never seen before! This was truly a banquet that offered abundance for every palate.

The Orchard Owner finished, put down the book, and picked up a giant loaf of crusty Italian bread. He broke the bread in half and gave one half to each side of the table. Each person took a piece and passed it to the next person.

When the bread had been distributed, he raised a glass and announced, "All preparations are complete and the food is served. Let the hungry eat and the thirsty drink! Dinner is served!" Everyone rose, lifted a glass, and toasted to friendship, to journeys shared, and to the host of the gracious feast that lay before them.

All the guests dug in with reckless abandon, Terrence included. Grace tasted a little of everything, letting the flavors linger in her mouth, overwhelmed by the fireworks going off in her senses. She sampled exotic food that normally she would have never tried. Everyone seemed caught up in rapturous ecstasy as they ate, drank, and shared stories. The light in the room was getting brighter, but not from any external source; it was emanating from the faces of those who were dining. The gracious meal was illuminating the grateful ragamuffins from the inside out.

Grace glanced over at the man in the purple-striped tie. He was eating his piece of the bread. He looked up at her, and they locked eyes.

In that moment Grace saw him for what he was: helpless and needy, just like her. In that moment, beholding the man instead of the offence, her anger disappeared.

He looked directly at Grace

His mouth formed the words, "I'm so sorry."

Grace gulped, knowing what she had to do. When the words came out, they weren't as hard as she imagined.

"I forgive you."

He smiled, and she smiled back. Grace felt a lightness come over her, as though a heavy burden had been removed from her shoulders.

It was finished.

Beautiful music was now playing from somewhere. Grace looked around the table at the faces of the honored guests. She saw the woman who had wiped the barbecue sauce from the Orchard Owner's feet. She saw some folks from the village with the sacred table. She recognized a few people from the EC, the godvernment, and several she believed were gamers from the carnival. Her heart skipped a beat when she noticed the girl from the Badlands who had asked her for food. People from every corner of god, regardless of background or prejudices, ate from the same table.

Bill had taken his glasses off and was laughing with Cal and Madeline. The old Wizard and his friend, reunited at last.

Grace looked down to pet Terrence and was shocked to see clean white clothes had somehow replaced the soiled ones she came in wearing. Looking around at the others, she saw the same thing had happened to everyone. Their filthy rags had been replaced with beautiful party attire.

At that moment the other friends looked up from their plates and locked eyes. Grace noticed that Tim had tears streaming down his cheeks with no eye drops in sight. Leona beamed. She had the most amazingly beautiful smile. Hayden's hat was gone, revealing hair that actually looked clean. He had the look of a man whose mind was at peace. Nothing needed to be spoken, for their faces told the story—they had all found what they were looking for.

Hayden spoke to Grace. "Thank you for rescuing me from the pole. I would probably still be sitting up there if you hadn't cared."

Grace smiled and said, "I don't know what I would have done without you. I don't know what I would have done without all of you." She looked at Leona then at Tim, who spoke up.

"We needed each other, and we stuck together."

"Of course we stuck together; we're family," Leona said, making no attempt to hold back the tears.

"Yes, to family!" Tim said, lifting his glass. The four toasted to what was behind them and to whatever lay ahead.

As the feast continued, the table appeared to be stretching out, expanding across the room as it went. The food never ran low; there was always an abundance, regardless of how much was eaten. The surreal had finally eclipsed the ordinary, and the supernatural was now seen as natural.

Suddenly, the room began to shake. Everyone went on eating, drinking, and laughing, unaffected.

Looking around the room once again, Grace spotted a woman sitting across the table beyond the man with the purple-striped tie. Her head was turned slightly, and she appeared to be chatting with someone.

Grace's heart jolted. She jumped up and started to make her way around the head of the table, her mind racing with thoughts of seeing the one she most longed to see. The room was shaking more violently now, but somehow the people seated were unmoved.

She was trying her best to hurry, but losing her balance, she was forced to hold onto the backs of chairs for support.

She had almost reached the end of the table when she looked up and saw the ceiling of the church crack open. Light streamed in, illuminating a blue sky. Cracks were appearing in the walls as well, and streams of water began pouring into the room. But all Grace thought of was reaching the other side of the table and the woman.

Finally reaching the head of the table, she ran into the Orchard Owner. He was standing next to his chair, holding Terrence. The building shook more violently, but nothing was falling on the people or the table. The Orchard Owner handed Terrence to Grace and smiled. She knew this was the end of their journey.

"No, I can't go now!" Grace said, clutching her dog and panting. "Is that…is that her? Is she really here? Is she okay? I couldn't be sure, 'cause it was so far away."

"Do you trust me, Grace?" asked the man.

She looked in his eyes. The Orchard Owner, The Barbecue Chef, The Baker, The Sandwich Cart Man, The Gracious Host. The One who feeds, and the One who loves.

Grace glanced quickly toward where the woman was seated. The shaking was growing stronger, and all that could be moved was being shaken.

She looked back at the Orchard Owner. He was smiling as usual.

"Don't be afraid. The food and drink I have given is unlike any other. It will remain *in* you, as an artesian spring of pure love that never runs dry. Your long journey to find your way home is over. Home is within you."

"It is time to go and your friends are waiting for you. Always remember, you need each other, as you can't dine alone. I'll see you at the table."

Grace believed, and was bathed in the brilliant light that streamed in through the cracks. All fear vanished in an instant, as she was enveloped in perfect peace.

The room was fading fast now, and she began to feel as if she was being pulled out of a dream. She instinctively wrapped herself into the arms of the Orchard Owner, closed her eyes, and hugged him with all her strength. Everything grew still for a moment, and she had the strangest sensation, as if his body was growing less tangible, somehow melting into hers, his energy and his love surging through her veins.

Home.

She felt herself falling. Then...

Darkness.

# CHAPTER 26

# HOME

*"Love doesn't just sit there, like a stone; it has to be made,
like bread; remade all the time, made new."*

— URSULA LE GUIN

A tiny beam of light pierced through the darkness. Grace's eyes fluttered open. She could hear shouts in the distance but couldn't understand the words. She didn't know where she was, but she felt safe, like she was being hugged. Terrence whimpered beside her. Then barked.

"Where are we, boy?"

Two things were certain: she was lying on the hard ground, and it was very dusty. She blinked again. It was pitch dark, besides the beam of light streaming above her. She looked to her left and perceived someone was lying next to her.

Tim?

"What happened?" Tim asked as he sat up

"I'm not sure," Grace whispered.

"Over here!" she heard someone yell. "I think I hear the dog!"

Terrence barked louder. Grace tried to sit up but realized whatever was causing the darkness was pressed up against her. It felt like wood.

"Here!" she heard a muffled voice say again, this time hovering over her.

"Lift this up!"

"Grace, are you down there? Grace!"

She recognized the voice of her Uncle Harry.

"I'm here, Uncle Harry!" she shouted.

"Oh, thank God!"

The large piece of wood that covered her was lifted off, and she squinted as the bright sunlight hit her face.

Uncle Harry along with several others stood peering down at her. Two of the men were firemen.

"There are two more of them! Alive!" shouted one of the firemen.

Grace looked around, confused.

"What happened?"

"Are you hurt?" Her Aunt Emily had now appeared and was kneeling beside her.

"I think I'm okay."

Both she and Tim were helped to their feet. They carefully made their way out of the pile of wreckage with the helpful hands of others.

"Are you sure you're okay?"

Grace noticed a fire truck and an ambulance in what she thought was once the church's driveway. *The church!* Looking behind her she saw that the old church had been completely destroyed and all that remained was a pile of debris.

"The storm," Grace said.

"It's a miracle, really!" Aunt Emily said, embracing her.

Just then, Grace saw Leona and Hayden walking quickly toward her and Tim.

"Leona! Hayden!" Grace exclaimed.

Her aunt looked puzzled.

"They were rescued from under the rubble right near you. They don't attend our church. Do you know them?"

Grace let go of her aunt and embraced the two, who were also covered in dust.

"Must be friends from her school," remarked Uncle Harry.

"It really is a miracle!" Aunt Emily insisted. "You should have all been smashed to pieces!"

"Well," Tim said, "sometimes you have to fall to pieces before you can fall into peace." Aunt Emily looked at him, puzzled.

The dusty travelers stood together once again, this time with no clear path before them. They all looked up at once and stared at each other in amazement. Spontaneous laughter broke out between them. .

After the laughter subsided, Grace spoke up.

"I see Him."

"Where?" Hayden began looking around. "Is He in the rubble?"

Grace smiled.

"Not in the rubble. In my friends."

"He asked me to be sure to always save Him a seat at the table," Leona responded.

"All He ever wanted to do was feed us," Hayden said, looking back and forth at his three friends. "It's so simple, not like I imagined enlightenment would come. But hey, it sure is good news!"

"Smart man!" Leona said, smiling, then she stepped forward and gave Hayden a huge hug.

Just then, Aunt Emily walked up holding a silver chalice engraved with an intricate design.

"I've never seen this before. Must've blown in with the storm," she said.

"Leftovers!" Hayden started looking around the debris.

"We will rebuild," remarked Uncle Harry confidently, walking up. "The important thing is that you all are happy, healthy, and wholesome."

Leona coughed.

Hayden laughed his ridiculous giggle, and the others joined him.

Grace's aunt and uncle looked at each other, not sure what to think.

"Yes," Grace said between laughter. "We will rebuild."

IT IS FINISHED.

45637239R00175

Made in the USA
Charleston, SC
30 August 2015